Anne of the Island

L. M. Montgomery

ANNE of the ISLAND

W. Books

This is a W. Books publication, a division of Grupo Ciranda Cultural.

Text: Lucy Maud Montgomery
First Publication: 1915
Graphic Design: Linea Editora
Cover Design and Illustrations: © Elena Distefano
© Sweet Cherry Publishing Limited, 2018

Dados Internacionais de Catalogação na Publicação (CIP) de acordo com ISBD

M787a Montgomery, Lucy Maud.

Anne of the Island / Lucy Maud Montgomery. - Jandira, SP : W. Books, 2025.
272 p. : 12,80cm x 19,70cm. - (Classics).

ISBN: 978-65-5294-080-3

1. Literatura canadense. 2. Romance. 3. Órfão. 4. Família. 5. Imaginação. 6. Amizade. 7. Canadá. I. Título. II. Série.

2025-2461 CDD 810
CDU 821.111(71)

Elaborada por Lucio Feitosa - CRB-8/8803

Índice para catálogo sistemático:
1. Literatura canadense 810
2. Literatura canadense 821.111(71)

www.cirandacultural.com.br

All precious things discovered late
To those that seek them issue forth,
For Love in sequel works with Fate,
And draws the veil from hidden worth.
—Tennyson

to
all the girls
all over the world
who have "wanted more"
about Anne

Contents

Chapter I.	The Shadow of Change	9
Chapter II.	Garlands of Autumn	18
Chapter III.	Greeting and Farewell	26
Chapter IV.	April's Lady	33
Chapter V.	Letters from Home	46
Chapter VI.	In the Park	54
Chapter VII.	Home Again	61
Chapter VIII.	Anne's First Proposal	70
Chapter IX.	An Unwelcome Lover and a Welcome Friend	75
Chapter X.	Patty's Place	83
Chapter XI.	The Round of Life	91
Chapter XII.	"Averil's Atonement"	100
Chapter XIII.	The Way of Transgressors	108
Chapter XIV.	The Summons	119
Chapter XV.	A Dream Turned Upside Down	127
Chapter XVI.	Adjusted Relationships	132
Chapter XVII.	A Letter from Davy	143
Chapter XVIII.	Miss Josephine Remembers the Anne-girl	147
Chapter XIX.	An Interlude	153

Chapter XX.	Gilbert Speaks	157
Chapter XXI.	Roses of Yesterday	163
Chapter XXII.	Spring and Anne Return to Green Gables	167
Chapter XXIII.	Paul Cannot Find the Rock People	172
Chapter XXIV.	Enter Jonas	176
Chapter XXV.	Enter Prince Charming	181
Chapter XXVI.	Enter Christine	188
Chapter XXVII.	Mutual Confidences	192
Chapter XXVIII.	A June Evening	198
Chapter XXIX.	Diana's Wedding	203
Chapter XXX.	Mrs. Skinner's Romance	207
Chapter XXXI.	Anne to Philippa	211
Chapter XXXII.	Tea with Mrs. Douglas	214
Chapter XXXIII.	"He Just Kept Coming and Coming"	219
Chapter XXXIV.	John Douglas Speaks at Last	223
Chapter XXXV.	The Last Redmond Year Opens	228
Chapter XXXVI.	The Gardners'Call	235
Chapter XXXVII.	Full-fledged B.A.'s	241
Chapter XXXVIII.	False Dawn	247
Chapter XXXIX.	Deals with Weddings	253
Chapter XL.	A Book of Revelation	261
Chapter XLI.	Love Takes Up the Glass of Time	266

Chapter I
The Shadow of Change

"Harvest is ended and summer is gone," quoted Anne Shirley, gazing across the shorn fields dreamily. She and Diana Barry had been picking apples in the Green Gables orchard, but were now resting from their labors in a sunny corner, where airy fleets of thistledown drifted by on the wings of a wind that was still summer-sweet with the incense of ferns in the Haunted Wood.

But everything in the landscape around them spoke of autumn. The sea was roaring hollowly in the distance, the fields were bare and sere, scarfed with golden rod, the brook valley below Green Gables overflowed with asters of ethereal purple, and the Lake of Shining Waters was blue—blue—blue; not the changeful blue of spring, nor the pale azure of summer, but a clear, steadfast, serene blue, as if the water were past all moods and tenses of emotion and had settled down to a tranquility unbroken by fickle dreams.

"It has been a nice summer," said Diana, twisting the new ring on her left hand with a smile. "And Miss Lavendar's wedding seemed to come as a sort of crown to it. I suppose Mr. and Mrs. Irving are on the Pacific coast now."

"It seems to me they have been gone long enough to go around the world," sighed Anne.

"I can't believe it is only a week since they were married. Everything has changed. Miss Lavendar and Mr. and Mrs. Allan gone—how lonely the manse looks with the shutters all closed! I went past it last night, and it made me feel as if everybody in it had died."

"We'll never get another minister as nice as Mr. Allan," said Diana, with gloomy conviction. "I suppose we'll have all kinds of supplies this winter, and half the Sundays no preaching at all. And you and Gilbert gone—it will be awfully dull."

"Fred will be here," insinuated Anne slyly.

"When is Mrs. Lynde going to move up?" asked Diana, as if she had not heard Anne's remark.

"Tomorrow. I'm glad she's coming—but it will be another change. Marilla and I cleared everything out of the spare room yesterday. Do you know, I hated to do it? Of course, it was silly—but it did seem as if we were committing sacrilege. That old spare room has always seemed like a shrine to me. When I was a child I thought it the most wonderful apartment in the world. You remember what a consuming desire I had to sleep in a spare room bed—but not the Green Gables spare room. Oh, no, never there! It would have been too terrible—I couldn't have slept a wink from awe. I never *walked* through that room when Marilla sent me in on an errand—no, indeed, I tiptoed through it and held my breath, as if I were in church, and felt relieved when I got out of it. The pictures of George Whitefield and the Duke of Wellington hung there, one on each side of the mirror, and frowned so sternly at me all the time I was in, especially if I dared peep in the mirror, which was the only one in the house that didn't twist my face a little. I always wondered how Marilla dared houseclean that room. And now it's not only cleaned but stripped bare. George Whitefield and the Duke have been relegated to the upstairs hall. 'So passes the glory of this world,'" concluded Anne, with a laugh in which there was a little note of regret. It is never pleasant to have our old shrines desecrated, even when we have outgrown them.

"I'll be so lonesome when you go," moaned Diana for the hundredth time. "And to think you go next week!"

"But we're together still," said Anne cheerily. "We mustn't let next week rob us of this week's joy. I hate the thought of going myself—home and I are such good friends. Talk of being lonesome! It's I who should groan. *You'll* be here with any number of your old friends—*and* Fred! While I shall be alone among strangers, not knowing a soul!"

"*Except* Gilbert—*and* Charlie Sloane," said Diana, imitating Anne's italics and slyness.

"Charlie Sloane will be a great comfort, of course," agreed Anne sarcastically; whereupon both those irresponsible damsels laughed. Diana knew exactly what Anne thought of Charlie Sloane; but, despite sundry confidential talks, she did not know just what Anne thought of Gilbert Blythe. To be sure, Anne herself did not know that.

"The boys may be boarding at the other end of Kingsport, for all I know," Anne went on. "I am glad I'm going to Redmond, and I am sure I shall like it after a while. But for the first few weeks I know I won't. I shan't even have the comfort of looking forward to the weekend visit home, as I had when I went to Queen's. Christmas will seem like a thousand years away."

"Everything is changing—or going to change," said Diana sadly. "I have a feeling that things will never be the same again, Anne."

"We have come to a parting of the ways, I suppose," said Anne thoughtfully. "We had to come to it. Do you think, Diana, that being grown up is really as nice as we used to imagine it would be when we were children?"

"I don't know—there are *some* nice things about it," answered Diana, again caressing her ring with that little smile which always had the effect of making Anne feel suddenly left out and inexperienced. "But there are so many puzzling things, too. Sometimes I feel as if being grown-up just frightened me—and then I would give anything to be a little girl again."

"I suppose we'll get used to being grownup in time," said Anne cheerfully. "There won't be so many unexpected things about it by and by—though, after all, I fancy it's the unexpected things that give spice to life. We're eighteen, Diana. In two more years we'll be twenty. When I was ten I thought twenty was a green old age. In no time you'll be a staid, middle-aged matron, and I shall be nice, old maid Aunt Anne, coming to visit you on vacations. You'll always keep a corner for me, won't you, Di darling? Not the spare room, of course—old maids can't aspire to spare rooms, and I shall be as 'umble as *Uriah Heep*, and quite content with a little over-the-porch or off-the-parlor cubby hole."

"What nonsense you do talk, Anne," laughed Diana. "You'll marry somebody splendid and handsome and rich—and no spare room in Avonlea will be half gorgeous enough for you—and you'll turn up your nose at all the friends of your youth."

"That would be a pity; my nose is quite nice, but I fear turning it up would spoil it," said Anne, patting that shapely organ. "I haven't so many good features that I could afford to spoil those I have; so, even if I should marry the King of the Cannibal Islands, I promise you I won't turn up my nose at you, Diana."

With another gay laugh the girls separated, Diana to return to Orchard Slope, Anne to walk to the Post Office. She found a letter awaiting her there, and when Gilbert Blythe overtook her on the bridge over the Lake of Shining Waters she was sparkling with the excitement of it.

"Priscilla Grant is going to Redmond, too," she exclaimed. "Isn't that splendid? I hoped she would, but she didn't think her father would consent. He has, however, and we're to board together. I feel that I can face an army with banners—or all the professors of Redmond in one fell phalanx—with a chum like Priscilla by my side."

"I think we'll like Kingsport," said Gilbert. "It's a nice old burg, they tell me, and has the finest natural park in the world. I've heard that the scenery in it is magnificent."

"I wonder if it will be—can be—any more beautiful than this," murmured Anne, looking around her with the loving, enraptured eyes of those to whom "home" must always be the loveliest spot in the world, no matter what fairer lands may lie under alien stars.

They were leaning on the bridge of the old pond, drinking deep of the enchantment of the dusk, just at the spot where Anne had climbed from her sinking Dory on the day Elaine floated down to Camelot. The fine, empurpling dye of sunset still stained the western skies, but the moon was rising and the water lay like a great, silver dream in her light. Remembrance wove a sweet and subtle spell over the two young creatures.

"You are very quiet, Anne," said Gilbert at last.

"I'm afraid to speak or move for fear all this wonderful beauty will vanish just like a broken silence," breathed Anne.

Gilbert suddenly laid his hand over the slender white one lying on the rail of the bridge. His hazel eyes deepened into darkness, his still boyish lips opened to say something of the dream and hope that thrilled his soul. But Anne snatched her hand away and turned quickly. The spell of the dusk was broken for her.

"I must go home," she exclaimed, with a rather overdone carelessness. "Marilla had a headache this afternoon, and I'm sure the twins will be in some dreadful mischief by this time. I really shouldn't have stayed away so long."

She chattered ceaselessly and inconsequently until they reached the Green Gables lane. Poor Gilbert hardly had a chance to get a word in edgewise. Anne felt rather relieved when they parted. There had been a new, secret self-consciousness in her heart with regard to Gilbert, ever since that fleeting moment of revelation in the garden of Echo Lodge. Something alien had intruded into the old, perfect, school-day comradeship—something that threatened to mar it.

"I never felt glad to see Gilbert go before," she thought, half-resentfully, half-sorrowfully, as she walked alone up the lane. "Our friendship will be spoiled if he goes on with this nonsense. It mustn't be spoiled—I won't let it. Oh, *why* can't boys be just sensible!"

Anne had an uneasy doubt that it was not strictly "sensible" that she should still feel on her hand the warm pressure of Gilbert's, as distinctly as she had felt it for the swift second his had rested there; and still less sensible that the sensation was far from being an unpleasant one—very different from that which had attended a similar demonstration on Charlie Sloane's part, when she had been sitting out a dance with him at a White Sands party three nights before. Anne shivered over the disagreeable recollection. But all problems connected with infatuated swains vanished from her mind when she entered the homely, unsentimental atmosphere of the Green Gables kitchen where an eight-year-old boy was crying grievously on the sofa.

"What is the matter, Davy?" asked Anne, taking him up in her arms. "Where are Marilla and Dora?"

"Marilla's putting Dora to bed," sobbed Davy, "and I'm crying 'cause Dora fell down the outside cellar steps, heels over head, and scraped all the skin off her nose, and—"

"Oh, well, don't cry about it, dear. Of course, you are sorry for her, but crying won't help her any. She'll be all right tomorrow. Crying never helps any one, Davy-boy, and—"

"I ain't crying 'cause Dora fell down cellar," said Davy, cutting short Anne's wellmeant preachment with increasing bitterness. "I'm crying, cause I wasn't there to see her fall. I'm always missing some fun or other, seems to me."

"Oh, Davy!" Anne choked back an unholy shriek of laughter. "Would you call it fun to see poor little Dora fall down the steps and get hurt?"

"She wasn't *much* hurt," said Davy, defiantly. "'Course, if she'd been killed I'd have been real sorry, Anne. But the Keiths ain't so easy killed. They're like the Blewetts, I guess. Herb Blewett fell off the hayloft last Wednesday, and rolled right down through the turnip chute into the box stall, where they had a fearful wild, cross horse, and rolled right under his heels. And still he got out alive, with only three bones broke. Mrs. Lynde says there are some folks you can't kill with a meat-axe. Is Mrs. Lynde coming here tomorrow, Anne?"

"Yes, Davy, and I hope you'll be always very nice and good to her."

"I'll be nice and good. But will she ever put me to bed at nights, Anne?"

"Perhaps. Why?"

"'Cause," said Davy very decidedly, "if she does I won't say my prayers before her like I do before you, Anne."

"Why not?"

"'Cause I don't think it would be nice to talk to God before strangers, Anne. Dora can say hers to Mrs. Lynde if she likes, but *I* won't. I'll wait till she's gone and then say 'em. Won't that be all right, Anne?"

"Yes, if you are sure you won't forget to say them, Davy-boy."

"Oh, I won't forget, you bet. I think saying my prayers is great fun. But it won't be as good fun saying them alone as saying them to you. I wish you'd stay home, Anne. I don't see what you want to go away and leave us for."

"I don't exactly *want* to, Davy, but I feel I ought to go."

"If you don't want to go you needn't. You're grown up. When *I*'m grown up I'm not going to do one single thing I don't want to do, Anne."

"All your life, Davy, you'll find yourself doing things you don't want to do."

"I won't," said Davy flatly. "Catch me! I have to do things I don't want to now 'cause you and Marilla'll send me to bed if I don't. But when I grow up you can't do that, and there'll be nobody to tell me not to do things. Won't I have the time! Say, Anne, Milty Boulter says his mother says you're going to college to see if you can catch a man. Are you, Anne? I want to know."

For a second Anne burned with resentment. Then she laughed, reminding herself that Mrs. Boulter's crude vulgarity of thought and speech could not harm her.

"No, Davy, I'm not. I'm going to study and grow and learn about many things."

"What things?"

> *"'Shoes and ships and sealing wax*
> *And cabbages and kings,'"*

quoted Anne.

"But if you *did* want to catch a man how would you go about it? I want to know," persisted Davy, for whom the subject evidently possessed a certain fascination.

"You'd better ask Mrs. Boulter," said Anne thoughtlessly. "I think it's likely she knows more about the process than I do."

"I will, the next time I see her," said Davy gravely.

"Davy! If you do!" cried Anne, realizing her mistake.

"But you just told me to," protested Davy aggrieved.

"It's time you went to bed," decreed Anne, by way of getting out of the scrape.

After Davy had gone to bed Anne wandered down to Victoria Island and sat there alone, curtained with fine-spun, moonlit gloom, while the water laughed around her in a duet of brook and wind. Anne had always loved that brook. Many a dream had she spun over its sparkling water in days gone by. She forgot lovelorn youths, and the cayenne speeches of malicious neighbors, and all the problems of her girlish existence. In imagination she sailed over storied seas that wash the distant shining shores of "faery lands forlorn," where lost Atlantis and Elysium lie, with the evening star for pilot, to the land of Heart's Desire. And she was richer in those dreams than in realities; for things seen pass away, but the things that are unseen are eternal.

Chapter II
Garlands of Autumn

The following week sped swiftly, crowded with innumerable "last things," as Anne called them. Good-bye calls had to be made and received, being pleasant or otherwise, according to whether callers and called-upon were heartily in sympathy with Anne's hopes, or thought she was too much puffed-up over going to college and that it was their duty to "take her down a peg or two."

The A.V.I.S. gave a farewell party in honor of Anne and Gilbert one evening at the home of Josie Pye, choosing that place, partly because Mr. Pye's house was large and convenient, partly because it was strongly suspected that the Pye girls would have nothing to do with the affair if their offer of the house for the party was not accepted. It was a very pleasant little time, for the Pye girls were gracious, and said and did nothing to mar the harmony of the occasion—which was not according to their wont. Josie was unusually amiable—so much so that she even remarked condescendingly to Anne,

"Your new dress is rather becoming to you, Anne. Really, you look *almost pretty* in it."

"How kind of you to say so," responded Anne, with dancing eyes. Her sense of humor was developing, and the speeches that would have hurt her at fourteen were becoming merely food for amusement now. Josie suspected that Anne was laughing at her behind those wicked eyes; but she contented herself with whispering to Gertie, as they went downstairs, that Anne Shirley would put on more airs than ever now that she was going to college—you'd see!

All the "old crowd" was there, full of mirth and zest and youthful lightheartedness. Diana Barry, rosy and dimpled, shadowed by the faithful Fred; Jane Andrews, neat and sensible and plain; Ruby Gillis, looking her handsomest and brightest in a cream silk blouse, with red geraniums in her golden hair; Gilbert Blythe and Charlie Sloane, both trying to keep as near the elusive Anne as possible; Carrie Sloane, looking pale and melancholy because, so it was reported, her father would not allow Oliver Kimball to come near the place; Moody Spurgeon MacPherson, whose round face and objectionable ears were as round and objectionable as ever; and Billy Andrews, who sat in a corner all the evening, chuckled when any one spoke to him, and watched Anne Shirley with a grin of pleasure on his broad, freckled countenance.

Anne had known beforehand of the party, but she had not known that she and Gilbert were, as the founders of the Society, to be presented with a very complimentary "address" and "tokens of respect"—in her case a volume of Shakespeare's plays, in Gilbert's a fountain pen. She was so taken by surprise and pleased by the nice things said in the address, read in Moody Spurgeon's most solemn and ministerial tones, that the tears quite drowned the sparkle of her big gray eyes. She had worked hard and faithfully for the A.V.I.S., and it warmed the cockles of her heart that the members appreciated her efforts so sincerely. And they were all so nice and friendly and jolly—even the Pye girls had their merits; at that moment Anne loved all the world.

She enjoyed the evening tremendously, but the end of it rather spoiled all. Gilbert again made the mistake of saying something sentimental to her as they ate their supper on the moonlit verandah; and Anne, to punish him, was gracious to Charlie Sloane and allowed the latter to walk home with her. She found, however, that revenge hurts nobody quite so much as the one who tries to inflict it. Gilbert walked airily off with Ruby Gillis, and Anne could hear them laughing and talking gaily as they loitered along in the still, crisp autumn air. They were evidently having the best of good times, while she was horribly bored by Charlie Sloane, who talked unbrokenly on, and never, even by accident, said one thing that was worth listening to. Anne gave an occasional absent "yes" or "no," and thought how beautiful Ruby had looked that night, how very goggly Charlie's eyes were in the moonlight—worse even than by daylight—and that the world, somehow, wasn't quite such a nice place as she had believed it to be earlier in the evening.

"I'm just tired out—that is what is the matter with me," she said, when she thankfully found herself alone in her own room. And she honestly believed it was. But a certain little gush of joy, as from some secret, unknown spring, bubbled up in her heart the next evening, when she saw Gilbert striding down through the Haunted Wood and crossing the old log bridge with that firm, quick step of his. So Gilbert was not going to spend this last evening with Ruby Gillis after all!

"You look tired, Anne," he said.

"I am tired, and, worse than that, I'm disgruntled. I'm tired because I've been packing my trunk and sewing all day. But I'm disgruntled because six women have been here to say good-bye to me, and every one of the six managed to say something that seemed to take the color right out of life and leave it as gray and dismal and cheerless as a November morning."

"Spiteful old cats!" was Gilbert's elegant comment.

"Oh, no, they weren't," said Anne seriously. "That is just the trouble. If they had been spiteful cats I wouldn't have minded them. But they are all nice, kind, motherly souls, who like me and whom I like, and that is why what they said, or hinted, had such undue weight with me. They let me see they thought I was crazy going to Redmond and trying to take a B.A., and ever since I've been wondering if I am. Mrs. Peter Sloane sighed and said she hoped my strength would hold out till I got through; and at once I saw myself a hopeless victim of nervous prostration at the end of my third year; Mrs. Eben Wright said it must cost an awful lot to put in four years at Redmond; and I felt all over me that it was unpardonable of me to squander Marilla's money and my own on such a folly. Mrs. Jasper Bell said she hoped I wouldn't let college spoil me, as it did some people; and I felt in my bones that the end of my four Redmond years would see me a most insufferable creature, thinking I knew it all, and looking down on everything and everybody in Avonlea; Mrs. Elisha Wright said she understood that Redmond girls, especially those who belonged to Kingsport, were 'dreadful dressy and stuck-up,' and she guessed I wouldn't feel much at home among them; and I saw myself, a snubbed, dowdy, humiliated country girl, shuffling through Redmond's classic halls in coppertoned boots."

Anne ended with a laugh and a sigh commingled. With her sensitive nature all disapproval had weight, even the disapproval of those for whose opinions she had scant respect. For the time being life was savorless, and ambition had gone out like a snuffed candle.

"You surely don't care for what they said," protested Gilbert. "You know exactly how narrow their outlook on life is, excellent creatures though they are. To do anything *they* have never done is anathema maranatha. You are the first Avonlea girl who has ever gone to college; and you know that all pioneers are considered to be afflicted with moonstruck madness."

"Oh, I know. But *feeling* is so different from *knowing*. My common sense tells me all you can say, but there are times when common sense has no power over me. Common nonsense takes possession of my soul. Really, after Mrs. Elisha went away I hardly had the heart to finish packing."

"You're just tired, Anne. Come, forget it all and take a walk with me—a ramble back through the woods beyond the marsh. There should be something there I want to show you."

"Should be! Don't you know if it is there?"

"No. I only know it should be, from something I saw there in spring. Come on. We'll pretend we are two children again and we'll go the way of the wind."

They started gaily off. Anne, remembering the unpleasantness of the preceding evening, was very nice to Gilbert; and Gilbert, who was learning wisdom, took care to be nothing save the schoolboy comrade again. Mrs. Lynde and Marilla watched them from the kitchen window.

"That'll be a match some day," Mrs. Lynde said approvingly.

Marilla winced slightly. In her heart she hoped it would, but it went against her grain to hear the matter spoken of in Mrs. Lynde's gossipy matter-of-fact way.

"They're only children yet," she said shortly.

Mrs. Lynde laughed good-naturedly.

"Anne is eighteen; I was married when I was that age. We old folks, Marilla, are too much given to thinking children never grow up, that's what. Anne is a young woman and Gilbert's a man, and he worships the ground she walks on, as any one can see. He's a fine fellow, and Anne can't do better. I hope she won't get any romantic nonsense into her head at Redmond. I don't approve of them coeducational places and never did, that's what. I don't believe," concluded Mrs. Lynde solemnly, "that the students at such colleges ever do much else than flirt."

"They must study a little," said Marilla, with a smile.

"Precious little," sniffed Mrs. Rachel. "However, I think Anne will. She never was flirtatious. But she doesn't appreciate Gilbert at his full value, that's what. Oh, I know girls! Charlie

Sloane is wild about her, too, but I'd never advise her to marry a Sloane. The Sloanes are good, honest, respectable people, of course. But when all's said and done, they're *Sloanes*."

Marilla nodded. To an outsider, the statement that Sloanes were Sloanes might not be very illuminating, but she understood. Every village has such a family; good, honest, respectable people they may be, but *Sloanes* they are and must ever remain, though they speak with the tongues of men and angels.

Gilbert and Anne, happily unconscious that their future was thus being settled by Mrs. Rachel, were sauntering through the shadows of the Haunted Wood. Beyond, the harvest hills were basking in an amber sunset radiance, under a pale, aerial sky of rose and blue. The distant spruce groves were burnished bronze, and their long shadows barred the upland meadows. But around them a little wind sang among the fir tassels, and in it there was the note of autumn.

"This wood really is haunted now—by old memories," said Anne, stooping to gather a spray of ferns, bleached to waxen whiteness by frost. "It seems to me that the little girls Diana and I used to be play here still, and sit by the Dryad's Bubble in the twilights, trysting with the ghosts. Do you know, I can never go up this path in the dusk without feeling a bit of the old fright and shiver? There was one especially horrifying phantom which we created—the ghost of the murdered child that crept up behind you and laid cold fingers on yours. I confess that, to this day, I cannot help fancying its little, furtive footsteps behind me when I come here after nightfall. I'm not afraid of the White Lady or the headless man or the skeletons, but I wish I had never imagined that baby's ghost into existence. How angry Marilla and Mrs. Barry were over that affair," concluded Anne, with reminiscent laughter.

The woods around the head of the marsh were full of purple vistas, threaded with gossamers. Past a dour plantation of gnarled spruces and a maple-fringed, sun-warm valley they found the "something" Gilbert was looking for.

"Ah, here it is," he said with satisfaction.

"An apple tree—and away back here!" exclaimed Anne delightedly.

"Yes, a veritable apple-bearing apple tree, too, here in the very midst of pines and beeches, a mile away from any orchard. I was here one day last spring and found it, all white with blossom. So I resolved I'd come again in the fall and see if it had been apples. See, it's loaded. They look good, too—tawny as russets but with a dusky red cheek. Most wild seedlings are green and uninviting."

"I suppose it sprang years ago from some chance-sown seed," said Anne dreamily. "And how it has grown and flourished and held its own here all alone among aliens, the brave determined thing!"

"Here's a fallen tree with a cushion of moss. Sit down, Anne—it will serve for a woodland throne. I'll climb for some apples. They all grow high—the tree had to reach up to the sunlight."

The apples proved to be delicious. Under the tawny skin was a white, white flesh, faintly veined with red; and, besides their own proper apple taste, they had a certain wild, delightful tang no orchard-grown apple ever possessed.

"The fatal apple of Eden couldn't have had a rarer flavor," commented Anne. "But it's time we were going home. See, it was twilight three minutes ago and now it's moonlight. What a pity we couldn't have caught the moment of transformation. But such moments never are caught, I suppose."

"Let's go back around the marsh and home by way of Lover's Lane. Do you feel as disgruntled now as when you started out, Anne?"

"Not I. Those apples have been as manna to a hungry soul. I feel that I shall love Redmond and have a splendid four years there."

"And after those four years—what?"

"Oh, there's another bend in the road at their end," answered Anne lightly. "I've no idea what may be around it—I don't want to have. It's nicer not to know."

Lover's Lane was a dear place that night, still and mysteriously dim in the pale radiance of the moonlight. They loitered through it in a pleasant chummy silence, neither caring to talk.

"If Gilbert were always as he has been this evening how nice and simple everything would be," reflected Anne.

Gilbert was looking at Anne, as she walked along. In her light dress, with her slender delicacy, she made him think of a white iris.

"I wonder if I can ever make her care for me," he thought, with a pang of self-distrust.

Chapter III
Greeting and Farewell

Charlie Sloane, Gilbert Blythe and Anne Shirley left Avonlea the following Monday morning. Anne had hoped for a fine day. Diana was to drive her to the station and they wanted this, their last drive together for some time, to be a pleasant one. But when Anne went to bed Sunday night the east wind was moaning around Green Gables with an ominous prophecy which was fulfilled in the morning. Anne awoke to find raindrops pattering against her window and shadowing the pond's gray surface with widening rings; hills and sea were hidden in mist, and the whole world seemed dim and dreary. Anne dressed in the cheerless gray dawn, for an early start was necessary to catch the boat train; she struggled against the tears that *would* well up in her eyes in spite of herself. She was leaving the home that was so dear to her, and something told her that she was leaving it forever, save as a holiday refuge. Things would never be the same again; coming back for vacations would not be living there. And oh, how dear and beloved everything was—that little white porch room, sacred to the dreams of girlhood, the old Snow Queen at the window, the brook in the hollow, the Dryad's Bubble, the Haunted Woods, and Lover's Lane—all the thousand and one dear spots where memories of the old years bided. Could she ever be really happy anywhere else?

Breakfast at Green Gables that morning was a rather doleful meal. Davy, for the first time in his life probably, could not eat, but blubbered shamelessly over his porridge. Nobody else seemed to have much appetite, save Dora, who tucked away her rations comfortably. Dora, like the immortal and most prudent Charlotte, who "went on cutting bread and butter" when her frenzied lover's body had been carried past on a shutter, was one of those fortunate creatures who are seldom disturbed by anything. Even at eight it took a great deal to ruffle Dora's placidity. She was sorry Anne was going away, of course, but was that any reason why she should fail to appreciate a poached egg on toast? Not at all. And, seeing that Davy could not eat his, Dora ate it for him.

Promptly on time Diana appeared with horse and buggy, her rosy face glowing above her raincoat. The good-byes had to be said then somehow. Mrs. Lynde came in from her quarters to give Anne a hearty embrace and warn her to be careful of her health, whatever she did. Marilla, brusque and tearless, pecked Anne's cheek and said she supposed they'd hear from her when she got settled. A casual observer might have concluded that Anne's going mattered very little to her—unless said observer had happened to get a good look in her eyes. Dora kissed Anne primly and squeezed out two decorous little tears; but Davy, who had been crying on the back porch step ever since they rose from the table, refused to say good-bye at all. When he saw Anne coming towards him he sprang to his feet, bolted up the back stairs, and hid in a clothes closet, out of which he would not come. His muffled howls were the last sounds Anne heard as she left Green Gables.

It rained heavily all the way to Bright River, to which station they had to go, since the branch line train from Carmody did not connect with the boat train. Charlie and Gilbert were on the station platform when they reached it, and the train was whistling. Anne had just time to get her ticket and trunk check, say a hurried farewell to Diana, and hasten on board. She wished she were going back with Diana to Avonlea; she knew she was going to die of homesickness. And oh, if only that dismal rain would stop pouring down as if the whole world were weeping over summer vanished and joys departed! Even Gilbert's presence brought her no comfort, for Charlie Sloane was there, too, and Sloanishness could be tolerated only in fine weather. It was absolutely insufferable in rain.

But when the boat steamed out of Charlottetown harbor things took a turn for the better. The rain ceased and the sun began to burst out goldenly now and again between the rents in the clouds, burnishing the gray seas with copper-hued radiance, and lighting up the mists that curtained the Island's red shores with gleams of gold foretokening a fine day after all. Besides, Charlie Sloane promptly became so seasick that he had to go below, and Anne and Gilbert were left alone on deck.

"I am very glad that all the Sloanes get seasick as soon as they go on water," thought Anne mercilessly. "I am sure I couldn't take my farewell look at the 'ould sod' with Charlie standing there pretending to look sentimentally at it, too."

"Well, we're off," remarked Gilbert unsentimentally.

"Yes, I feel like Byron's 'Childe Harold'—only it isn't really my 'native shore' that I'm watching," said Anne, winking her gray eyes vigorously. "Nova Scotia is that, I suppose. But one's native shore is the land one loves the best, and that's good old P.E.I. for me. I can't believe I didn't always live here. Those eleven years before I came seem like a bad dream. It's seven years since I crossed on this boat—the evening Mrs. Spencer brought me over from Hopetown. I can see myself, in that dreadful old wincey dress and faded sailor hat, exploring decks and cabins with enraptured curiosity. It was a fine evening; and how those red Island shores did gleam in the sunshine. Now I'm crossing the strait again. Oh, Gilbert, I do hope I'll like Redmond and Kingsport, but I'm sure I won't!"

"Where's all your philosophy gone, Anne?"

"It's all submerged under a great, swamping wave of loneliness and homesickness. I've longed for three years to go to Redmond—and now I'm going—and I wish I weren't! Never mind! I shall be cheerful and philosophical again after I have just one good cry. I *must* have that, 'as a went'—and I'll have to wait until I get into my boardinghouse bed tonight, wherever it may be, before I can have it. Then Anne will be herself again. I wonder if Davy has come out of the closet yet."

It was nine that night when their train reached Kingsport, and they found themselves in the blue-white glare of the crowded station. Anne felt horribly bewildered, but a moment later she was seized by Priscilla Grant, who had come to Kingsport on Saturday.

"Here you are, beloved! And I suppose you're as tired as I was when I got here Saturday night."

"Tired! Priscilla, don't talk of it. I'm tired, and green, and provincial, and only about ten years old. For pity's sake take your poor, broken-down chum to some place where she can hear herself think."

"I'll take you right up to our boardinghouse. I've a cab ready outside."

"It's such a blessing you're here, Prissy. If you weren't I think I should just sit down on my suitcase, here and now, and weep bitter tears. What a comfort one familiar face is in a howling wilderness of strangers!"

"Is that Gilbert Blythe over there, Anne? How he has grown up this past year! He was only a schoolboy when I taught in Carmody. And of course that's Charlie Sloane. *He* hasn't changed—couldn't! He looked just like that when he was born, and he'll look like that when he's eighty. This way, dear. We'll be home in twenty minutes."

"Home!" groaned Anne. "You mean we'll be in some horrible boardinghouse, in a still more horrible hall bedroom, looking out on a dingy back yard."

"It isn't a horrible boardinghouse, Anne-girl. Here's our cab. Hop in—the driver will get your trunk. Oh, yes, the boardinghouse—it's really a very nice place of its kind, as you'll admit tomorrow morning when a good night's sleep has turned your blues rosy pink. It's a big, old-fashioned, gray stone house on St. John Street, just a nice little constitutional from Redmond. It used to be the 'residence' of great folk, but fashion has deserted St. John Street and its houses only dream now of better days. They're so big that people living in them have to take boarders just to fill up. At least, that is the reason our landladies are very anxious to impress on us. They're delicious, Anne—our landladies, I mean."

"How many are there?"

"Two. Miss Hannah Harvey and Miss Ada Harvey. They were born twins about fifty years ago."

"I can't get away from twins, it seems," smiled Anne. "Wherever I go they confront me."

"Oh, they're not twins now, dear. After they reached the age of thirty they never were twins again. Miss Hannah has grown old, not too gracefully, and Miss Ada has stayed thirty, less gracefully still. I don't know whether Miss Hannah can smile or not; I've never caught her at it so far, but Miss Ada smiles all the time and that's worse. However, they're nice, kind souls, and they take two boarders every year because Miss Hannah's economical soul cannot bear to 'waste room space'—not because they need to or have to, as Miss Ada has told me seven times since Saturday night. As for our rooms, I admit they are hall bedrooms, and mine does look out on the back yard. Your room is a front one and looks out on Old St. John's graveyard, which is just across the street."

"That sounds gruesome," shivered Anne. "I think I'd rather have the back yard view."

"Oh, no, you wouldn't. Wait and see. Old St. John's is a darling place. It's been a graveyard so long that it's ceased to be one and has become one of the sights of Kingsport. I was all through it yesterday for a pleasure exertion. There's a big stone wall and a row of enormous trees all around it, and rows of trees all through it, and the queerest old tombstones, with the queerest and quaintest inscriptions. You'll go there to study, Anne, see if you don't. Of course, nobody is ever buried there now. But a few years ago they put up a beautiful monument to the memory of Nova Scotian soldiers who fell in the Crimean War. It is just opposite the entrance gates and there's 'scope for imagination' in it, as you used to say. Here's your trunk at last—and the boys coming to say good night. Must I really shake hands with Charlie Sloane, Anne? His hands are always so cold and fishy-feeling. We must ask them to call occasionally. Miss Hannah gravely told me we could have 'young gentlemen callers' two evenings in the week, if they went away at a reasonable hour; and Miss Ada asked me, smiling, please to be sure they didn't sit on her beautiful cushions. I promised to see to it; but goodness knows where else they *can* sit, unless they sit on the floor, for there are cushions on *everything*. Miss Ada even has an elaborate Battenburg one on top of the piano."

Anne was laughing by this time. Priscilla's gay chatter had the intended effect of cheering her up; homesickness vanished for the time being, and did not even return in full force when she finally found herself alone in her little bedroom. She went to her window and looked out. The street below was dim and quiet. Across it the moon was shining above the trees in Old St. John's, just behind the great dark head of the lion on the monument. Anne wondered if it could have been only that morning that she had left Green Gables. She had the sense of a long passage of time which one day of change and travel gives.

"I suppose that very moon is looking down on Green Gables now," she mused. "But I won't think about it—that way homesickness lies. I'm not even going to have my good cry. I'll put that off to a more convenient season, and just now I'll go calmly and sensibly to bed and to sleep."

Chapter IV
April's Lady

Kingsport is a quaint old town, hearking back to early Colonial days, and wrapped in its ancient atmosphere, as some fine old dame in garments fashioned like those of her youth. Here and there it sprouts out into modernity, but at heart it is still unspoiled; it is full of curious relics, and haloed by the romance of many legends of the past. Once it was a mere frontier station on the fringe of the wilderness, and those were the days when Indians kept life from being monotonous to the settlers. Then it grew to be a bone of contention between the British and the French, being occupied now by the one and now by the other, emerging from each occupation with some fresh scar of battling nations branded on it.

It has in its park a martello tower, autographed all over by tourists, a dismantled old French fort on the hills beyond the town, and several antiquated cannon in its public squares. It has other historic spots also, which may be hunted out by the curious, and none is more quaint and delightful than Old St. John's Cemetery at the very core of the town, with streets of quiet, old-time houses on two sides, and busy, bustling, modern thoroughfares on the others. Every citizen of Kingsport feels a thrill of possessive pride in Old St. John's, for, if he be of any pretensions at all, he has an ancestor buried there, with a queer, crooked slab at his head, or else sprawling protectively over the grave, on which all the main facts of his history are recorded. For the most part no great art or skill was lavished on those old tombstones. The larger number are of roughly chiselled brown or gray native stone, and only in a few cases is there any attempt at ornamentation. Some are adorned with skull and cross-bones, and this grizzly decoration is frequently coupled with a cherub's head. Many are prostrate and in ruins. Into almost all Time's tooth has been gnawing, until some inscriptions have been completely effaced, and others can only be deciphered with difficulty. The graveyard is very full and very bowery, for it is surrounded and intersected by rows of elms and willows, beneath whose shade the sleepers must lie very dreamlessly, forever crooned to by the winds and leaves over them, and quite undisturbed by the clamor of traffic just beyond.

Anne took the first of many rambles in Old St. John's the next afternoon. She and Priscilla had gone to Redmond in the forenoon and registered as students, after which there was nothing more to do that day. The girls gladly made their escape, for it was not exhilarating to be surrounded by crowds of strangers, most of whom had a rather alien appearance, as if not quite sure where they belonged.

The "freshettes" stood about in detached groups of two or three, looking askance at each other; the "freshies," wiser in their day and generation, had banded themselves together on the big staircase of the entrance hall, where they were shouting out glees with all the vigor of youthful lungs, as a species of defiance to their traditional enemies, the Sophomores, a few of whom were prowling loftily about, looking properly disdainful of the "unlicked cubs" on the stairs. Gilbert and Charlie were nowhere to be seen.

"Little did I think the day would ever come when I'd be glad of the sight of a Sloane," said Priscilla, as they crossed the campus, "but I'd welcome Charlie's goggle eyes almost ecstatically. At least, they'd be familiar eyes."

"Oh," sighed Anne. "I can't describe how I felt when I was standing there, waiting my turn to be registered—as insignificant as the teeniest drop in a most enormous bucket. It's bad enough to feel insignificant, but it's unbearable to have it grained into your soul that you will never, can never, be anything but insignificant, and that is how I did feel—as if I were invisible to the naked eye and some of those Sophs might step on me. I knew I would go down to my grave unwept, unhonored and unsung."

"Wait till next year," comforted Priscilla. "Then we'll be able to look as bored and sophisticated as any Sophomore of them all. No doubt it is rather dreadful to feel insignificant; but I think it's better than to feel as big and awkward as I did—as if I were sprawled all over Redmond. That's how I felt—I suppose because I was a good two inches taller than any one else in the crowd. I wasn't afraid a Soph might walk over me; I was afraid they'd take me for an elephant, or an overgrown sample of a potato-fed Islander."

"I suppose the trouble is we can't forgive big Redmond for not being little Queen's," said Anne, gathering about her the shreds of her old cheerful philosophy to cover her nakedness of spirit. "When we left Queen's we knew everybody and had a place of our own. I suppose we have been unconsciously expecting to take life up at Redmond just where we left off at Queen's, and now we feel as if the ground had slipped from under our feet. I'm thankful that neither Mrs. Lynde nor Mrs. Elisha Wright know, or ever will know, my state of mind at present. They would exult in saying 'I told you so,' and be convinced it was the beginning of the end. Whereas it is just the end of the beginning."

"Exactly. That sounds more Anneish. In a little while we'll be acclimated and acquainted, and all will be well. Anne, did you notice the girl who stood alone just outside the door of the coeds' dressing room all the morning—the pretty one with the brown eyes and crooked mouth?"

"Yes, I did. I noticed her particularly because she seemed the only creature there who *looked* as lonely and friendless as I *felt*. I had *you*, but she had no one."

"I think she felt pretty all-by-herselfish, too. Several times I saw her make a motion as if to cross over to us, but she never did it—too shy, I suppose. I wished she would come. If I hadn't felt so much like the aforesaid elephant I'd have gone to her. But I couldn't lumber across that big hall with all those boys howling on the stairs. She was the prettiest freshette I saw today, but probably favor is deceitful and even beauty is vain on your first day at Redmond," concluded Priscilla with a laugh.

"I'm going across to Old St. John's after lunch," said Anne. "I don't know that a graveyard is a very good place to go to get cheered up, but it seems the only get-at-able place where there are trees, and trees I must have. I'll sit on one of those old slabs and shut my eyes and imagine I'm in the Avonlea woods."

Anne did not do that, however, for she found enough of interest in Old St. John's to keep her eyes wide open. They went in by the entrance gates, past the simple, massive, stone arch surmounted by the great lion of England.

> "'*And on Inkerman yet the wild bramble is gory,*
> *And those bleak heights henceforth shall be famous*
> *in story,*'"

quoted Anne, looking at it with a thrill. They found themselves in a dim, cool, green place where winds were fond of purring. Up and down the long grassy aisles they wandered, reading the quaint, voluminous epitaphs, carved in an age that had more leisure than our own.

"'Here lieth the body of Albert Crawford, Esq.,'" read Anne from a worn, gray slab, "'for many years Keeper of His Majesty's Ordnance at Kingsport. He served in the army till the peace of

1763, when he retired from bad health. He was a brave officer, the best of husbands, the best of fathers, the best of friends. He died October 29th, 1792, aged 84 years.' There's an epitaph for you, Prissy. There is certainly some 'scope for imagination' in it. How full such a life must have been of adventure! And as for his personal qualities, I'm sure human eulogy couldn't go further. I wonder if they told him he was all those best things while he was alive."

"Here's another," said Priscilla. "Listen—

'To the memory of Alexander Ross, who died on the 22nd of September, 1840, aged 43 years. This is raised as a tribute of affection by one whom he served so faithfully for 27 years that he was regarded as a friend, deserving the fullest confidence and attachment.'"

"A very good epitaph," commented Anne thoughtfully. "I wouldn't wish a better. We are all servants of some sort, and if the fact that we are faithful can be truthfully inscribed on our tombstones nothing more need be added. Here's a sorrowful little gray stone, Prissy—'to the memory of a favorite child.' And here is another 'erected to the memory of one who is buried elsewhere.' I wonder where that unknown grave is. Really, Pris, the graveyards of today will never be as interesting as this. You were right—I shall come here often. I love it already. I see we're not alone here—there's a girl down at the end of this avenue."

"Yes, and I believe it's the very girl we saw at Redmond this morning. I've been watching her for five minutes. She has started to come up the avenue exactly half a dozen times, and half a dozen times has she turned and gone back. Either she's dreadfully shy or she has got something on her conscience. Let's go and meet her. It's easier to get acquainted in a graveyard than at Redmond, I believe."

They walked down the long grassy arcade towards the stranger, who was sitting on a gray slab under an enormous willow.

She was certainly very pretty, with a vivid, irregular, bewitching type of prettiness. There was a gloss as of brown nuts on her satin-smooth hair and a soft, ripe glow on her round cheeks. Her eyes were big and brown and velvety, under oddly-pointed black brows, and her crooked mouth was rose-red. She wore a smart brown suit, with two very modish little shoes peeping from beneath it; and her hat of dull pink straw, wreathed with golden-brown poppies, had the indefinable, unmistakable air which pertains to the "creation" of an artist in millinery. Priscilla had a sudden stinging consciousness that her own hat had been trimmed by her village store milliner, and Anne wondered uncomfortably if the blouse she had made herself, and which Mrs. Lynde had fitted, looked *very* countrified and home-made besides the stranger's smart attire. For a moment both girls felt like turning back.

But they had already stopped and turned towards the gray slab. It was too late to retreat, for the brown-eyed girl had evidently concluded that they were coming to speak to her. Instantly she sprang up and came forward with outstretched hand and a gay, friendly smile in which there seemed not a shadow of either shyness or burdened conscience.

"Oh, I want to know who you two girls are," she exclaimed eagerly. "I've been *dying* to know. I saw you at Redmond this morning. Say, wasn't it *awful* there? For the time I wished I had stayed home and got married."

Anne and Priscilla both broke into unconstrained laughter at this unexpected conclusion. The brown-eyed girl laughed, too.

"I really did. I *could* have, you know. Come, let's all sit down on this gravestone and get acquainted. It won't be hard. I know we're going to adore each other—I knew it as soon as I saw you at Redmond this morning. I wanted so much to go right over and hug you both."

"Why didn't you?" asked Priscilla.

"Because I simply couldn't make up my mind to do it. I never can make up my mind about anything myself—I'm always afflicted with indecision. Just as soon as I decide to do something I feel in my bones that another course would be the correct one. It's a dreadful misfortune, but I was born that way, and there is no use in blaming me for it, as some people do. So I couldn't make up my mind to go and speak to you, much as I wanted to."

"We thought you were too shy," said Anne.

"No, no, dear. Shyness isn't among the many failings—or virtues—of Philippa Gordon—Phil for short. Do call me Phil right off. Now, what are your handles?"

"She's Priscilla Grant," said Anne, pointing.

"And *she's* Anne Shirley," said Priscilla, pointing in turn.

"And we're from the Island," said both together.

"I hail from Bolingbroke, Nova Scotia," said Philippa.

"Bolingbroke!" exclaimed Anne. "Why, that is where I was born."

"Do you really mean it? Why, that makes you a Bluenose after all."

"No, it doesn't," retorted Anne. "Wasn't it Dan O'Connell who said that if a man was born in a stable it didn't make him a horse? I'm Island to the core."

"Well, I'm glad you were born in Bolingbroke anyway. It makes us kind of neighbors, doesn't it? And I like that, because when I tell you secrets it won't be as if I were telling them to a stranger. I have to tell them. I can't keep secrets—it's no use to try. That's my worst failing—that, and indecision, as aforesaid. Would you believe it?—it took me half an hour to decide which hat to wear when I was coming here—*here*, to a graveyard! At first I inclined to my brown one with the feather; but as soon as I put it on I thought this pink one with the floppy brim would be more becoming. When I got *it* pinned in place I liked the brown one better. At last I put them close together on the bed, shut my eyes, and jabbed with a hat pin. The pin speared the pink one, so I put it on. It is becoming, isn't it? Tell me, what do you think of my looks?"

At this naive demand, made in a perfectly serious tone, Priscilla laughed again. But Anne said, impulsively squeezing Philippa's hand,

"We thought this morning that you were the prettiest girl we saw at Redmond."

Philippa's crooked mouth flashed into a bewitching, crooked smile over very white little teeth.

"I thought that myself," was her next astounding statement, "but I wanted some one else's opinion to bolster mine up. I can't decide even on my own appearance. Just as soon as I've decided that I'm pretty I begin to feel miserably that I'm not. Besides, have a horrible old great-aunt who is always saying to me, with a mournful sigh, 'You were such a pretty baby. It's strange how children change when they grow up.' I adore aunts, but I detest great-aunts. Please tell me quite often that I am pretty, if you don't mind. I feel so much more comfortable when I can believe I'm pretty. And I'll be just as obliging to you if you want me to—I *can* be, with a clear conscience."

"Thanks," laughed Anne, "but Priscilla and I are so firmly convinced of our own good looks that we don't need any assurance about them, so you needn't trouble."

"Oh, you're laughing at me. I know you think I'm abominably vain, but I'm not. There really isn't one spark of vanity in me. And I'm never a bit grudging about paying compliments to other girls when they deserve them. I'm so glad I know you folks. I came up on Saturday and I've nearly died of homesickness ever since. It's a horrible feeling, isn't it? In Bolingbroke I'm an important personage, and in Kingsport I'm just nobody! There were times when I could feel my soul turning a delicate blue. Where do you hang out?"

"Thirty-eight St. John's Street."

"Better and better. Why, I'm just around the corner on Wallace Street. I don't like my boardinghouse, though. It's bleak and lonesome, and my room looks out on such an unholy back yard. It's the ugliest place in the world. As for cats—well, surely *all* the Kingsport cats can't congregate there at night, but half of them must. I adore cats on hearth rugs, snoozing before nice, friendly fires, but cats in back yards at midnight are totally different animals. The first night I was here I cried all night, and so did the cats. You should have seen my nose in the morning. How I wished I had never left home!"

"I don't know how you managed to make up your mind to come to Redmond at all, if you are really such an undecided person," said amused Priscilla.

"Bless your heart, honey, I didn't. It was father who wanted me to come here. His heart was set on it—why, I don't know. It seems perfectly ridiculous to think of me studying for a B.A. degree, doesn't it? Not but what I can do it, all right. I have heaps of brains."

"Oh!" said Priscilla vaguely.

"Yes. But it's such hard work to use them. And B.A.'s are such learned, dignified, wise, solemn creatures—they must be. No, *I* didn't want to come to Redmond. I did it just to oblige father. He *is* such a duck. Besides, I knew if I stayed home I'd have to get married. Mother wanted that—wanted it decidedly. Mother has plenty of decision. But I really hated the thought of being married for a few years yet. I want to have heaps of fun before I settle down. And, ridiculous as the idea of my being a B.A. is, the idea of my being an old married woman is still more absurd, isn't it? I'm only eighteen. No, I concluded I would rather come to Redmond than be married. Besides, how could I ever have made up my mind which man to marry?"

"Were there so many?" laughed Anne.

"Heaps. The boys like me awfully—they really do. But there were only two that mattered. The rest were all too young and too poor. I must marry a rich man, you know."

"Why must you?"

"Honey, you couldn't imagine *me* being a poor man's wife, could you? I can't do a single useful thing, and I am *very* extravagant. Oh, no, my husband must have heaps of money. So that narrowed them down to two. But I couldn't decide between two any easier than between two hundred. I knew perfectly well that whichever one I chose I'd regret all my life that I hadn't married the other."

"Didn't you—love—either of them?" asked Anne, a little hesitatingly. It was not easy for her to speak to a stranger of the great mystery and transformation of life.

"Goodness, no. *I* couldn't love anybody. It isn't in me. Besides I wouldn't want to. Being in love makes you a perfect slave, *I* think. And it would give a man such power to hurt you. I'd be afraid. No, no, Alec and Alonzo are two dear boys, and I like them both so much that I really don't know which I like the better. That is the trouble. Alec is the best looking, of course, and I simply couldn't marry a man who wasn't handsome. He is good-tempered too, and has lovely, curly, black hair. He's rather too perfect—I don't believe I'd like a perfect husband—somebody I could never find fault with."

"Then why not marry Alonzo?" asked Priscilla gravely.

"Think of marrying a name like Alonzo!" said Phil dolefully. "I don't believe I could endure it. But he has a classic nose, and it *would* be a comfort to have a nose in the family that could be depended on. I can't depend on mine. So far, it takes after the Gordon pattern, but I'm so afraid it will develop Byrne tendencies as I grow older. I examine it every day anxiously to make sure it's still Gordon. Mother was a Byrne and has the Byrne nose in the Byrnest degree. Wait till you see it. I adore nice noses. Your nose is awfully nice, Anne Shirley. Alonzo's nose nearly turned the balance in his favor. But *Alonzo!* No, I couldn't decide. If I could have done as I did with the hats—stood them both up together, shut my eyes, and jabbed with a hatpin—it would have been quite easy."

"What did Alec and Alonzo feel like when you came away?" queried Priscilla.

"Oh, they still have hope. I told them they'd have to wait till I could make up my mind. They're quite willing to wait. They both worship me, you know. Meanwhile, I intend to have a good time. I expect I shall have heaps of beaux at Redmond. I can't be happy unless I have, you know. But don't you think the freshmen are fearfully homely? I saw only one really handsome fellow among them. He went away before you came. I heard his chum call him Gilbert. His chum had eyes that stuck out *that far*. But you're not going yet, girls? Don't go yet."

"I think we must," said Anne, rather coldly. "It's getting late, and I've some work to do."

"But you'll both come to see me, won't you?" asked Philippa, getting up and putting an arm around each. "And let me come to see you. I want to be chummy with you. I've taken such a fancy to you both. And I haven't quite disgusted you with my frivolity, have I?"

"Not quite," laughed Anne, responding to Phil's squeeze, with a return of cordiality.

"Because I'm not half so silly as I seem on the surface, you know. You just accept Philippa Gordon, as the Lord made her, with all her faults, and I believe you'll come to like her. Isn't this graveyard a sweet place? I'd love to be buried here. Here's a grave I didn't see before—this one in the iron railing—oh, girls, look, see—the stone says it's the grave of a middy who was killed in the fight between the Shannon and the Chesapeake. Just fancy!"

Anne paused by the railing and looked at the worn stone, her pulses thrilling with sudden excitement. The old graveyard, with its over-arching trees and long aisles of shadows, faded from her sight. Instead, she saw the Kingsport Harbor of nearly a century agone. Out of the mist came slowly a great frigate, brilliant with "the meteor flag of England." Behind her was another, with a still, heroic form, wrapped in his own starry flag, lying on the quarter deck—the gallant Lawrence. Time's finger had turned back his pages, and that was the Shannon sailing triumphant up the bay with the Chesapeake as her prize.

"Come back, Anne Shirley—come back," laughed Philippa, pulling her arm. "You're a hundred years away from us. Come back."

Anne came back with a sigh; her eyes were shining softly.

"I've always loved that old story," she said, "and although the English won that victory, I think it was because of the brave, defeated commander I love it. This grave seems to bring it so near and make it so real. This poor little middy was only eighteen. He 'died of desperate wounds received in gallant action'—so reads his epitaph. It is such as a soldier might wish for."

Before she turned away, Anne unpinned the little cluster of purple pansies she wore and dropped it softly on the grave of the boy who had perished in the great sea-duel.

"Well, what do you think of our new friend?" asked Priscilla, when Phil had left them.

"I like her. There is something very lovable about her, in spite of all her nonsense. I believe, as she says herself, that she isn't half as silly as she sounds. She's a dear, kissable baby—and I don't know that she'll ever really grow up."

"I like her, too," said Priscilla, decidedly. "She talks as much about boys as Ruby Gillis does. But it always enrages or sickens me to hear Ruby, whereas I just wanted to laugh good-naturedly at Phil. Now, what is the why of that?"

"There is a difference," said Anne meditatively. "I think it's because Ruby is really so *conscious* of boys. She plays at love and love-making. Besides, you feel, when she is boasting of her beaux that she is doing it to rub it well into you that you haven't half so many. Now, when Phil talks of her beaux it sounds as if she was just speaking of chums. She really looks upon boys as good comrades, and she is pleased when she has dozens of them tagging round, simply because she likes to be popular and to be thought popular. Even Alex and Alonzo—I'll never be able to think of those two names separately after this—are to her just two playfellows who want her to play with them all their lives. I'm glad we met her, and I'm glad we went to Old St. John's. I believe I've put forth a tiny soul-root into Kingsport soil this afternoon. I hope so. I hate to feel transplanted."

Chapter V
Letters from Home

For the next three weeks Anne and Priscilla continued to feel as strangers in a strange land. Then, suddenly, everything seemed to fall into focus—Redmond, professors, classes, students, studies, social doings. Life became homogeneous again, instead of being made up of detached fragments. The Freshmen, instead of being a collection of unrelated individuals, found themselves a class, with a class spirit, a class yell, class interests, class antipathies and class ambitions. They won the day in the annual "Arts Rush" against the Sophomores, and thereby gained the respect of all the classes, and an enormous, confidence-giving opinion of themselves. For three years the Sophomores had won in the "rush"; that the victory of this year perched upon the Freshmen's banner was attributed to the strategic generalship of Gilbert Blythe, who marshalled the campaign and originated certain new tactics, which demoralized the Sophs and swept the Freshmen to triumph. As a reward of merit he was elected president of the Freshman Class, a position of honor and responsibility—from a Fresh point of view, at least—coveted by many. He was also invited to join the "Lambs"—Redmondese for Lamba Theta—a compliment rarely paid to a Freshman. As a preparatory initiation ordeal he had to parade the principal business streets of Kingsport for a whole day wearing a sunbonnet and a voluminous kitchen apron of gaudily flowered calico.

This he did cheerfully, doffing his sunbonnet with courtly grace when he met ladies of his acquaintance. Charlie Sloane, who had not been asked to join the Lambs, told Anne he did not see how Blythe could do it, and *he*, for his part, could never humiliate himself so.

"Fancy Charlie Sloane in a 'caliker' apron and a 'sunbunnit,'" giggled Priscilla. "He'd look exactly like his old Grandmother Sloane. Gilbert, now, looked as much like a man in them as in his own proper habiliments."

Anne and Priscilla found themselves in the thick of the social life of Redmond. That this came about so speedily was due in great measure to Philippa Gordon. Philippa was the daughter of a rich and well-known man, and belonged to an old and exclusive "Bluenose" family. This, combined with her beauty and charm—a charm acknowledged by all who met her—promptly opened the gates of all cliques, clubs and classes in Redmond to her; and where she went Anne and Priscilla went, too. Phil "adored" Anne and Priscilla, especially Anne. She was a loyal little soul, crystal-free from any form of snobbishness. "Love me, love my friends" seemed to be her unconscious motto. Without effort, she took them with her into her ever widening circle of acquaintanceship, and the two Avonlea girls found their social pathway at Redmond made very easy and pleasant for them, to the envy and wonderment of the other freshettes, who, lacking Philippa's sponsorship, were doomed to remain rather on the fringe of things during their first college year.

To Anne and Priscilla, with their more serious views of life, Phil remained the amusing, lovable baby she had seemed on their first meeting. Yet, as she said herself, she had "heaps" of brains. When or where she found time to study was a mystery, for she seemed always in demand for some kind of "fun," and her home evenings were crowded with callers. She had all the "beaux" that heart could desire, for nine-tenths of the Freshmen and a big fraction of all the other classes were rivals for her smiles. She was naively delighted over this, and gleefully recounted each new conquest to Anne and Priscilla, with comments that might have made the unlucky lover's ears burn fiercely.

"Alec and Alonzo don't seem to have any serious rival yet," remarked Anne, teasingly.

"Not one," agreed Philippa. "I write them both every week and tell them all about my young men here. I'm sure it must amuse them. But, of course, the one I like best I can't get. Gilbert Blythe won't take any notice of me, except to look at me as if I were a nice little kitten he'd like to pat. Too well I know the reason. I owe you a grudge, Queen Anne. I really ought to hate you and instead I love you madly, and I'm miserable if I don't see you every day. You're different from any girl I ever knew before. When you look at me in a certain way I feel what an insignificant, frivolous little beast I am, and I long to be better and wiser and stronger. And then I make good resolutions; but the first nice-looking mannie who comes my way knocks them all out of my head. Isn't college life magnificent? It's so funny to think I hated it that first day. But if I hadn't I might never got really acquainted with you. Anne, please tell me over again that you like me a little bit. I yearn to hear it."

"I like you a big bit—and I think you're a dear, sweet, adorable, velvety, clawless, little—kitten," laughed Anne, "but I don't see when you ever get time to learn your lessons."

Phil must have found time for she held her own in every class of her year. Even the grumpy old professor of Mathematics, who detested coeds, and had bitterly opposed their admission to Redmond, couldn't floor her. She led the freshettes everywhere, except in English, where Anne Shirley left her far behind. Anne herself found the studies of her Freshman year very easy, thanks in great part to the steady work she and Gilbert had put in during those two past years in Avonlea. This left her more time for a social life which she thoroughly enjoyed. But never for a moment did she forget Avonlea and the friends there. To her, the happiest moments in each week were those in which letters came from home. It was not until she had got her first letters that she began to think she could ever like Kingsport or feel at home there. Before they came, Avonlea had seemed thousands of miles away; those letters brought it near and linked the old life to the new so closely that they began to seem one and the same, instead of two hopelessly segregated existences. The first batch contained six letters, from Jane Andrews, Ruby Gillis, Diana Barry, Marilla, Mrs. Lynde and Davy. Jane's was a copperplate production, with every "t" nicely crossed and every "i" precisely dotted, and not an interesting sentence in it. She never mentioned the school, concerning which Anne was avid to hear; she never answered one of the questions Anne had asked in her letter. But she told Anne how many yards of lace she had recently crocheted, and the kind of weather they were having in Avonlea, and how she intended to have her new dress made, and the way she felt when her head ached. Ruby Gillis wrote a gushing epistle deploring Anne's absence, assuring her she was horribly missed in everything, asking what the Redmond "fellows" were like, and filling the rest with accounts of her own harrowing experiences with her numerous admirers. It was a silly, harmless letter, and Anne would have laughed over it had it not been for the postscript. "Gilbert seems to be enjoying Redmond, judging from his letters," wrote Ruby. "I don't think Charlie is so stuck on it."

So Gilbert was writing to Ruby! Very well. He had a perfect right to, of course. Only—!! Anne did not know that Ruby had written the first letter and that Gilbert had answered it from mere courtesy. She tossed Ruby's letter aside contemptuously. But it took all Diana's breezy, newsy, delightful epistle to banish the sting of Ruby's postscript. Diana's letter contained a little too much Fred, but was otherwise crowded and crossed with items of interest, and Anne almost felt herself back in Avonlea while reading it. Marilla's was a rather prim and colorless epistle, severely innocent of gossip or emotion. Yet somehow it conveyed to Anne a whiff of the wholesome, simple life at Green Gables, with its savor of ancient peace, and the steadfast abiding love that was there for her. Mrs. Lynde's letter was full of church news. Having broken up housekeeping, Mrs. Lynde had more time than ever to devote to church affairs and had flung herself into them heart and soul. She was at present much worked up over the poor "supplies" they were having in the vacant Avonlea pulpit.

"I don't believe any but fools enter the ministry nowadays," she wrote bitterly. "Such candidates as they have sent us, and such stuff as they preach! Half of it ain't true, and, what's worse, it ain't sound doctrine. The one we have now is the worst of the lot. He mostly takes a text and preaches about something else. And he says he doesn't believe all the heathen will be eternally lost. The idea! If they won't all the money we've been giving to Foreign Missions will be clean wasted, that's what! Last Sunday night he announced that next Sunday he'd preach on the axehead that swam. I think he'd better confine himself to the Bible and leave sensational subjects alone. Things have come to a pretty pass if a minister can't find enough in Holy Writ to preach about, that's what. What church do you attend, Anne? I hope you go regularly. People are apt to get so careless about church-going away from home, and I understand college students are great sinners in this respect. I'm told many of them actually study their lessons on Sunday. I hope you'll never sink that low, Anne. Remember how you were brought up. And be very careful what friends you make. You never know what sort of creatures are in them colleges. Outwardly they may be as whited sepulchers and inwardly as ravening wolves, that's what. You'd better not have anything to say to any young man who isn't from the Island.

"I forgot to tell you what happened the day the minister called here. It was the funniest thing I ever saw. I said to Marilla, 'If Anne had been here wouldn't she have had a laugh?' Even Marilla laughed. You know he's a very short, fat little man with bow legs. Well, that old pig of Mr. Harrison's—the big, tall one—had wandered over here that day again and broke into the yard, and it got into the back porch, unbeknowns to us, and it was there when the minister appeared in the doorway. It made one wild bolt to get out, but there was nowhere to bolt to except between them bow legs. So there it went, and, being as it was so big and the minister so little, it took him clean off his feet and carried him away. His hat went one way and his cane another, just as Marilla and I got to the door. I'll never forget the look of him. And that poor pig was near scared to death. I'll never be able to read that account in the Bible of the swine that rushed madly down the steep place into the sea without seeing Mr. Harrison's pig careering down the hill with that minister. I guess the pig thought he had the Old Boy on his back instead of inside of him. I was thankful the twins weren't about. It wouldn't have been the right thing for them to have seen a minister in such an undignified predicament. Just before they got to the brook the minister jumped off or fell off. The pig rushed through the brook like mad and up through the woods. Marilla and I run down and helped the minister get up and brush his coat. He wasn't hurt, but he was mad. He seemed to hold Marilla and me responsible for it all, though we told him the pig didn't belong to us, and had been pestering us all summer. Besides, what did he come to the back door for? You'd never have caught Mr. Allan doing that. It'll be a long time before we get a man like Mr. Allan. But it's an ill wind that blows no good. We've never seen hoof or hair of that pig since, and it's my belief we never will.

"Things is pretty quiet in Avonlea. I don't find Green Gables as lonesome as I expected. I think I'll start another cotton warp quilt this winter. Mrs. Silas Sloane has a handsome new apple-leaf pattern.

"When I feel that I must have some excitement I read the murder trials in that Boston paper my niece sends me. I never used to do it, but they're real interesting. The States must be an awful place. I hope you'll never go there, Anne. But the way girls roam over the earth now is something terrible. It always makes me think of Satan in the Book of Job, going to and fro and walking up and down. I don't believe the Lord ever intended it, that's what.

"Davy has been pretty good since you went away. One day he was bad and Marilla punished him by making him wear Dora's apron all day, and then he went and cut all Dora's aprons up. I spanked him for that and then he went and chased my rooster to death.

"The MacPhersons have moved down to my place. She's a great housekeeper and very particular. She's rooted all my June lilies up because she says they make a garden look so untidy. Thomas set them lilies out when we were married. Her husband seems a nice sort of a man, but she can't get over being an old maid, that's what.

"Don't study too hard, and be sure and put your winter underclothes on as soon as the weather gets cool. Marilla worries a lot about you, but I tell her you've got a lot more sense than I ever thought you would have at one time, and that you'll be all right."

Davy's letter plunged into a grievance at the start.

"Dear anne, please write and tell marilla not to tie me to the rale of the bridge when I go fishing the boys make fun of me when she does. Its awful lonesome here without you but grate fun in school. Jane andrews is crosser than you. I scared mrs. lynde with a jacky lantern last nite. She was offel mad and she was mad cause I chased her old rooster round the yard till he fell down ded. I didn't mean to make him fall down ded. What made him die, anne, I want to know. mrs. lynde threw him into the pig pen she mite of sold him to mr. blair. mr. blair is giving 50 sense apeace for good ded roosters now. I herd mrs. lynde asking the minister to pray for her. What did she do that was so bad, anne, I want to know. I've got a kite with a magnificent tail, anne. Milty bolter told me a grate story in school yesterday. it is troo. old Joe Mosey and Leon were playing cards one nite last week in the woods. The cards were on a stump and a big black man bigger than the trees come along and grabbed the cards and the stump and disapered with a noys like thunder. Ill bet they were skared. Milty says the black man was the old harry. was he, anne, I want to know. Mr. kimball over at spenservale is very sick and will have to go to the hospitable. please excuse me while I ask marilla if thats spelled rite. Marilla says its the silem he has to go to not the other place. He thinks he has a snake inside of him. whats it like to have a snake inside of you, anne. I want to know. mrs. lawrence bell is sick to. mrs. lynde says that all that is the matter with her is that she thinks too much about her insides."

"I wonder," said Anne, as she folded up her letters, "what Mrs. Lynde would think of Philippa."

Chapter VI
In the Park

"What are you going to do with yourselves today, girls?" asked Philippa, popping into Anne's room one Saturday afternoon.

"We are going for a walk in the park," answered Anne. "I ought to stay in and finish my blouse. But I couldn't sew on a day like this. There's something in the air that gets into my blood and makes a sort of glory in my soul. My fingers would twitch and I'd sew a crooked seam. So it's ho for the park and the pines."

"Does 'we' include any one but yourself and Priscilla?"

"Yes, it includes Gilbert and Charlie, and we'll be very glad if it will include you, also."

"But," said Philippa dolefully, "if I go I'll have to be gooseberry, and that will be a new experience for Philippa Gordon."

"Well, new experiences are broadening. Come along, and you'll be able to sympathize with all poor souls who have to play gooseberry often. But where are all the victims?"

"Oh, I was tired of them all and simply couldn't be bothered with any of them today. Besides, I've been feeling a little blue—just a pale, elusive azure. It isn't serious enough for anything darker. I wrote Alec and Alonzo last week. I put the letters into envelopes and addressed them, but I didn't seal them up. That evening something funny happened. That is, Alec would think it funny, but Alonzo wouldn't be likely to. I was in a hurry, so I snatched Alec's letter—as I thought—out of the envelope and scribbled down a postscript. Then I mailed both letters. I got Alonzo's reply this morning. Girls, I had put that postscript to his letter and he was furious. Of course he'll get over it—and I don't care if he doesn't—but it spoiled my day. So I thought I'd come to you darlings to get cheered up. After the football season opens I won't have any spare Saturday afternoons. I adore football. I've got the most gorgeous cap and sweater striped in Redmond colors to wear to the games. To be sure, a little way off I'll look like a walking barber's pole. Do you know that that Gilbert of yours has been elected Captain of the Freshman football team?"

"Yes, he told us so last evening," said Priscilla, seeing that outraged Anne would not answer. "He and Charlie were down. We knew they were coming, so we painstakingly put out of sight or out of reach all Miss Ada's cushions. That very elaborate one with the raised embroidery I dropped on the floor in the corner behind the chair it was on. I thought it would be safe there. But would you believe it? Charlie Sloane made for that chair, noticed the cushion behind it, solemnly fished it up, and sat on it the whole evening. Such a wreck of a cushion as it was! Poor Miss Ada asked me today, still smiling, but oh, so reproachfully, why I had allowed it to be sat upon. I told her I hadn't—that it was a matter of predestination coupled with inveterate Sloanishness and I wasn't a match for both combined."

"Miss Ada's cushions are really getting on my nerves," said Anne. "She finished two new ones last week, stuffed and embroidered within an inch of their lives. There being absolutely no other cushionless place to put them she stood them up against the wall on the stair landing. They topple over half the time and if we come up or down the stairs in the dark we fall over them. Last Sunday, when Dr. Davis prayed for all those exposed to the perils of the sea, I added in thought 'and for all those who live in houses where cushions are loved not wisely but too well!' There! we're ready, and I see the boys coming through Old St. John's.

Do you cast in your lot with us, Phil?"

"I'll go, if I can walk with Priscilla and Charlie. That will be a bearable degree of gooseberry. That Gilbert of yours is a darling, Anne, but why does he go around so much with Goggle-eyes?"

Anne stiffened. She had no great liking for Charlie Sloane; but he was of Avonlea, so no outsider had any business to laugh at him.

"Charlie and Gilbert have always been friends," she said coldly. "Charlie is a nice boy. He's not to blame for his eyes."

"Don't tell me that! He is! He must have done something dreadful in a previous existence to be punished with such eyes. Pris and I are going to have such sport with him this afternoon. We'll make fun of him to his face and he'll never know it."

Doubtless, "the abandoned P's," as Anne called them, did carry out their amiable intentions. But Sloane was blissfully ignorant; he thought he was quite a fine fellow to be walking with two such coeds, especially Philippa Gordon, the class beauty and belle. It must surely impress Anne. She would see that some people appreciated him at his real value.

Gilbert and Anne loitered a little behind the others, enjoying the calm, still beauty of the autumn afternoon under the pines of the park, on the road that climbed and twisted round the harbor shore.

"The silence here is like a prayer, isn't it?" said Anne, her face upturned to the shining sky. "How I love the pines! They seem to strike their roots deep into the romance of all the ages. It is so comforting to creep away now and then for a good talk with them. I always feel so happy out here."

"'And so in mountain solitudes o'ertaken
As by some spell divine,
Their cares drop from them like the needles shaken
From out the gusty pine,'"

quoted Gilbert.

"They make our little ambitions seem rather petty, don't they, Anne?"

"I think, if ever any great sorrow came to me, I would come to the pines for comfort," said Anne dreamily.

"I hope no great sorrow ever will come to you, Anne," said Gilbert, who could not connect the idea of sorrow with the vivid, joyous creature beside him, unwitting that those who can soar to the highest heights can also plunge to the deepest depths, and that the natures which enjoy most keenly are those which also suffer most sharply.

"But there must—sometime," mused Anne. "Life seems like a cup of glory held to my lips just now. But there must be some bitterness in it—there is in every cup. I shall taste mine some day. Well, I hope I shall be strong and brave to meet it. And I hope it won't be through my own fault that it will come. Do you remember what Dr. Davis said last Sunday evening—that the sorrows God sent us brought comfort and strength with them, while the sorrows we brought on ourselves, through folly or wickedness, were by far the hardest to bear? But we mustn't talk of sorrow on an afternoon like this. It's meant for the sheer joy of living, isn't it?"

"If I had my way I'd shut everything out of your life but happiness and pleasure, Anne," said Gilbert in the tone that meant "danger ahead."

"Then you would be very unwise," rejoined Anne hastily. "I'm sure no life can be properly developed and rounded out without some trial and sorrow—though I suppose it is only when we are pretty comfortable that we admit it. Come—the others have got to the pavilion and are beckoning to us."

They all sat down in the little pavilion to watch an autumn sunset of deep red fire and pallid gold. To their left lay Kingsport, its roofs and spires dim in their shroud of violet smoke. To their right lay the harbor, taking on tints of rose and copper as it stretched out into the sunset. Before them the water shimmered, satin smooth and silver gray, and beyond, clean shaven William's Island loomed out of the mist, guarding the town like a sturdy bulldog. Its lighthouse beacon flared through the mist like a baleful star, and was answered by another in the far horizon.

"Did you ever see such a strong-looking place?" asked Philippa. "I don't want William's Island especially, but I'm sure I couldn't get it if I did. Look at that sentry on the summit of the fort, right beside the flag. Doesn't he look as if he had stepped out of a romance?"

"Speaking of romance," said Priscilla, "we've been looking for heather—but, of course, we couldn't find any. It's too late in the season, I suppose."

"Heather!" exclaimed Anne. "Heather doesn't grow in America, does it?"

"There are just two patches of it in the whole continent," said Phil, "one right here in the park, and one somewhere else in Nova Scotia, I forget where. The famous Highland Regiment, the Black Watch, camped here one year, and, when the men shook out the straw of their beds in the spring, some seeds of heather took root."

"Oh, how delightful!" said enchanted Anne.

"Let's go home around by Spofford Avenue," suggested Gilbert. "We can see all 'the handsome houses where the wealthy nobles dwell.' Spofford Avenue is the finest residential street in Kingsport. Nobody can build on it unless he's a millionaire."

"Oh, do," said Phil. "There's a perfectly killing little place I want to show you, Anne. *it* wasn't built by a millionaire. It's the first place after you leave the park, and must have grown while Spofford Avenue was still a country road. It *did* grow—it wasn't built! I don't care for the houses on the Avenue. They're too brand new and plateglassy. But this little spot is a dream—and its name—but wait till you see it."

They saw it as they walked up the pine-fringed hill from the park. Just on the crest, where Spofford Avenue petered out into a plain road, was a little white frame house with groups of pines on either side of it, stretching their arms protectingly over its low roof. It was covered with red and gold vines, through which its green-shuttered windows peeped. Before it was a tiny garden, surrounded by a low stone wall. October though it was, the garden was still very sweet with dear, old-fashioned, unworldly flowers and shrubs—sweet may, southern-wood, lemon verbena, alyssum, petunias, marigolds and chrysanthemums. A tiny brick wall, in herring-bone pattern, led from the gate to the front porch. The whole place might have been transplanted from some remote country village; yet there was something about it that made its nearest neighbor, the big lawn-encircled palace of a tobacco king, look exceedingly crude and showy and ill-bred by contrast. As Phil said, it was the difference between being born and being made.

"It's the dearest place I ever saw," said Anne delightedly. "It gives me one of my old, delightful funny aches. It's dearer and quainter than even Miss Lavendar's stone house."

"It's the name I want you to notice especially," said Phil. "Look—in white letters, around the archway over the gate. 'Patty's Place.' Isn't that killing? Especially on this Avenue of Pinehursts and Elmwolds and Cedarcrofts? 'Patty's Place,' if you please! I adore it."

"Have you any idea who Patty is?" asked Priscilla.

"Patty Spofford is the name of the old lady who owns it, I've discovered. She lives there with her niece, and they've lived there for hundreds of years, more or less—maybe a little less, Anne. Exaggeration is merely a flight of poetic fancy. I understand that wealthy folk have tried to buy the lot time and again—it's really worth a small fortune now, you know—but 'Patty' won't sell upon any consideration. And there's an apple orchard behind the house in place of a back yard—you'll see it when we get a little past—a real apple orchard on Spofford Avenue!"

"I'm going to dream about 'Patty's Place' tonight," said Anne. "Why, I feel as if I belonged to it. I wonder if, by any chance, we'll ever see the inside of it."

"It isn't likely," said Priscilla.

Anne smiled mysteriously.

"No, it isn't likely. But I believe it will happen. I have a queer, creepy, crawly feeling—you can call it a presentiment, if you like—that 'Patty's Place' and I are going to be better acquainted yet."

Chapter VII
Home Again

Those first three weeks at Redmond had seemed long; but the rest of the term flew by on wings of wind. Before they realized it the Redmond students found themselves in the grind of Christmas examinations, emerging therefrom more or less triumphantly. The honor of leading in the Freshman classes fluctuated between Anne, Gilbert and Philippa; Priscilla did very well; Charlie Sloane scraped through respectably, and comported himself as complacently as if he had led in everything.

"I can't really believe that this time tomorrow I'll be in Green Gables," said Anne on the night before departure. "But I shall be. And you, Phil, will be in Bolingbroke with Alec and Alonzo."

"I'm longing to see them," admitted Phil, between the chocolate she was nibbling. "They really are such dear boys, you know. There's to be no end of dances and drives and general jamborees. I shall never forgive you, Queen Anne, for not coming home with me for the holidays."

"'Never' means three days with you, Phil. It was dear of you to ask me—and I'd love to go to Bolingbroke some day. But I can't go this year—I *must* go home. You don't know how my heart longs for it."

"You won't have much of a time," said Phil scornfully. "There'll be one or two quilting parties, I suppose; and all the old gossips will talk you over to your face and behind your back. You'll die of lonesomeness, child."

"In Avonlea?" said Anne, highly amused.

"Now, if you'd come with me you'd have a perfectly gorgeous time. Bolingbroke would go wild over you, Queen Anne—your hair and your style and, oh, everything! You're so *different*. You'd be such a success—and I would bask in reflected glory—'not the rose but near the rose.' Do come, after all, Anne."

"Your picture of social triumphs is quite fascinating, Phil, but I'll paint one to offset it. I'm going home to an old country farmhouse, once green, rather faded now, set among leafless apple orchards. There is a brook below and a December fir wood beyond, where I've heard harps swept by the fingers of rain and wind. There is a pond nearby that will be gray and brooding now. There will be two oldish ladies in the house, one tall and thin, one short and fat; and there will be two twins, one a perfect model, the other what Mrs. Lynde calls a 'holy terror.' There will be a little room upstairs over the porch, where old dreams hang thick, and a big, fat, glorious feather bed which will almost seem the height of luxury after a boardinghouse mattress. How do you like my picture, Phil?"

"It seems a very dull one," said Phil, with a grimace.

"Oh, but I've left out the transforming thing," said Anne softly. "There'll be love there, Phil—faithful, tender love, such as I'll never find anywhere else in the world—love that's waiting for me. That makes my picture a masterpiece, doesn't it, even if the colors are not very brilliant?"

Phil silently got up, tossed her box of chocolates away, went up to Anne, and put her arms about her.

"Anne, I wish I was like you," she said soberly.

Diana met Anne at the Carmody station the next night, and they drove home together under silent, star-sown depths of sky. Green Gables had a very festal appearance as they drove up the lane. There was a light in every window, the glow breaking out through the darkness like flame-red blossoms swung against the dark background of the Haunted Wood. And in the yard was a brave bonfire with two gay little figures dancing around it, one of which gave an unearthly yell as the buggy turned in under the poplars.

"Davy means that for an Indian war-whoop," said Diana. "Mr. Harrison's hired boy taught it to him, and he's been practicing it up to welcome you with. Mrs. Lynde says it has worn her nerves to a frazzle. He creeps up behind her, you know, and then lets go. He was determined to have a bonfire for you, too. He's been piling up branches for a fortnight and pestering Marilla to be let pour some kerosene oil over it before setting it on fire. I guess she did, by the smell, though Mrs. Lynde said up to the last that Davy would blow himself and everybody else up if he was let."

Anne was out of the buggy by this time, and Davy was rapturously hugging her knees, while even Dora was clinging to her hand.

"Isn't that a bully bonfire, Anne? Just let me show you how to poke it—see the sparks? I did it for you, Anne, 'cause I was so glad you were coming home."

The kitchen door opened and Marilla's spare form darkened against the inner light. She preferred to meet Anne in the shadows, for she was horribly afraid that she was going to cry with joy—she, stern, repressed Marilla, who thought all display of deep emotion unseemly. Mrs. Lynde was behind her, sonsy, kindly, matronly, as of yore. The love that Anne had told Phil was waiting for her surrounded her and enfolded her with its blessing and its sweetness. Nothing, after all, could compare with old ties, old friends, and old Green Gables! How starry Anne's eyes were as they sat down to the loaded supper table, how pink her cheeks, how silver-clear her laughter! And Diana was going to stay all night, too. How like the dear old times it was! And the rose-bud tea-set graced the table! With Marilla the force of nature could no further go.

"I suppose you and Diana will now proceed to talk all night," said Marilla sarcastically, as the girls went upstairs. Marilla was always sarcastic after any self-betrayal.

"Yes," agreed Anne gaily, "but I'm going to put Davy to bed first. He insists on that."

"You bet," said Davy, as they went along the hall. "I want somebody to say my prayers to again. It's no fun saying them alone."

"You don't say them alone, Davy. God is always with you to hear you."

"Well, I can't see Him," objected Davy. "I want to pray to somebody I can see, but I *won't* say them to Mrs. Lynde or Marilla, there now!"

Nevertheless, when Davy was garbed in his gray flannel nighty, he did not seem in a hurry to begin. He stood before Anne, shuffling one bare foot over the other, and looked undecided.

"Come, dear, kneel down," said Anne.

Davy came and buried his head in Anne's lap, but he did not kneel down.

"Anne," he said in a muffled voice. "I don't feel like praying after all. I haven't felt like it for a week now. I—I *didnt't* pray last night nor the night before."

"Why not, Davy?" asked Anne gently.

"You—you won't be mad if I tell you?" implored Davy.

Anne lifted the little gray-flannelled body on her knee and cuddled his head on her arm.

"Do I ever get 'mad' when you tell me things, Davy?"

"No-o-o, you never do. But you get sorry, and that's worse. You'll be awful sorry when I tell you this, Anne—and you'll be 'shamed of me, I s'pose."

"Have you done something naughty, Davy, and is that why you can't say your prayers?"

"No, I haven't done anything naughty—yet. But I want to do it."

"What is it, Davy?"

"I—I want to say a bad word, Anne," blurted out Davy, with a desperate effort. "I heard Mr. Harrison's hired boy say it one day last week, and ever since I've been wanting to say it *all* the time—even when I'm saying my prayers."

"Say it then, Davy."

Davy lifted his flushed face in amazement.

"But, Anne, it's an *awful* bad word."

"*Say it!*"

Davy gave her another incredulous look, then in a low voice he said the dreadful word. The next minute his face was burrowing against her.

"Oh, Anne, I'll never say it again—never. I'll never *want* to say it again. I knew it was bad, but I didn't s'pose it was so—so—I didn't s'pose it was like *that*."

"No, I don't think you'll ever want to say it again, Davy—or think it, either. And I wouldn't go about much with Mr. Harrison's hired boy if I were you."

"He can make bully war-whoops," said Davy a little regretfully.

"But you don't want your mind filled with bad words, do you, Davy—words that will poison it and drive out all that is good and manly?"

"No," said Davy, owl-eyed with introspection.

"Then don't go with those people who use them. And now do you feel as if you could say your prayers, Davy?"

"Oh, yes," said Davy, eagerly wriggling down on his knees, "I can say them now all right. I ain't scared now to say 'if I should die before I wake,' like I was when I was wanting to say that word."

Probably Anne and Diana did empty out their souls to each other that night, but no record of their confidences has been preserved. They both looked as fresh and bright-eyed at breakfast as only youth can look after unlawful hours of revelry and confession. There had been no snow up to this time, but as Diana crossed the old log bridge on her homeward way the white flakes were beginning to flutter down over the fields and woods, russet and gray in their dreamless sleep. Soon the far-away slopes and hills were dim and wraith-like through their gauzy scarfing, as if pale autumn had flung a misty bridal veil over her hair and was waiting for her wintry bridegroom. So they had a white Christmas after all, and a very pleasant day it was. In the forenoon letters and gifts came from Miss Lavendar and Paul; Anne opened them in the cheerful Green Gables kitchen, which was filled with what Davy, sniffing in ecstasy, called "pretty smells."

"Miss Lavendar and Mr. Irving are settled in their new home now," reported Anne. "I am sure Miss Lavendar is perfectly happy—I know it by the general tone of her letter—but there's a note from Charlotta the Fourth. She doesn't like Boston at all, and she is fearfully homesick. Miss Lavendar wants me to go through to Echo Lodge some day while I'm home and light a fire to air it, and see that the cushions aren't getting moldy. I think I'll get Diana to go over with me next week, and we can spend the evening with Theodora Dix. I want to see Theodora. By the way, is Ludovic Speed still going to see her?"

"They say so," said Marilla, "and he's likely to continue it. Folks have given up expecting that that courtship will ever arrive anywhere."

"I'd hurry him up a bit, if I was Theodora, that's what," said Mrs. Lynde. And there is not the slightest doubt but that she would.

There was also a characteristic scrawl from Philippa, full of Alec and Alonzo, what they said and what they did, and how they looked when they saw her.

"But I can't make up my mind yet which to marry," wrote Phil. "I do wish you had come with me to decide for me. Some one will have to. When I saw Alec my heart gave a great thump and I thought, 'He might be the right one.' And then, when Alonzo came, thump went my heart again. So that's no guide, though it should be, according to all the novels I've ever read. Now, Anne, *your* heart wouldn't thump for anybody but the genuine Prince Charming, would it? There must be something radically wrong with mine. But I'm having a perfectly gorgeous time. How I wish you were here! It's snowing today, and I'm rapturous. I was so afraid we'd have a green Christmas and I loathe them. You know, when Christmas is a dirty grayey-browney affair, looking as if it had been left over a hundred years ago and had been in soak ever since, it is called a *green* Christmas! Don't ask me why. As Lord Dundreary says, 'there are thome thingth no fellow can underthtand.'

"Anne, did you ever get on a street car and then discover that you hadn't any money with you to pay your fare? I did, the other day. It's quite awful. I had a nickel with me when I got on the car. I thought it was in the left pocket of my coat. When I got settled down comfortably I felt for it. It wasn't there. I had a cold chill. I felt in the other pocket. Not there. I had another chill. Then I felt in a little inside pocket. All in vain. I had two chills at once.

"I took off my gloves, laid them on the seat, and went over all my pockets again. It was not there. I stood up and shook myself, and then looked on the floor. The car was full of people, who were going home from the opera, and they all stared at me, but I was past caring for a little thing like that.

"But I could not find my fare. I concluded I must have put it in my mouth and swallowed it inadvertently.

"I didn't know what to do. Would the conductor, I wondered, stop the car and put me off in ignominy and shame? Was it possible that I could convince him that I was merely the victim of my own absentmindedness, and not an unprincipled creature trying to obtain a ride upon false pretenses? How I wished that Alec or Alonzo were there. But they weren't because I wanted them. If I *hadn't* wanted them they would have been there by the dozen. And I couldn't decide what to say to the conductor when he came around. As soon as I got one sentence of explanation mapped out in my mind I felt nobody could believe it and I must compose another. It seemed there was nothing to do but trust in Providence, and for all the comfort that gave me I might as well have been the old lady who, when told by the captain during a storm that she must put her trust in the Almighty exclaimed, 'Oh, Captain, is it as bad as that?'

"Just at the conventional moment, when all hope had fled, and the conductor was holding out his box to the passenger next to me, I suddenly remembered where I had put that wretched coin of the realm. I hadn't swallowed it after all. I meekly fished it out of the index finger of my glove and poked it in the box. I smiled at everybody and felt that it was a beautiful world."

The visit to Echo Lodge was not the least pleasant of many pleasant holiday outings. Anne and Diana went back to it by the old way of the beech woods, carrying a lunch basket with them. Echo Lodge, which had been closed ever since Miss Lavendar's wedding, was briefly thrown open to wind and sunshine once more, and firelight glimmered again in the little rooms. The perfume of Miss Lavendar's rose bowl still filled the air. It was hardly possible to believe that Miss Lavendar would not come tripping in presently, with her brown eyes a-star with welcome, and that Charlotta the Fourth, blue of bow and wide of smile, would not pop through the door. Paul, too, seemed hovering around, with his fairy fancies.

"It really makes me feel a little bit like a ghost revisiting the old time glimpses of the moon," laughed Anne. "Let's go out and see if the echoes are at home. Bring the old horn. It is still behind the kitchen door."

The echoes were at home, over the white river, as silver-clear and multitudinous as ever; and when they had ceased to answer the girls locked up Echo Lodge again and went away in the perfect half hour that follows the rose and saffron of a winter sunset.

Chapter VIII
Anne's First Proposal

The old year did not slip away in a green twilight, with a pinky-yellow sunset. Instead, it went out with a wild, white bluster and blow. It was one of the nights when the storm-wind hurtles over the frozen meadows and black hollows, and moans around the eaves like a lost creature, and drives the snow sharply against the shaking panes.

"Just the sort of night people like to cuddle down between their blankets and count their mercies," said Anne to Jane Andrews, who had come up to spend the afternoon and stay all night. But when they were cuddled between their blankets, in Anne's little porch room, it was not her mercies of which Jane was thinking.

"Anne," she said very solemnly, "I want to tell you something. May I"

Anne was feeling rather sleepy after the party Ruby Gillis had given the night before. She would much rather have gone to sleep than listen to Jane's confidences, which she was sure would bore her. She had no prophetic inkling of what was coming. Probably Jane was engaged, too; rumor averred that Ruby Gillis was engaged to the Spencervale schoolteacher, about whom all the girls were said to be quite wild.

"I'll soon be the only fancy-free maiden of our old quartet," thought Anne, drowsily. Aloud she said, "Of course."

"Anne," said Jane, still more solemnly, "what do you think of my brother Billy?"

Anne gasped over this unexpected question, and floundered helplessly in her thoughts. Goodness, what *did* she think of Billy Andrews? She had never thought *anything* about him—round-faced, stupid, perpetually smiling, good-natured Billy Andrews. Did *anybody* ever think about Billy Andrews?

"I—I don't understand, Jane," she stammered. "What do you mean—exactly?"

"Do you like Billy?" asked Jane bluntly.

"Why—why—yes, I like him, of course," gasped Anne, wondering if she were telling the literal truth. Certainly she did not *dis*like Billy. But could the indifferent tolerance with which she regarded him, when he happened to be in her range of vision, be considered positive enough for liking? *What* was Jane trying to elucidate?

"Would you like him for a husband?" asked Jane calmly.

"A husband!" Anne had been sitting up in bed, the better to wrestle with the problem of her exact opinion of Billy Andrews. Now she fell flatly back on her pillows, the very breath gone out of her. "Whose husband?"

"Yours, of course," answered Jane. "Billy wants to marry you. He's always been crazy about you—and now father has given him the upper farm in his own name and there's nothing to prevent him from getting married. But he's so shy he couldn't ask you himself if you'd have him, so he got me to do it. I'd rather not have, but he gave me no peace till I said I would, if I got a good chance. What do you think about it, Anne?"

Was it a dream? Was it one of those nightmare things in which you find yourself engaged or married to some one you hate or don't know, without the slightest idea how it ever came about? No, she, Anne Shirley, was lying there, wide awake, in her own bed, and Jane Andrews was beside her, calmly proposing for her brother Billy. Anne did not know whether she wanted to writhe or laugh; but she could do neither, for Jane's feelings must not be hurt.

"I—I couldn't marry Bill, you know, Jane," she managed to gasp. "Why, such an idea never occurred to me—never!"

"I don't suppose it did," agreed Jane. "Billy has always been far too shy to think of courting. But you might think it over, Anne. Billy is a good fellow. I must say that, if he is my brother. He has no bad habits and he's a great worker, and you can depend on him. 'A bird in the hand is worth two in the bush.' He told me to tell you he'd be quite willing to wait till you got through college, if you insisted, though he'd *rather* get married this spring before the planting begins. He'd always be very good to you, I'm sure, and you know, Anne, I'd love to have you for a sister."

"I can't marry Billy," said Anne decidedly. She had recovered her wits, and was even feeling a little angry. It was all so ridiculous. "There is no use thinking of it, Jane. I don't care anything for him in that way, and you must tell him so."

"Well, I didn't suppose you would," said Jane with a resigned sigh, feeling that she had done her best. "I told Billy I didn't believe it was a bit of use to ask you, but he insisted. Well, you've made your decision, Anne, and I hope you won't regret it."

Jane spoke rather coldly. She had been perfectly sure that the enamored Billy had no chance at all of inducing Anne to marry him. Nevertheless, she felt a little resentment that Anne Shirley, who was, after all, merely an adopted orphan, without kith or kin, should refuse her brother—one of the Avonlea Andrews. Well, pride sometimes goes before a fall, Jane reflected ominously.

Anne permitted herself to smile in the darkness over the idea that she might ever regret not marrying Billy Andrews.

"I hope Billy won't feel very badly over it," she said nicely.

Jane made a movement as if she were tossing her head on her pillow.

"Oh, he won't break his heart. Billy has too much good sense for that. He likes Nettie Blewett pretty well, too, and mother would rather he married her than any one. She's such a good manager and saver. I think, when Billy is once sure you won't have him, he'll take Nettie. Please don't mention this to any one, will you, Anne?"

"Certainly not," said Anne, who had no desire whatever to publish abroad the fact that Billy Andrews wanted to marry her, preferring her, when all was said and done, to Nettie Blewett. Nettie Blewett!

"And now I suppose we'd better go to sleep," suggested Jane.

To sleep went Jane easily and speedily; but, though very unlike MacBeth in most respects, she had certainly contrived to murder sleep for Anne. That proposed-to damsel lay on a wakeful pillow until the wee sma's, but her meditations were far from being romantic. It was not, however, until the next morning that she had an opportunity to indulge in a good laugh over the whole affair. When Jane had gone home—still with a hint of frost in voice and manner because Anne had declined so ungratefully and decidedly the honor of an alliance with the House of Andrews—Anne retreated to the porch room, shut the door, and had her laugh out at last.

"If I could only share the joke with some one!" she thought. "But I can't. Diana is the only one I'd want to tell, and, even if I hadn't sworn secrecy to Jane, I can't tell Diana things now. She tells everything to Fred—I know she does. Well, I've had my first proposal. I supposed it would come some day—but I certainly never thought it would be by proxy. It's awfully funny—and yet there's a sting in it, too, somehow."

Anne knew quite well wherein the sting consisted, though she did not put it into words. She had had her secret dreams of the first time some one should ask her the great question. And it had, in those dreams, always been very romantic and beautiful: and the "some one" was to be very handsome and dark-eyed and distinguished-looking and eloquent, whether he were Prince Charming to be enraptured with "yes," or one to whom a regretful, beautifully worded, but hopeless refusal must be given. If the latter, the refusal was to be expressed so delicately that it would be next best thing to acceptance, and he would go away, after kissing her hand, assuring her of his unalterable, life-long devotion. And it would always be a beautiful memory, to be proud of and a little sad about, also.

And now, this thrilling experience had turned out to be merely grotesque. Billy Andrews had got his sister to propose for him because his father had given him the upper farm; and if Anne wouldn't "have him" Nettie Blewett would. There was romance for you, with a vengeance! Anne laughed—and then sighed. The bloom had been brushed from one little maiden dream. Would the painful process go on until everything became prosaic and hum-drum?

Chapter IX
An Unwelcome Lover and a Welcome Friend

The second term at Redmond sped as quickly as had the first—"actually whizzed away," Philippa said. Anne enjoyed it thoroughly in all its phases—the stimulating class rivalry, the making and deepening of new and helpful friendships, the gay little social stunts, the doings of the various societies of which she was a member, the widening of horizons and interests. She studied hard, for she had made up her mind to win the Thorburn Scholarship in English. This being won, meant that she could come back to Redmond the next year without trenching on Marilla's small savings—something Anne was determined she would not do.

Gilbert, too, was in full chase after a scholarship, but found plenty of time for frequent calls at Thirty-eight, St. John's. He was Anne's escort at nearly all the college affairs, and she knew that their names were coupled in Redmond gossip. Anne raged over this but was helpless; she could not cast an old friend like Gilbert aside, especially when he had grown suddenly wise and wary, as behooved him in the dangerous proximity of more than one Redmond youth who would gladly have taken his place by the side of the slender, red-haired coed, whose gray eyes were as alluring as stars of evening. Anne was never attended by the crowd of willing victims who hovered around Philippa's conquering march through her Freshman year; but there was a lanky, brainy Freshie, a jolly, little, round Sophomore, and a tall, learned Junior who all liked to call at Thirty-eight, St. John's, and talk over 'ologies and 'isms, as well as lighter subjects, with Anne, in the becushioned parlor of that domicile. Gilbert did not love any of them, and he was exceedingly careful to give none of them the advantage over him by any untimely display of his real feelings Anne-ward. To her he had become again the boy-comrade of Avonlea days, and as such could hold his own against any smitten swain who had so far entered the lists against him. As a companion, Anne honestly acknowledged nobody could be so satisfactory as Gilbert; she was very glad, so she told herself, that he had evidently dropped all nonsensical ideas—though she spent considerable time secretly wondering why.

Only one disagreeable incident marred that winter. Charlie Sloane, sitting bolt upright on Miss Ada's most dearly beloved cushion, asked Anne one night if she would promise "to become Mrs. Charlie Sloane some day." Coming after Billy Andrews' proxy effort, this was not quite the shock to Anne's romantic sensibilities that it would otherwise have been; but it was certainly another heart-rending disillusion. She was angry, too, for she felt that she had never given Charlie the slightest encouragement to suppose such a thing possible. But what could you expect of a Sloane, as Mrs. Rachel Lynde would ask scornfully? Charlie's whole attitude, tone, air, words, fairly reeked with Sloanishness. "He was conferring a great honor—no doubt whatever about that. And when Anne, utterly insensible to the honor, refused him, as delicately and considerately as she could—for even a Sloane had feelings which ought not to be unduly lacerated—Sloanishness still further betrayed itself. Charlie certainly did not take his dismissal as Anne's imaginary rejected suitors did.

Instead, he became angry, and showed it; he said two or three quite nasty things; Anne's temper flashed up mutinously and she retorted with a cutting little speech whose keenness pierced even Charlie's protective Sloanishness and reached the quick; he caught up his hat and flung himself out of the house with a very red face; Anne rushed upstairs, falling twice over Miss Ada's cushions on the way, and threw herself on her bed, in tears of humiliation and rage. Had she actually stooped to quarrel with a Sloane? Was it possible anything Charlie Sloane could say had power to make her angry? Oh, this was degradation, indeed—worse even than being the rival of Nettie Blewett!

"I wish I need never see the horrible creature again," she sobbed vindictively into her pillows.

She could not avoid seeing him again, but the outraged Charlie took care that it should not be at very close quarters. Miss Ada's cushions were henceforth safe from his depredations, and when he met Anne on the street, or in Redmond's halls, his bow was icy in the extreme. Relations between these two old schoolmates continued to be thus strained for nearly a year! Then Charlie transferred his blighted affections to a round, rosy, snub-nosed, blue-eyed, little Sophomore who appreciated them as they deserved, whereupon he forgave Anne and condescended to be civil to her again; in a patronizing manner intended to show her just what she had lost.

One day Anne scurried excitedly into Priscilla's room.

"Read that," she cried, tossing Priscilla a letter. "It's from Stella—and she's coming to Redmond next year—and what do you think of her idea? I think it's a perfectly splendid one, if we can only carry it out. Do you suppose we can, Pris?"

"I'll be better able to tell you when I find out what it is," said Priscilla, casting aside a Greek lexicon and taking up Stella's letter. Stella Maynard had been one of their chums at Queen's Academy and had been teaching school ever since.

"But I'm going to give it up, Anne dear," she wrote, "and go to college next year. As I took the third year at Queen's I can enter the Sophomore year. I'm tired of teaching in a back country school. Some day I'm going to write a treatise on 'The Trials of a Country Schoolmarm.' It will be a harrowing bit of realism. It seems to be the prevailing impression that we live in clover, and have nothing to do but draw our quarter's salary. My treatise shall tell the truth about us. Why, if a week should pass without some one telling me that I am doing easy work for big pay I would conclude that I might as well order my ascension robe 'immediately and to onct.' 'Well, you get your money easy,' some rate-payer will tell me, condescendingly. 'All you have to do is to sit there and hear lessons.' I used to argue the matter at first, but I'm wiser now. Facts are stubborn things, but as some one has wisely said, not half so stubborn as fallacies. So I only smile loftily now in eloquent silence. Why, I have nine grades in my school and I have to teach a little of everything, from investigating the interiors of earthworms to the study of the solar system. My youngest pupil is four—his mother sends him to school to 'get him out of the way'—and my oldest twenty—it 'suddenly struck him' that it would be easier to go to school and get an education than follow the plough any longer. In the wild effort to cram all sorts of research into six hours a day I don't wonder if the children feel like the little boy who was taken to see the biograph. 'I have to look for what's coming next before I know what went last,' he complained. I feel like that myself.

"And the letters I get, Anne! Tommy's mother writes me that Tommy is not coming on in arithmetic as fast as she would like. He is only in simple reduction yet, and Johnny Johnson is in fractions, and Johnny isn't half as smart as her Tommy, and she can't understand it. And Susy's father wants to know why Susy can't write a letter without misspelling half the words, and Dick's aunt wants me to change his seat, because that bad Brown boy he is sitting with is teaching him to say naughty words.

"As to the financial part—but I'll not begin on that. Those whom the gods wish to destroy they first make country schoolmarms!

"There, I feel better, after that growl. After all, I've enjoyed these past two years. But I'm coming to Redmond.

"And now, Anne, I've a little plan. You know how I loathe boarding. I've boarded for four years and I'm so tired of it. I don't feel like enduring three years more of it.

"Now, why can't you and Priscilla and I club together, rent a little house somewhere in Kingsport, and board ourselves? It would be cheaper than any other way. Of course, we would have to have a housekeeper and I have one ready on the spot. You've heard me speak of Aunt Jamesina? She's the sweetest aunt that ever lived, in spite of her name. She can't help that! She was called Jamesina because her father, whose name was James, was drowned at sea a month before she was born. I always call her Aunt Jimsie. Well, her only daughter has recently married and gone to the foreign mission field. Aunt Jamesina is left alone in a great big house, and she is horribly lonesome. She will come to Kingsport and keep house for us if we want her, and I know you'll both love her. The more I think of the plan the more I like it. We could have such good, independent times.

"Now, if you and Priscilla agree to it, wouldn't it be a good idea for you, who are on the spot, to look around and see if you can find a suitable house this spring? That would be better than leaving it till the fall. If you could get a furnished one so much the better, but if not, we can scare up a few sticks of finiture between us and old family friends with attics. Anyhow, decide as soon as you can and write me, so that Aunt Jamesina will know what plans to make for next year."

"I think it's a good idea," said Priscilla.

"So do I," agreed Anne delightedly. "Of course, we have a nice boardinghouse here, but, when all's said and done, a boardinghouse isn't home. So let's go house-hunting at once, before exams come on."

"I'm afraid it will be hard enough to get a really suitable house," warned Priscilla. "Don't expect too much, Anne. Nice houses in nice localities will probably be away beyond our means. We'll likely have to content ourselves with a shabby little place on some street whereon live people whom to know is to be unknown, and make life inside compensate for the outside."

Accordingly they went house-hunting, but to find just what they wanted proved even harder than Priscilla had feared. Houses there were galore, furnished and unfurnished; but one was too big, another too small; this one too expensive, that one too far from Redmond. Exams were on and over; the last week of the term came and still their "house o'dreams," as Anne called it, remained a castle in the air.

"We shall have to give up and wait till the fall, I suppose," said Priscilla wearily, as they rambled through the park on one of April's darling days of breeze and blue, when the harbor was creaming and shimmering beneath the pearl-hued mists floating over it. "We may find some shack to shelter us then; and if not, boardinghouses we shall have always with us."

"I'm not going to worry about it just now, anyway, and spoil this lovely afternoon," said Anne, gazing around her with delight. The fresh chill air was faintly charged with the aroma of pine balsam, and the sky above was crystal clear and blue—a great inverted cup of blessing. "Spring is singing in my blood today, and the lure of April is abroad on the air. I'm seeing visions and dreaming dreams, Pris. That's because the wind is from the west. I do love the west wind. It sings of hope and gladness, doesn't it? When the east wind blows I always think of sorrowful rain on the eaves and sad waves on a gray shore. When I get old I shall have rheumatism when the wind is east."

"And isn't it jolly when you discard furs and winter garments for the first time and sally forth, like this, in spring attire?" laughed Priscilla. "Don't you feel as if you had been made over new?"

"Everything is new in the spring," said Anne. "Springs themselves are always so new, too. No spring is ever just like any other spring. It always has something of its own to be its own peculiar sweetness. See how green the grass is around that little pond, and how the willow buds are bursting."

"And exams are over and gone—the time of Convocation will come soon—next Wednesday. This day next week we'll be home."

"I'm glad," said Anne dreamily. "There are so many things I want to do. I want to sit on the back porch steps and feel the breeze blowing down over Mr. Harrison's fields. I want to hunt ferns in the Haunted Wood and gather violets in Violet Vale. Do you remember the day of our golden picnic, Priscilla? I want to hear the frogs singing and the poplars whispering. But I've learned to love Kingsport, too, and I'm glad I'm coming back next fall. If I hadn't won the Thorburn I don't believe I could have. I *couldn't* take any of Marilla's little hoard."

"If we could only find a house!" sighed Priscilla. "Look over there at Kingsport, Anne—houses, houses everywhere, and not one for us."

"Stop it, Pris. 'The best is yet to be.' Like the old Roman, we'll find a house or build one. On a day like this there's no such word as fail in my bright lexicon."

They lingered in the park until sunset, living in the amazing miracle and glory and wonder of the springtide; and they went home as usual, by way of Spofford Avenue, that they might have the delight of looking at Patty's Place.

"I feel as if something mysterious were going to happen right away—'by the pricking of my thumbs,'" said Anne, as they went up the slope. "It's a nice story-bookish feeling. Why—why—why! Priscilla Grant, look over there and tell me if it's true, or am I seein' things?"

Priscilla looked. Anne's thumbs and eyes had not deceived her. Over the arched gateway of Patty's Place dangled a little, modest sign. It said "To Let, Furnished. Inquire Within."

"Priscilla," said Anne, in a whisper, "do you suppose it's possible that we could rent Patty's Place?"

"No, I don't," averred Priscilla. "It would be too good to be true. Fairy tales don't happen nowadays. I won't hope, Anne. The disappointment would be too awful to bear. They're sure to want more for it than we can afford. Remember, it's on Spofford Avenue."

"We must find out anyhow," said Anne resolutely. "It's too late to call this evening, but we'll come tomorrow. Oh, Pris, if we can get this darling spot! I've always felt that my fortunes were linked with Patty's Place, ever since I saw it first."

Chapter X
Patty's Place

The next evening found them treading resolutely the herring-bone walk through the tiny garden. The April wind was filling the pine trees with its roundelay, and the grove was alive with robins—great, plump, saucy fellows, strutting along the paths. The girls rang rather timidly, and were admitted by a grim and ancient handmaiden. The door opened directly into a large living-room, where by a cheery little fire sat two other ladies, both of whom were also grim and ancient. Except that one looked to be about seventy and the other fifty, there seemed little difference between them. Each had amazingly big, light-blue eyes behind steel-rimmed spectacles; each wore a cap and a gray shawl; each was knitting without haste and without rest; each rocked placidly and looked at the girls without speaking; and just behind each sat a large white china dog, with round green spots all over it, a green nose and green ears. Those dogs captured Anne's fancy on the spot; they seemed like the twin guardian deities of Patty's Place.

For a few minutes nobody spoke. The girls were too nervous to find words, and neither the ancient ladies nor the china dogs seemed conversationally inclined. Anne glanced about the room. What a dear place it was! Another door opened out of it directly into the pine grove and the robins came boldly up on the very step. The floor was spotted with round, braided mats, such as

Marilla made at Green Gables, but which were considered out of date everywhere else, even in Avonlea. And yet here they were on Spofford Avenue! A big, polished grandfather's clock ticked loudly and solemnly in a corner. There were delightful little cupboards over the mantelpiece, behind whose glass doors gleamed quaint bits of china. The walls were hung with old prints and silhouettes. In one corner the stairs went up, and at the first low turn was a long window with an inviting seat. It was all just as Anne had known it must be.

By this time the silence had grown too dreadful, and Priscilla nudged Anne to intimate that she must speak.

"We—we—saw by your sign that this house is to let," said Anne faintly, addressing the older lady, who was evidently Miss Patty Spofford.

"Oh, yes," said Miss Patty. "I intended to take that sign down today."

"Then—then we are too late," said Anne sorrowfully. "You've let it to some one else?"

"No, but we have decided not to let it at all."

"Oh, I'm so sorry," exclaimed Anne impulsively. "I love this place so. I did hope we could have got it."

Then did Miss Patty lay down her knitting, take off her specs, rub them, put them on again, and for the first time look at Anne as at a human being. The other lady followed her example so perfectly that she might as well have been a reflection in a mirror.

"You *love* it," said Miss Patty with emphasis. "Does that mean that you really *love* it? Or that you merely like the looks of it? The girls nowadays indulge in such exaggerated statements that one never can tell what they *do* mean. It wasn't so in my young days. *Then* a girl did not say she *loved* turnips, in just the same tone as she might have said she loved her mother or her Savior."

Anne's conscience bore her up.

"I really do love it," she said gently. "I've loved it ever since I saw it last fall. My two college chums and I want to keep house next year instead of boarding, so we are looking for a little place to rent; and when I saw that this house was to let I was so happy."

"If you love it, you can have it," said Miss Patty. "Maria and I decided today that we would not let it after all, because we did not like any of the people who have wanted it. We don't *have* to let it. We can afford to go to Europe even if we don't let it. It would help us out, but not for gold will I let my home pass into the possession of such people as have come here and looked at it. *You* are different. I believe you do love it and will be good to it. You can have it."

"If—if we can afford to pay what you ask for it," hesitated Anne.

Miss Patty named the amount required. Anne and Priscilla looked at each other. Priscilla shook her head.

"I'm afraid we can't afford quite so much," said Anne, choking back her disappointment. "You see, we are only college girls and we are poor."

"What were you thinking you could afford?" demanded Miss Patty, ceasing not to knit.

Anne named her amount. Miss Patty nodded gravely.

"That will do. As I told you, it is not strictly necessary that we should let it at all. We are not rich, but we have enough to go to Europe on. I have never been in Europe in my life, and never expected or wanted to go. But my niece there, Maria Spofford, has taken a fancy to go. Now, you know a young person like Maria can't go globetrotting alone."

"No—I—I suppose not," murmured Anne, seeing that Miss Patty was quite solemnly in earnest.

"Of course not. So I have to go along to look after her. I expect to enjoy it, too; I'm seventy years old, but I'm not tired of living yet. I daresay I'd have gone to Europe before if the idea had occurred to me. We shall be away for two years, perhaps three. We sail in June and we shall send you the key, and leave all in order for you to take possession when you choose. We shall pack away a few things we prize especially, but all the rest will be left."

"Will you leave the china dogs?" asked Anne timidly.

"Would you like me to?"

"Oh, indeed, yes. They are delightful."

A pleased expression came into Miss Patty's face.

"I think a great deal of those dogs," she said proudly. "They are over a hundred years old, and they have sat on either side of this fireplace ever since my brother Aaron brought them from London fifty years ago. Spofford Avenue was called after my brother Aaron."

"A fine man he was," said Miss Maria, speaking for the first time. "Ah, you don't see the like of him nowadays."

"He was a good uncle to you, Maria," said Miss Patty, with evident emotion. "You do well to remember him."

"I shall always remember him," said Miss Maria solemnly. "I can see him, this minute, standing there before that fire, with his hands under his coat-tails, beaming on us."

Miss Maria took out her handkerchief and wiped her eyes; but Miss Patty came resolutely back from the regions of sentiment to those of business.

"I shall leave the dogs where they are, if you will promise to be very careful of them," she said. "Their names are Gog and Magog. Gog looks to the right and Magog to the left. And there's just one thing more. You don't object, I hope, to this house being called Patty's Place?"

"No, indeed. We think that is one of the nicest things about it."

"You have sense, I see," said Miss Patty in a tone of great satisfaction. "Would you believe it? All the people who came here to rent the house wanted to know if they couldn't take the name off the gate during their occupation of it. I told them roundly that the name went with the house. This has been Patty's Place ever since my brother Aaron left it to me in his will, and Patty's Place it shall remain until I die and Maria dies. After that happens the next possessor can call it any fool name he likes," concluded Miss Patty, much as she might have said, "After that—the deluge." "And now, wouldn't you like to go over the house and see it all before we consider the bargain made?"

Further exploration still further delighted the girls. Besides the big living-room, there was a kitchen and a small bedroom downstairs. Upstairs were three rooms, one large and two small. Anne took an especial fancy to one of the small ones, looking out into the big pines, and hoped it would be hers. It was papered in pale blue and had a little, old-timey toilet table with sconces for candles. There was a diamond-paned window with a seat under the blue muslin frills that would be a satisfying spot for studying or dreaming.

"It's all so delicious that I know we are going to wake up and find it a fleeting vision of the night," said Priscilla as they went away.

"Miss Patty and Miss Maria are hardly such stuff as dreams are made of," laughed Anne. "Can you fancy them 'globe-trotting'—especially in those shawls and caps?"

"I suppose they'll take them off when they really begin to trot," said Priscilla, "but I know they'll take their knitting with them everywhere. They simply couldn't be parted from it. They will walk about Westminster Abbey and knit, I feel sure. Meanwhile, Anne, we shall be living in Patty's Place—and on Spofford Avenue. I feel like a millionairess even now."

"I feel like one of the morning stars that sang for joy," said Anne.

Phil Gordon crept into Thirty-eight, St John's, that night and flung herself on Anne's bed.

"Girls, dear, I'm tired to death. I feel like the man without a country—or was it without a shadow? I forget which. Anyway, I've been packing up."

"And I suppose you are worn out because you couldn't decide which things to pack first, or where to put them," laughed Priscilla.

"E-zackly. And when I had got everything jammed in somehow, and my landlady and her maid had both sat on it while I locked it, I discovered I had packed a whole lot of things I wanted for Convocation at the very bottom. I had to unlock the old thing and poke and dive into it for an hour before I fished out what I wanted. I would get hold of something that felt like what I was looking for, and I'd yank it up, and it would be something else. No, Anne, I did *not* swear."

"I didn't say you did."

"Well, you looked it. But I admit my thoughts verged on the profane. And I have such a cold in the head—I can do nothing but sniffle, sigh and sneeze. Isn't that alliterative agony for you? Queen Anne, do say something to cheer me up."

"Remember that next Thursday night, you'll be back in the land of Alec and Alonzo," suggested Anne.

Phil shook her head dolefully.

"More alliteration. No, I don't want Alec and Alonzo when I have a cold in the head. But what has happened you two? Now that I look at you closely you seem all lighted up with an internal iridescence. Why, you're actually *shining*! What's up?"

"We are going to live in Patty's Place next winter," said Anne triumphantly. "Live, mark you, not board! We've rented it, and Stella Maynard is coming, and her aunt is going to keep house for us."

Phil bounced up, wiped her nose, and fell on her knees before Anne.

"Girls—girls—let me come, too. Oh, I'll be so good. If

there's no room for me I'll sleep in the little doghouse in the orchard—I've seen it. Only let me come."

"Get up, you goose."

"I won't stir off my marrow bones till you tell me I can live with you next winter."

Anne and Priscilla looked at each other. Then Anne said slowly, "Phil dear, we'd love to have you. But we may as well speak plainly. I'm poor—Pris is poor—Stella Maynard is poor—our housekeeping will have to be very simple and our table plain. You'd have to live as we would. Now, you are rich and your boardinghouse fare attests the fact."

"Oh, what do I care for that?" demanded Phil tragically. "Better a dinner of herbs where your chums are than a stalled ox in a lonely boardinghouse. Don't think I'm *all* stomach, girls. I'll be willing to live on bread and water—with just a *leetle* jam—if you'll let me come."

"And then," continued Anne, "there will be a good deal of work to be done. Stella's aunt can't do it all. We all expect to have our chores to do. Now, you—"

"Toil not, neither do I spin," finished Philippa. "But I'll learn to do things. You'll only have to show me once. I *can* make my own bed to begin with. And remember that, though I can't cook, I *can* keep my temper. That's something. And I *never* growl about the weather. That's more. Oh, please, please! I never wanted anything so much in my life—and this floor is awfully hard."

"There's just one more thing," said Priscilla resolutely. "You, Phil, as all Redmond knows, entertain callers almost every evening. Now, at Patty's Place we can't do that. We have decided that we shall be at home to our friends on Friday evenings only. If you come with us you'll have to abide by that rule."

"Well, you don't think I'll mind that, do you? Why, I'm glad of it. I knew I should have had some such rule myself, but I hadn't enough decision to make it or stick to it. When I can shuffle off the responsibility on you it will be a real relief. If you won't let me cast in my lot with you I'll die of the disappointment and then I'll come back and haunt you. I'll camp on the very doorstep of Patty's Place and you won't be able to go out or come in without falling over my spook."

Again Anne and Priscilla exchanged eloquent looks.

"Well," said Anne, "of course we can't promise to take you until we've consulted with Stella; but I don't think she'll object, and, as far as we are concerned, you may come and glad welcome."

"If you get tired of our simple life you can leave us, and no questions asked," added Priscilla.

Phil sprang up, hugged them both jubilantly, and went on her way rejoicing.

"I hope things will go right," said Priscilla soberly.

"We must *make* them go right," avowed Anne. "I think Phil will fit into our 'appy little 'ome very well."

"Oh, Phil's a dear to rattle round with and be chums. And, of course, the more there are of us the easier it will be on our slim purses. But how will she be to live with? You have to summer and winter with any one before you know if she's *livable* or not."

"Oh, well, we'll all be put to the test, as far as that goes. And we must quit us like sensible folk, living and let live. Phil isn't selfish, though she's a little thoughtless, and I believe we will all get on beautifully in Patty's Place."

Chapter XI
The Round of Life

Anne was back in Avonlea with the luster of the Thorburn Scholarship on her brow. People told her she hadn't changed much, in a tone which hinted they were surprised and a little disappointed she hadn't. Avonlea had not changed, either. At least, so it seemed at first. But as Anne sat in the Green Gables pew, on the first Sunday after her return, and looked over the congregation, she saw several little changes which, all coming home to her at once, made her realize that time did not quite stand still, even in Avonlea. A new minister was in the pulpit. In the pews more than one familiar face was missing forever. Old "Uncle Abe," his prophesying over and done with, Mrs. Peter Sloane, who had sighed, it was to be hoped, for the last time, Timothy Cotton, who, as Mrs. Rachel Lynde said "had actually managed to die at last after practicing at it for twenty years," and old Josiah Sloane, whom nobody knew in his coffin because he had his whiskers neatly trimmed, were all sleeping in the little graveyard behind the church. And Billy Andrews was married to Nettie Blewett! They "appeared out" that Sunday. When Billy, beaming with pride and happiness, showed his be-plumed and be-silked bride into the Harmon Andrews' pew, Anne dropped her lids to hide her dancing eyes. She recalled the stormy winter night of the Christmas holidays when Jane had proposed for Billy. He certainly had not broken his heart over his rejection. Anne wondered if Jane had also proposed to Nettie for him, or if he had mustered enough spunk to ask the fateful question himself. All the Andrews family seemed to share in his pride and pleasure, from Mrs. Harmon in the pew to Jane in the choir. Jane had resigned from the Avonlea school and intended to go West in the fall.

"Can't get a beau in Avonlea, that's what," said Mrs. Rachel Lynde scornfully. "*Says* she thinks she'll have better health out West. I never heard her health was poor before."

"Jane is a nice girl," Anne had said loyally. "She never tried to attract attention, as some did."

"Oh, she never chased the boys, if that's what you mean," said Mrs. Rachel. "But she'd like to be married, just as much as anybody, that's what. What else would take her out West to some forsaken place whose only recommendation is that men are plenty and women scarce? Don't you tell me!"

But it was not at Jane, Anne gazed that day in dismay and surprise. It was at Ruby Gillis, who sat beside her in the choir. What had happened to Ruby? She was even handsomer than ever; but her blue eyes were too bright and lustrous, and the color of her cheeks was hectically brilliant; besides, she was very thin; the hands that held her hymn-book were almost transparent in their delicacy.

"Is Ruby Gillis ill?" Anne asked of Mrs. Lynde, as they went home from church.

"Ruby Gillis is dying of galloping consumption," said Mrs. Lynde bluntly. "Everybody knows it except herself and her *family*. They won't give in. If you ask *them*, she's perfectly well. She hasn't been able to teach since she had that attack of congestion in the winter, but she says she's going to teach again in the fall, and she's after the White Sands school. She'll be in her grave, poor girl, when White Sands school opens, that's what."

Anne listened in shocked silence. Ruby Gillis, her old school-chum, dying? Could it be possible? Of late years they had grown apart; but the old tie of school-girl intimacy was there, and made itself felt sharply in the tug the news gave at Anne's heartstrings. Ruby, the brilliant, the merry, the coquettish! It was impossible to associate the thought of her with anything like death. She had greeted Anne with gay cordiality after church, and urged her to come up the next evening.

"I'll be away Tuesday and Wednesday evenings," she had whispered triumphantly. "There's a concert at Carmody and a party at White Sands. Herb Spencer's going to take me. He's my *latest*. Be sure to come up tomorrow. I'm dying for a good talk with you. I want to hear all about your doings at Redmond."

Anne knew that Ruby meant that she wanted to tell Anne all about her own recent flirtations, but she promised to go, and Diana offered to go with her.

"I've been wanting to go to see Ruby for a long while," she told Anne, when they left Green Gables the next evening, "but I really couldn't go alone. It's so awful to hear Ruby rattling on as she does, and pretending there is nothing the matter with her, even when she can hardly speak for coughing. She's fighting so hard for her life, and yet she hasn't any chance at all, they say."

The girls walked silently down the red, twilit road. The robins were singing vespers in the high treetops, filling the golden air with their jubilant voices. The silver fluting of the frogs came from marshes and ponds, over fields where seeds were beginning to stir with life and thrill to the sunshine and rain that had drifted over them. The air was fragrant with the wild, sweet, wholesome smell of young raspberry copses. White mists were hovering in the silent hollows and violet stars were shining bluely on the brooklands.

"What a beautiful sunset," said Diana. "Look, Anne, it's just like a land in itself, isn't it? That long, low back of purple cloud is the shore, and the clear sky further on is like a golden sea."

"If we could sail to it in the moonshine boat Paul wrote of in his old composition—you remember?—how nice it would be," said Anne, rousing from her reverie. "Do you think we could find all our yesterdays there, Diana—all our old springs and blossoms? The beds of flowers that Paul saw there are the roses that have bloomed for us in the past?"

"Don't!" said Diana. "You make me feel as if we were old women with everything in life behind us."

"I think I've almost felt as if we were since I heard about poor Ruby," said Anne. "If it is true that she is dying any other sad thing might be true, too."

"You don't mind calling in at Elisha Wright's for a moment, do you?" asked Diana. "Mother asked me to leave this little dish of jelly for Aunt Atossa."

"Who is Aunt Atossa?"

"Oh, haven't you heard? She's Mrs. Samson Coates of Spencervale—Mrs. Elisha Wright's aunt. She's father's aunt, too. Her husband died last winter and she was left very poor and lonely, so the Wrights took her to live with them. Mother thought we ought to take her, but father put his foot down. Live with Aunt Atossa he would not."

"Is she so terrible?" asked Anne absently.

"You'll probably see what she's like before we can get away," said Diana significantly. "Father says she has a face like a hatchet—it cuts the air. But her tongue is sharper still."

Late as it was Aunt Atossa was cutting potato sets in the Wright kitchen. She wore a faded old wrapper, and her gray hair was decidedly untidy. Aunt Atossa did not like being "caught in a kilter," so she went out of her way to be disagreeable.

"Oh, so you're Anne Shirley?" she said, when Diana introduced Anne. "I've heard of you." Her tone implied that she had heard nothing good. "Mrs. Andrews was telling me you were home. She said you had improved a good deal."

There was no doubt Aunt Atossa thought there was plenty of room for further improvement. She ceased not from cutting sets with much energy.

"Is it any use to ask you to sit down?" she inquired sarcastically. "Of course, there's nothing very entertaining here for you. The rest are all away."

"Mother sent you this little pot of rhubarb jelly," said Diana pleasantly. "She made it today and thought you might like some."

"Oh, thanks," said Aunt Atossa sourly. "I never fancy your mother's jelly—she always makes it too sweet. However, I'll try to worry some down. My appetite's been dreadful poor this spring. I'm far from well," continued Aunt Atossa solemnly, "but still I keep a-doing. People who can't work aren't wanted here. If it isn't too much trouble will you be condescending enough to set the jelly in the pantry? I'm in a hurry to get these spuds done tonight. I suppose you two *ladies* never do anything like this. You'd be afraid of spoiling your hands."

"I used to cut potato sets before we rented the farm," smiled Anne.

"I do it yet," laughed Diana. "I cut sets three days last week. Of course," she added teasingly, "I did my hands up in lemon juice and kid gloves every night after it."

Aunt Atossa sniffed.

"I suppose you got that notion out of some of those silly magazines you read so many of. I wonder your mother allows you. But she always spoiled you. We all thought when George married her she wouldn't be a suitable wife for him."

Aunt Atossa sighed heavily, as if all forebodings upon the occasion of George Barry's marriage had been amply and darkly fulfilled.

"Going, are you?" she inquired, as the girls rose. "Well, I suppose you can't find much amusement talking to an old woman like me. It's such a pity the boys ain't home."

"We want to run in and see Ruby Gillis a little while," explained Diana.

"Oh, anything does for an excuse, of course," said Aunt Atossa, amiably. "Just whip in and whip out before you have time to say how-do decently. It's college airs, I s'pose. You'd be wiser to keep away from Ruby Gillis. The doctors say consumption's catching. I always knew Ruby'd get something, gadding off to Boston last fall for a visit. People who ain't content to stay home always catch something."

"People who don't go visiting catch things, too. Sometimes they even die," said Diana solemnly.

"Then they don't have themselves to blame for it," retorted Aunt Atossa triumphantly. "I hear you are to be married in June, Diana."

"There is no truth in that report," said Diana, blushing.

"Well, don't put it off too long," said Aunt Atossa significantly. "You'll fade soon—you're all complexion and hair. And the Wrights are terrible fickle. You ought to wear a hat, *Miss Shirley*. Your nose is freckling scandalous. My, but you *are* redheaded! Well, I s'pose we're all as the Lord made us! Give Marilla Cuthbert my respects. She's never been to see me since I come to Avonlea, but I s'pose I oughtn't to complain. The Cuthberts always did think themselves a cut higher than any one else round here."

"Oh, isn't she dreadful?" gasped Diana, as they escaped down the lane.

"She's worse than Miss Eliza Andrews," said Anne. "But then think of living all your life with a name like Atossa! Wouldn't it sour almost any one? She should have tried to imagine her name was Cordelia. It might have helped her a great deal. It certainly helped me in the days when I didn't like *Anne*."

"Josie Pye will be just like her when she grows up," said Diana. "Josie's mother and Aunt Atossa are cousins, you know. Oh, dear, I'm glad that's over. She's so malicious—she seems to put a bad flavor in everything. Father tells such a funny story about her. One time they had a minister in Spencervale who was a very good, spiritual man but very deaf. He couldn't hear any ordinary conversation at all. Well, they used to have a prayer meeting on Sunday evenings, and all the church members present would get up and pray in turn, or say a few words on some Bible verse. But one evening Aunt Atossa bounced up. She didn't either pray or preach. Instead, she lit into everybody else in the church and gave them a fearful raking down, calling them right out by name and telling them how they all had behaved, and casting up all the quarrels and scandals of the past ten years. Finally she wound up by saying that she was disgusted with Spencervale church and she never meant to darken its door again, and she hoped a fearful judgment would come upon it. Then she sat down out of breath, and the minister, who hadn't heard a word she said, immediately remarked, in a very devout voice, 'amen! The Lord grant our dear sister's prayer!' You ought to hear father tell the story."

"Speaking of stories, Diana," remarked Anne, in a significant, confidential tone, "do you know that lately I have been wondering if I could write a short story—a story that would be good enough to be published?"

"Why, of course you could," said Diana, after she had grasped the amazing suggestion. "You used to write perfectly thrilling stories years ago in our old Story Club."

"Well, I hardly meant one of that kind of stories," smiled Anne. "I've been thinking about it a little of late, but I'm almost afraid to try, for, if I should fail, it would be too humiliating."

"I heard Priscilla say once that all Mrs. Morgan's first stories were rejected. But I'm sure yours wouldn't be, Anne, for it's likely editors have more sense nowadays."

"Margaret Burton, one of the Junior girls at Redmond, wrote a story last winter and it was published in the *Canadian Woman*. I really do think I could write one at least as good."

"And will you have it published in the *Canadian Woman?*"

"I might try one of the bigger magazines first. It all depends on what kind of a story I write."

"What is it to be about?"

"I don't know yet. I want to get hold of a good plot. I believe this is very necessary from an editor's point of view. The only thing I've settled on is the heroine's name. It is to be *Averil Lester*. Rather pretty, don't you think? Don't mention this to any one, Diana. I haven't told anybody but you and Mr. Harrison. *He* wasn't very encouraging—he said there was far too much trash written nowadays as it was, and he'd expected something better of me, after a year at college."

"What does Mr. Harrison know about it?" demanded Diana scornfully.

They found the Gillis home gay with lights and callers. Leonard Kimball, of Spencervale, and Morgan Bell, of Carmody, were glaring at each other across the parlor. Several merry girls had dropped in. Ruby was dressed in white and her eyes and cheeks were very brilliant. She laughed and chattered incessantly, and after the other girls had gone she took Anne upstairs to display her new summer dresses.

"I've a blue silk to make up yet, but it's a little heavy for summer wear. I think I'll leave it until the fall. I'm going to teach in White Sands, you know. How do you like my hat? That one you had on in church yesterday was real dinky. But I like something brighter for myself. Did you notice those two ridiculous boys downstairs? They've both come determined to sit each other out. I don't care a single bit about either of them, you know. Herb Spencer is the one I like. Sometimes I really do think he's *Mr. Right*. At Christmas I thought the Spencervale schoolmaster was that. But I found out something about him that turned me against him. He nearly went insane when I turned him down. I wish those two boys hadn't come tonight. I wanted to have a nice good talk with you, Anne, and tell you such heaps of things. You and I were always good chums, weren't we?"

Ruby slipped her arm about Anne's waist with a shallow little laugh. But just for a moment their eyes met, and, behind all the luster of Ruby's, Anne saw something that made her heart ache.

"Come up often, won't you, Anne?" whispered Ruby. "Come alone—I want you."

"Are you feeling quite well, Ruby?"

"Me! Why, I'm perfectly well. I never felt better in my life. Of course, that congestion last winter pulled me down a little. But just see my color. I don't look much like an invalid, I'm sure."

Ruby's voice was almost sharp. She pulled her arm away from Anne, as if in resentment, and ran downstairs, where she was gayer than ever, apparently so much absorbed in bantering her two swains that Diana and Anne felt rather out of it and soon went away.

Chapter XII
"Averil's Atonement"

"What are you dreaming of, Anne?"

The two girls were loitering one evening in a fairy hollow of the brook. Ferns nodded in it, and little grasses were green, and wild pears hung finely-scented, white curtains around it.

Anne roused herself from her reverie with a happy sigh.

"I was thinking out my story, Diana."

"Oh, have you really begun it?" cried Diana, all alight with eager interest in a moment.

"Yes, I have only a few pages written, but I have it all pretty well thought out. I've had such a time to get a suitable plot. None of the plots that suggested themselves suited a girl named *Averil*."

"Couldn't you have changed her name?"

"No, the thing was impossible. I tried to, but I couldn't do it, any more than I could change yours. *Averil* was so real to me that no matter what other name I tried to give her I just thought of her as *Averil* behind it all. But finally I got a plot that matched her. Then came the excitement of choosing names for all my characters. You have no idea how fascinating that is. I've lain awake for hours thinking over those names. The hero's name is *Perceval Dalrymple*."

"Have you named *all* the characters?" asked Diana wistfully. "If you hadn't I was going to ask you to let me name one—just some unimportant person. I'd feel as if I had a share in the story then."

"You may name the little hired boy who lived with the *Lesters*," conceded Anne. "He is not very important, but he is the only one left unnamed."

"Call him *Raymond Fitzosborne*," suggested Diana, who had a store of such names laid away in her memory, relics of the old "Story Club," which she and Anne and Jane Andrews and Ruby Gillis had had in their schooldays.

Anne shook her head doubtfully.

"I'm afraid that is too aristocratic a name for a chore boy, Diana. I couldn't imagine a Fitzosborne feeding pigs and picking up chips, could you?"

Diana didn't see why, if you had an imagination at all, you couldn't stretch it to that extent; but probably Anne knew best, and the chore boy was finally christened *Robert Ray*, to be called *Bobby* should occasion require.

"How much do you suppose you'll get for it?" asked Diana.

But Anne had not thought about this at all. She was in pursuit of fame, not filthy lucre, and her literary dreams were as yet untainted by mercenary considerations.

"You'll let me read it, won't you?" pleaded Diana.

"When it is finished I'll read it to you and Mr. Harrison, and I shall want you to criticize it *severely*. No one else shall see it until it is published."

"How are you going to end it—happily or unhappily?"

"I'm not sure. I'd like it to end unhappily, because that would be so much more romantic. But I understand editors have a prejudice against sad endings. I heard Professor Hamilton say once that nobody but a genius should try to write an unhappy ending. And," concluded Anne modestly, "I'm anything but a genius."

"Oh I like happy endings best. You'd better let him marry

her," said Diana, who, especially since her engagement to Fred, thought this was how every story should end.

"But you like to cry over stories?"

"Oh, yes, in the middle of them. But I like everything to come right at last."

"I must have one pathetic scene in it," said Anne thoughtfully. "I might let *Robert Ray* be injured in an accident and have a death scene."

"No, you mustn't kill *Bobby* off," declared Diana, laughing. "He belongs to me and I want him to live and flourish. Kill somebody else if you have to."

For the next fortnight Anne writhed or reveled, according to mood, in her literary pursuits. Now she would be jubilant over a brilliant idea, now despairing because some contrary character would *not* behave properly. Diana could not understand this.

"*Make* them do as you want them to," she said.

"I can't," mourned Anne. "Averil is such an unmanageable heroine. She *will* do and say things I never meant her to. Then that spoils everything that went before and I have to write it all over again."

Finally, however, the story was finished, and Anne read it to Diana in the seclusion of the porch gable. She had achieved her "pathetic scene" without sacrificing *Robert Ray*, and she kept a watchful eye on Diana as she read it. Diana rose to the occasion and cried properly; but, when the end came, she looked a little disappointed.

"Why did you kill *Maurice Lennox?*" she asked reproachfully.

"He was the villain," protested Anne. "He had to be punished."

"I like him best of them all," said unreasonable Diana.

"Well, he's dead, and he'll have to stay dead," said Anne, rather resentfully. "If I had let him live he'd have gone on persecuting *Averil* and *Perceval*."

"Yes—unless you had reformed him."

"That wouldn't have been romantic, and, besides, it would have made the story too long."

"Well, anyway, it's a perfectly elegant story, Anne, and will make you famous, of that I'm sure. Have you got a title for it?"

"Oh, I decided on the title long ago. I call it *Averil's atonement*. Doesn't that sound nice and alliterative? Now, Diana, tell me candidly, do you see any faults in my story?"

"Well," hesitated Diana, "that part where *Averil* makes the cake doesn't seem to me quite romantic enough to match the rest. It's just what anybody might do. Heroines shouldn't do cooking, *I* think."

"Why, that is where the humor comes in, and it's one of the best parts of the whole story," said Anne. And it may be stated that in this she was quite right.

Diana prudently refrained from any further criticism, but Mr. Harrison was much harder to please. First he told her there was entirely too much description in the story.

"Cut out all those flowery passages," he said unfeelingly.

Anne had an uncomfortable conviction that Mr. Harrison was right, and she forced herself to expunge most of her beloved descriptions, though it took three re-writings before the story could be pruned down to please the fastidious Mr. Harrison.

"I've left out *all* the descriptions but the sunset," she said at last. "I simply *couldn't* let it go. It was the best of them all."

"It hasn't anything to do with the story," said Mr. Harrison, "and you shouldn't have laid the scene among rich city people. What do you know of them? Why didn't you lay it right here in Avonlea—changing the name, of course, or else Mrs. Rachel Lynde would probably think she was the heroine."

"Oh, that would never have done," protested Anne. "Avonlea is the dearest place in the world, but it isn't quite romantic enough for the scene of a story."

"I daresay there's been many a romance in Avonlea—and many a tragedy, too," said Mr. Harrison drily. "But your folks ain't like real folks anywhere. They talk too much and use too high-flown language. There's one place where that *Dalrymple* chap talks even on for two pages, and never lets the girl get a word in edgewise. If he'd done that in real life she'd have pitched him."

"I don't believe it," said Anne flatly. In her secret soul she thought that the beautiful, poetical things said to *Averil* would win any girl's heart completely. Besides, it was gruesome to hear of *Averil*, the stately, queen-like *Averil*, "pitching" any one. *Averil* "declined her suitors."

"Anyhow," resumed the merciless Mr. Harrison, "I don't see why *Maurice Lennox* didn't get her. He was twice the man the other is. He did bad things, but he did them. Perceval hadn't time for anything but mooning."

"Mooning." That was even worse than "pitching!"

"*Maurice Lennox* was the villain," said Anne indignantly. "I don't see why every one likes him better than *Perceval*."

"Perceval is too good. He's aggravating. Next time you write about a hero put a little spice of human nature in him."

"*Averil* couldn't have married *Maurice*. He was bad."

"She'd have reformed him. You can reform a man; you can't reform a jelly-fish, of course. Your story isn't bad—it's kind of interesting, I'll admit. But you're too young to write a story that would be worth while. Wait ten years."

Anne made up her mind that the next time she wrote a story she wouldn't ask anybody to criticize it. It was too discouraging. She would not read the story to Gilbert, although she told him about it.

"If it is a success you'll see it when it is published, Gilbert, but if it is a failure nobody shall ever see it."

Marilla knew nothing about the venture. In imagination

Anne saw herself reading a story out of a magazine to Marilla, entrapping her into praise of it—for in imagination all things are possible—and then triumphantly announcing herself the author.

One day Anne took to the Post Office a long, bulky envelope, addressed, with the delightful confidence of youth and inexperience, to the very biggest of the "big" magazines. Diana was as excited over it as Anne herself.

"How long do you suppose it will be before you hear from it?" she asked.

"It shouldn't be longer than a fortnight. Oh, how happy and proud I shall be if it is accepted!"

"Of course it will be accepted, and they will likely ask you to send them more. You may be as famous as Mrs. Morgan some day, Anne, and then how proud I'll be of knowing you," said Diana, who possessed, at least, the striking merit of an unselfish admiration of the gifts and graces of her friends.

A week of delightful dreaming followed, and then came a bitter awakening. One evening Diana found Anne in the porch gable, with suspicious-looking eyes. On the table lay a long envelope and a crumpled manuscript.

"Anne, your story hasn't come back?" cried Diana incredulously.

"Yes, it has," said Anne shortly.

"Well, that editor must be crazy. What reason did he give?"

"No reason at all. There is just a printed slip saying that it wasn't found acceptable."

"I never thought much of that magazine, anyway," said Diana hotly. "The stories in it are not half as interesting as those in the *Canadian Woman*, although it costs so much more. I suppose the editor is prejudiced against any one who isn't a Yankee. Don't be discouraged, Anne. Remember how Mrs. Morgan's stories came back. Send yours to the *Canadian Woman*."

"I believe I will," said Anne, plucking up heart. "And if it is published I'll send that American editor a marked copy. But I'll cut the sunset out. I believe Mr. Harrison was right."

Out came the sunset; but in spite of this heroic mutilation the editor of the *Canadian Woman* sent Averil's Atonement back so promptly that the indignant Diana declared that it couldn't have been read at all, and vowed she was going to stop her subscription immediately. Anne took this second rejection with the calmness of despair. She locked the story away in the garret trunk where the old Story Club tales reposed; but first she yielded to Diana's entreaties and gave her a copy.

"This is the end of my literary ambitions," she said bitterly.

She never mentioned the matter to Mr. Harrison, but one evening he asked her bluntly if her story had been accepted.

"No, the editor wouldn't take it," she answered briefly.

Mr. Harrison looked sidewise at the flushed, delicate profile.

"Well, I suppose you'll keep on writing them," he said encouragingly.

"No, I shall never try to write a story again," declared Anne, with the hopeless finality of nineteen when a door is shut in its face.

"I wouldn't give up altogether," said Mr. Harrison reflectively. "I'd write a story once in a while, but I wouldn't pester editors with it. I'd write of people and places like I knew, and I'd make my characters talk everyday English; and I'd let the sun rise and set in the usual quiet way without much fuss over the fact. If I had to have villains at all, I'd give them a chance, Anne—I'd give them a chance. There are some terrible bad men in the world, I suppose, but you'd have to go a long piece to find them—though Mrs. Lynde believes we're all bad. But most of us have got a little decency somewhere in us. Keep on writing, Anne."

"No. It was very foolish of me to attempt it. When I'm through Redmond I'll stick to teaching. I can teach. I can't write stories."

"It'll be time for you to be getting a husband when you're through Redmond," said Mr. Harrison. "I don't believe in putting marrying off too long—like I did."

Anne got up and marched home. There were times when Mr. Harrison was really intolerable. "Pitching," "mooning," and "getting a husband." Ow!!

Chapter XIII
The Way of Transgressors

Davy and Dora were ready for Sunday School. They were going alone, which did not often happen, for Mrs. Lynde always attended Sunday School. But Mrs. Lynde had twisted her ankle and was lame, so she was staying home this morning. The twins were also to represent the family at church, for Anne had gone away the evening before to spend Sunday with friends in Carmody, and Marilla had one of her headaches.

Davy came downstairs slowly. Dora was waiting in the hall for him, having been made ready by Mrs. Lynde. Davy had attended to his own preparations. He had a cent in his pocket for the Sunday School collection, and a five-cent piece for the church collection; he carried his Bible in one hand and his Sunday School quarterly in the other; he knew his lesson and his Golden Text and his catechism question perfectly. Had he not studied them—perforce—in Mrs. Lynde's kitchen, all last Sunday afternoon? Davy, therefore, should have been in a placid frame of mind. As a matter of fact, despite text and catechism, he was inwardly as a ravening wolf.

Mrs. Lynde limped out of her kitchen as he joined Dora.

"Are you clean?" she demanded severely.

"Yes—all of me that shows," Davy answered with a defiant scowl.

Mrs. Rachel sighed. She had her suspicions about Davy's

neck and ears. But she knew that if she attempted to make a personal examination Davy would likely take to his heels and she could not pursue him today.

"Well, be sure you behave yourselves," she warned them. "Don't walk in the dust. Don't stop in the porch to talk to the other children. Don't squirm or wriggle in your places. Don't forget the Golden Text. Don't lose your collection or forget to put it in. Don't whisper at prayer time, and don't forget to pay attention to the sermon."

Davy deigned no response. He marched away down the lane, followed by the meek Dora. But his soul seethed within. Davy had suffered, or thought he had suffered, many things at the hands and tongue of Mrs. Rachel Lynde since she had come to Green Gables, for Mrs. Lynde could not live with anybody, whether they were nine or ninety, without trying to bring them up properly. And it was only the preceding afternoon that she had interfered to influence Marilla against allowing Davy to go fishing with the Timothy Cottons. Davy was still boiling over this.

As soon as he was out of the lane Davy stopped and twisted his countenance into such an unearthly and terrific contortion that Dora, although she knew his gifts in that respect, was honestly alarmed lest he should never in the world be able to get it straightened out again.

"Darn her," exploded Davy.

"Oh, Davy, don't swear," gasped Dora in dismay.

"'Darn' isn't swearing—not real swearing. And I don't care if it is," retorted Davy recklessly.

"Well, if you *must* say dreadful words don't say them on Sunday," pleaded Dora.

Davy was as yet far from repentance, but in his secret soul he felt that, perhaps, he had gone a little too far.

"I'm going to invent a swear word of my own," he declared.

"God will punish you if you do," said Dora solemnly.

"Then I think God is a mean old scamp," retorted Davy. "Doesn't He know a fellow must have some way of 'spressing his feelings?"

"Davy!!!" said Dora. She expected that Davy would be struck down dead on the spot. But nothing happened.

"Anyway, I ain't going to stand any more of Mrs. Lynde's bossing," spluttered Davy. "Anne and Marilla may have the right to boss me, but *she* hasn't. I'm going to do every single thing she told me not to do. You watch me."

In grim, deliberate silence, while Dora watched him with the fascination of horror, Davy stepped off the green grass of the roadside, ankle deep into the fine dust which four weeks of rainless weather had made on the road, and marched along in it, shuffling his feet viciously until he was enveloped in a hazy cloud.

"That's the beginning," he announced triumphantly. "And I'm going to stop in the porch and talk as long as there's anybody there to talk to. I'm going to squirm and wriggle and whisper, and I'm going to say I don't know the Golden Text. And I'm going to throw away both of my collections *right now*."

And Davy hurled cent and nickel over Mr. Barry's fence with fierce delight.

"Satan made you do that," said Dora reproachfully.

"He didn't," cried Davy indignantly. "I just thought it out for myself. And I've thought of something else. I'm not going to Sunday School or church at all. I'm going up to play with the Cottons. They told me yesterday they weren't going to Sunday School today, 'cause their mother was away and there was nobody to make them. Come along, Dora, we'll have a great time."

"I don't want to go," protested Dora.

"You've got to," said Davy. "If you don't come I'll tell Marilla that Frank Bell kissed you in school last Monday."

"I couldn't help it. I didn't know he was going to," cried Dora, blushing scarlet.

"Well, you didn't slap him or seem a bit cross," retorted Davy. "I'll tell her *that*, too, if you don't come. We'll take the short cut up this field."

"I'm afraid of those cows," protested poor Dora, seeing a prospect of escape.

"The very idea of your being scared of those cows," scoffed Davy. "Why, they're both younger than you."

"They're bigger," said Dora.

"They won't hurt you. Come along, now. This is great. When I grow up I ain't going to bother going to church at all. I believe I can get to heaven by myself."

"You'll go to the other place if you break the Sabbath day," said unhappy Dora, following him sorely against her will.

But Davy was not scared—yet. Hell was very far off, and the delights of a fishing expedition with the Cottons were very near. He wished Dora had more spunk. She kept looking back as if she were going to cry every minute, and that spoiled a fellow's fun. Hang girls, anyway. Davy did not say "darn" this time, even in thought. He was not sorry—yet—that he had said it once, but it might be as well not to tempt the Unknown Powers too far on one day.

The small Cottons were playing in their back yard, and hailed Davy's appearance with whoops of delight. Pete, Tommy, Adolphus, and Mirabel Cotton were all alone. Their mother and older sisters were away. Dora was thankful Mirabel was there, at least. She had been afraid she would be alone in a crowd of boys. Mirabel was almost as bad as a boy—she was so noisy and sunburned and reckless. But at least she wore dresses.

"We've come to go fishing," announced Davy.

"Whoop," yelled the Cottons. They rushed away to dig worms at once, Mirabel leading the van with a tin can. Dora could have sat down and cried. Oh, if only that hateful Frank Bell had never kissed her! Then she could have defied Davy, and gone to her beloved Sunday School.

They dared not, of course, go fishing on the pond, where they would be seen by people going to church. They had to resort to the brook in the woods behind the Cotton house. But it was full of trout, and they had a glorious time that morning—at least the Cottons certainly had, and Davy seemed to have it. Not being entirely bereft of prudence, he had discarded boots and stockings and borrowed Tommy Cotton's overalls. Thus accoutered, bog and marsh and undergrowth had no terrors for him. Dora was frankly and manifestly miserable. She followed the others in their peregrinations from pool to pool, clasping her Bible and quarterly tightly and thinking with bitterness of soul of her beloved class where she should be sitting that very moment, before a teacher she adored. Instead, here she was roaming the woods with those half-wild Cottons, trying to keep her boots clean and her pretty white dress free from rents and stains. Mirabel had offered the loan of an apron but Dora had scornfully refused.

The trout bit as they always do on Sundays. In an hour the transgressors had all the fish they wanted, so they returned to the house, much to Dora's relief. She sat primly on a hencoop in the yard while the others played an uproarious game of tag; and then they all climbed to the top of the pig-house roof and cut their initials on the saddleboard. The flat-roofed henhouse and a pile of straw beneath gave Davy another inspiration. They spent a splendid half hour climbing on the roof and diving off into the straw with whoops and yells.

But even unlawful pleasures must come to an end. When the rumble of wheels over the pond bridge told that people were going home from church Davy knew they must go. He discarded Tommy's overalls, resumed his own rightful attire, and turned away from his string of trout with a sigh. No use to think of taking them home.

"Well, hadn't we a splendid time?" he demanded defiantly, as they went down the hill field.

"I hadn't," said Dora flatly. "And I don't believe you had—really—either," she added, with a flash of insight that was not to be expected of her.

"I had so," cried Davy, but in the voice of one who doth protest too much. "No wonder you hadn't—just sitting there like a—like a mule."

"I ain't going to, 'sociate with the Cottons," said Dora loftily.

"The Cottons are all right," retorted Davy. "And they have far better times than we have. They do just as they please and say just what they like before everybody. *I*'m going to do that, too, after this."

"There are lots of things you wouldn't dare say before everybody," averred Dora.

"No, there isn't."

"There is, too. Would you," demanded Dora gravely, "would you say 'tomcat' before the minister?"

This was a staggerer. Davy was not prepared for such a concrete example of the freedom of speech. But one did not have to be consistent with Dora.

"Of course not," he admitted sulkily.

"'Tomcat' isn't a holy word. I wouldn't mention such an animal before a minister at all."

"But if you had to?" persisted Dora.

"I'd call it a Thomas pussy," said Davy.

"*I* think 'gentleman cat' would be more polite," reflected Dora.

"*You* thinking!" retorted Davy with withering scorn.

Davy was not feeling comfortable, though he would have died before he admitted it to Dora. Now that the exhilaration of truant delights had died away, his conscience was beginning to give him salutary twinges. After all, perhaps it would have been better to have gone to Sunday School and church. Mrs. Lynde might be bossy; but there was always a box of cookies in her kitchen cupboard and she was not stingy. At this inconvenient moment Davy remembered that when he had torn his new school pants the week before, Mrs. Lynde had mended them beautifully and never said a word to Marilla about them.

But Davy's cup of iniquity was not yet full. He was to discover that one sin demands another to cover it. They had dinner with Mrs. Lynde that day, and the first thing she asked Davy was,

"Were all your class in Sunday School today?"

"Yes'm," said Davy with a gulp. "All were there—'cept one."

"Did you say your Golden Text and catechism?"

"Yes'm."

"Did you put your collection in?"

"Yes'm."

"Was Mrs. Malcolm MacPherson in church?"

"I don't know." This, at least, was the truth, thought wretched Davy.

"Was the Ladies' Aid announced for next week?"

"Yes'm"—quakingly.

"Was prayer-meeting?"

"I—I don't know."

"*You* should know. You should listen more attentively to the announcements. What was Mr. Harvey's text?"

Davy took a frantic gulp of water and swallowed it and

the last protest of conscience together. He glibly recited an old Golden Text learned several weeks ago. Fortunately Mrs. Lynde now stopped questioning him; but Davy did not enjoy his dinner.

He could only eat one helping of pudding.

"What's the matter with you?" demanded justly astonished Mrs. Lynde. "Are you sick?"

"No," muttered Davy.

"You look pale. You'd better keep out of the sun this afternoon," admonished Mrs. Lynde.

"Do you know how many lies you told Mrs. Lynde?" asked Dora reproachfully, as soon as they were alone after dinner.

Davy, goaded to desperation, turned fiercely.

"I don't know and I don't care," he said. "You just shut up, Dora Keith."

Then poor Davy betook himself to a secluded retreat behind the woodpile to think over the way of transgressors.

Green Gables was wrapped in darkness and silence when Anne reached home. She lost no time going to bed, for she was very tired and sleepy. There had been several Avonlea jollifications the preceding week, involving rather late hours. Anne's head was hardly on her pillow before she was half asleep; but just then her door was softly opened and a pleading voice said, "Anne."

Anne sat up drowsily.

"Davy, is that you? What is the matter?"

A white-clad figure flung itself across the floor and on to the bed.

"Anne," sobbed Davy, getting his arms about her neck. "I'm awful glad you're home. I couldn't go to sleep till I'd told somebody."

"Told somebody what?"

"How mis'rubul I am."

"Why are you miserable, dear?"

"'Cause I was so bad today, Anne. Oh, I was awful bad—badder'n I've ever been yet."

"What did you do?"

"Oh, I'm afraid to tell you. You'll never like me again, Anne. I couldn't say my prayers tonight. I couldn't tell God what I'd done. I was 'shamed to have Him know."

"But He knew anyway, Davy."

"That's what Dora said. But I thought p'raps He mightn't have noticed just at the time. Anyway, I'd rather tell you first."

"*What* is it you did?"

Out it all came in a rush.

"I run away from Sunday School—and went fishing with the Cottons—and I told ever so many whoppers to Mrs. Lynde—oh! 'most half a dozen—and—and—I—I said a swear word, Anne—a pretty near swear word, anyhow—and I called God names."

There was silence. Davy didn't know what to make of it. Was Anne so shocked that she never would speak to him again?

"Anne, what are you going to do to me?" he whispered.

"Nothing, dear. You've been punished already, I think."

"No, I haven't. Nothing's been done to me."

"You've been very unhappy ever since you did wrong, haven't you?"

"You bet!" said Davy emphatically.

"That was your conscience punishing you, Davy."

"What's my conscience? I want to know."

"It's something in you, Davy, that always tells you when you are doing wrong and makes you unhappy if you persist in doing it. Haven't you noticed that?"

"Yes, but I didn't know what it was. I wish I didn't have it. I'd have lots more fun. Where is my conscience, Anne? I want to know. Is it in my stomach?"

"No, it's in your soul," answered Anne, thankful for the darkness, since gravity must be preserved in serious matters.

"I s'pose I can't get clear of it then," said Davy with a sigh. "Are you going to tell Marilla and Mrs. Lynde on me, Anne?"

"No, dear, I'm not going to tell any one. You are sorry you were naughty, aren't you?"

"You bet!"

"And you'll never be bad like that again."

"No, but—" added Davy cautiously, "I might be bad some other way."

"You won't say naughty words, or run away on Sundays, or tell falsehoods to cover up your sins?"

"No. It doesn't pay," said Davy.

"Well, Davy, just tell God you are sorry and ask Him to forgive you."

"Have *you* forgiven me, Anne?"

"Yes, dear."

"Then," said Davy joyously, "I don't care much whether God does or not."

"Davy!"

"Oh—I'll ask Him—I'll ask Him," said Davy quickly, scrambling off the bed, convinced by Anne's tone that he must have said something dreadful. "I don't mind asking Him, Anne.—Please, God, I'm awful sorry I behaved bad today and I'll try to be good on Sundays always and please forgive me.—There now, Anne."

"Well, now, run off to bed like a good boy."

"All right. Say, I don't feel mis'rubul any more. I feel fine. Good night."

"Good night."

Anne slipped down on her pillows with a sigh of relief. Oh—how sleepy—she was! In another second—

"Anne!" Davy was back again by her bed. Anne dragged her eyes open.

"What is it now, dear?" she asked, trying to keep a note of impatience out of her voice.

"Anne, have you ever noticed how Mr. Harrison spits? Do you s'pose, if I practice hard, I can learn to spit just like him?"

Anne sat up.

"Davy Keith," she said, "go straight to your bed and don't let me catch you out of it again tonight! Go, now!"

Davy went, and stood not upon the order of his going.

Chapter XIV
The Summons

Anne was sitting with Ruby Gillis in the Gillis' garden after the day had crept lingeringly through it and was gone. It had been a warm, smoky summer afternoon. The world was in a splendor of out-flowering. The idle valleys were full of hazes. The woodways were pranked with shadows and the fields with the purple of the asters.

Anne had given up a moonlight drive to the White Sands beach that she might spend the evening with Ruby. She had so spent many evenings that summer, although she often wondered what good it did any one, and sometimes went home deciding that she could not go again.

Ruby grew paler as the summer waned; the White Sands school was given up—"her father thought it better that she shouldn't teach till New Year's"—and the fancy work she loved oftener and oftener fell from hands grown too weary for it. But she was always gay, always hopeful, always chattering and whispering of her beaux, and their rivalries and despairs. It was this that made Anne's visits hard for her. What had once been silly or amusing was gruesome, now; it was death peering through a wilful mask of life. Yet Ruby seemed to cling to her, and never let her go until she had promised to come again soon. Mrs. Lynde grumbled about Anne's frequent visits, and declared she would catch consumption; even Marilla was dubious.

"Every time you go to see Ruby you come home looking tired out," she said.

"It's so very sad and dreadful," said Anne in a low tone. "Ruby doesn't seem to realize her condition in the least. And yet I somehow feel she needs help—craves it—and I want to give it to her and can't. All the time I'm with her I feel as if I were watching her struggle with an invisible foe—trying to push it back with such feeble resistance as she has. That is why I come home tired."

But tonight Anne did not feel this so keenly. Ruby was strangely quiet. She said not a word about parties and drives and dresses and "fellows." She lay in the hammock, with her untouched work beside her, and a white shawl wrapped about her thin shoulders. Her long yellow braids of hair—how Anne had envied those beautiful braids in old schooldays!—lay on either side of her. She had taken the pins out—they made her head ache, she said. The hectic flush was gone for the time, leaving her pale and childlike.

The moon rose in the silvery sky, empearling the clouds around her. Below, the pond shimmered in its hazy radiance. Just beyond the Gillis homestead was the church, with the old graveyard beside it. The moonlight shone on the white stones, bringing them out in clear-cut relief against the dark trees behind.

"How strange the graveyard looks by moonlight!" said Ruby suddenly. "How ghostly!" she shuddered. "Anne, it won't be long now before I'll be lying over there. You and Diana and all the rest will be going about, full of life—and I'll be there—in the old graveyard—dead!"

The surprise of it bewildered Anne. For a few moments she could not speak.

"You know it's so, don't you?" said Ruby insistently.

"Yes, I know," answered Anne in a low tone. "Dear Ruby, I know."

"Everybody knows it," said Ruby bitterly. "I know it—I've known it all summer, though I wouldn't give in. And, oh, Anne"—she reached out and caught Anne's hand pleadingly, impulsively—"I don't want to die. I'm *afraid* to die."

"Why should you be afraid, Ruby?" asked Anne quietly.

"Because—because—oh, I'm not afraid but that I'll go to heaven, Anne. I'm a church member. But—it'll be all so different. I think—and think—and I get so frightened—and—and—homesick. Heaven must be very beautiful, of course, the Bible says so—but, Anne, *it won't be what 've been used to*."

Through Anne's mind drifted an intrusive recollection of a funny story she had heard Philippa Gordon tell—the story of some old man who had said very much the same thing about the world to come. It had sounded funny then—she remembered how she and Priscilla had laughed over it. But it did not seem in the least humorous now, coming from Ruby's pale, trembling lips. It was sad, tragic—and true! Heaven could not be what Ruby had been used to. There had been nothing in her gay, frivolous life, her shallow ideals and aspirations, to fit her for that great change, or make the life to come seem to her anything but alien and unreal and undesirable. Anne wondered helplessly what she could say that would help her. Could she say anything? "I think, Ruby," she began hesitatingly—for it was difficult for Anne to speak to any one of the deepest thoughts of her heart, or the new ideas that had vaguely begun to shape themselves in her mind, concerning the great mysteries of life here and hereafter, superseding her old childish conceptions, and it was hardest of all to speak of them to such as Ruby Gillis—"I think, perhaps, we have very mistaken ideas about heaven—what it is and what it holds for us. I don't think it can be so very different from life here as most people seem to think. I believe we'll just go on living, a good deal as we live here and be *ourselves* just the same—only it will be easier to be good and to—follow the highest. All the hindrances and perplexities will be taken away, and we shall see clearly. Don't be afraid, Ruby."

"I can't help it," said Ruby pitifully. "Even if what you say about heaven is true—and you can't be sure—it may be only that imagination of yours—it won't be *just* the same. It *can't* be. I want to go on living *here*. I'm so young, Anne. I haven't had my life. I've fought so hard to live—and it isn't any use—I have to die—and leave *everything* I care for." Anne sat in a pain that was almost intolerable. She could not tell comforting falsehoods; and all that Ruby said was so horribly true. She *was* leaving everything she cared for. She had laid up her treasures on earth only; she had lived solely for the little things of life—the things that pass—forgetting the great things that go onward into eternity, bridging the gulf between the two lives and making of death a mere passing from one dwelling to the other—from twilight to unclouded day. God would take care of her there—Anne believed—she would learn—but now it was no wonder her soul clung, in blind helplessness, to the only things she knew and loved.

Ruby raised herself on her arm and lifted up her bright, beautiful blue eyes to the moonlit skies.

"I want to live," she said, in a trembling voice. "I want to live like other girls. I—I want to be married, Anne—and—and—have little children. You know I always loved babies, Anne. I couldn't say this to any one but you. I know you understand. And then poor Herb—he—he loves me and I love him, Anne. The others meant nothing to me, but *he* does—and if I could live I would be his wife and be so happy. Oh, Anne, it's hard."

Ruby sank back on her pillows and sobbed convulsively. Anne pressed her hand in an agony of sympathy—silent sympathy, which perhaps helped Ruby more than broken, imperfect words could have done; for presently she grew calmer and her sobs ceased.

"I'm glad I've told you this, Anne," she whispered. "It has helped me just to say it all out. I've wanted to all summer—every time you came. I wanted to talk it over with you—but I *couldn't*. It seemed as if it would make death so *sure* if I *said* I was going to die, or if any one else said it or hinted it. I wouldn't say it, or even think it. In the daytime, when people were around me and everything was cheerful, it wasn't so hard to keep from thinking of it. But in the night, when I couldn't sleep—it was so dreadful, Anne. I couldn't get away from it then. Death just came and stared me in the face, until I got so frightened I could have screamed.

"But you won't be frightened any more, Ruby, will you? You'll be brave, and believe that all is going to be well with you."

"I'll try. I'll think over what you have said, and try to believe it. And you'll come up as often as you can, won't you, Anne?"

"Yes, dear."

"It—it won't be very long now, Anne. I feel sure of that. And I'd rather have you than any one else. I always liked you best of all the girls I went to school with. You were never jealous, or mean, like some of them were. Poor Em White was up to see me yesterday. You remember Em and I were such chums for three years when we went to school? And then we quarrelled the time of the school concert. We've never spoken to each other since. Wasn't it silly? Anything like that seems silly *now*. But Em and I made up the old quarrel yesterday. She said she'd have spoken years ago, only she thought I wouldn't. And I never spoke to her because I was sure she wouldn't speak to me. Isn't it strange how people misunderstand each other, Anne?"

"Most of the trouble in life comes from misunderstanding, I think," said Anne. "I must go now, Ruby. It's getting late—and you shouldn't be out in the damp."

"You'll come up soon again."

"Yes, very soon. And if there's anything I can do to help you I'll be so glad."

"I know. You *have* helped me already. Nothing seems quite so dreadful now. Good night, Anne."

"Good night, dear."

Anne walked home very slowly in the moonlight. The evening had changed something for her. Life held a different meaning, a deeper purpose. On the surface it would go on just the same; but the deeps had been stirred. It must not be with her as with poor butterfly Ruby. When she came to the end of one life it must not be to face the next with the shrinking terror of something wholly different—something for which accustomed thought and ideal and aspiration had unfitted her. The little things of life, sweet and excellent in their place, must not be the things lived for; the highest must be sought and followed; the life of heaven must be begun here on earth.

That good night in the garden was for all time. Anne never saw Ruby in life again. The next night the A.V.I.S. gave a farewell party to Jane Andrews before her departure for the West. And, while light feet danced and bright eyes laughed and merry tongues chattered, there came a summons to a soul in Avonlea that might not be disregarded or evaded. The next morning the word went from house to house that Ruby Gillis was dead. She had died in her sleep, painlessly and calmly, and on her face was a smile—as if, after all, death had come as a kindly friend to lead her over the threshold, instead of the grisly phantom she had dreaded.

Mrs. Rachel Lynde said emphatically after the funeral that Ruby Gillis was the handsomest corpse she ever laid eyes on. Her loveliness, as she lay, white-clad, among the delicate flowers that Anne had placed about her, was remembered and talked of for years in Avonlea. Ruby had always been beautiful; but her beauty had been of the earth, earthy; it had had a certain insolent quality in it, as if it flaunted itself in the beholder's eye; spirit had never shone through it, intellect had never refined it. But death had touched it and consecrated it, bringing out delicate modelings and purity of outline never seen before—doing what life and love and great sorrow and deep womanhood joys might have done for Ruby. Anne, looking down through a mist of tears, at her old playfellow, thought she saw the face God had meant Ruby to have, and remembered it so always.

Mrs. Gillis called Anne aside into a vacant room before the funeral procession left the house, and gave her a small packet.

"I want you to have this," she sobbed. "Ruby would have liked you to have it. It's the embroidered centerpiece she was working at. It isn't quite finished—the needle is sticking in it just where her poor little fingers put it the last time she laid it down, the afternoon before she died."

"There's always a piece of unfinished work left," said Mrs. Lynde, with tears in her eyes. "But I suppose there's always some one to finish it."

"How difficult it is to realize that one we have always known can really be dead," said Anne, as she and Diana walked home. "Ruby is the first of our schoolmates to go. One by one, sooner or later, all the rest of us must follow."

"Yes, I suppose so," said Diana uncomfortably. She did not want to talk of that. She would have preferred to have discussed the details of the funeral—the splendid white velvet casket Mr. Gillis had insisted on having for Ruby—"the Gillises must always make a splurge, even at funerals," quoth Mrs. Rachel Lynde—Herb Spencer's sad face, the uncontrolled, hysteric grief of one of Ruby's sisters—but Anne would not talk of these things. She seemed wrapped in a reverie in which Diana felt lonesomely that she had neither lot nor part.

"Ruby Gillis was a great girl to laugh," said Davy suddenly. "Will she laugh as much in heaven as she did in Avonlea, Anne? I want to know."

"Yes, I think she will," said Anne.

"Oh, Anne," protested Diana, with a rather shocked smile.

"Well, why not, Diana?" asked Anne seriously. "Do you think we'll never laugh in heaven?"

"Oh—I—I don't know" floundered Diana. "It doesn't seem just right, somehow. You know it's rather dreadful to laugh in church."

"But heaven won't be like church—all the time," said Anne.

"I hope it ain't," said Davy emphatically. "If it is I don't want to go. Church is awful dull. Anyway, I don't mean to go for ever so long. I mean to live to be a hundred years old, like Mr. Thomas Blewett of White Sands. He says he's lived so long 'cause he always smoked tobacco and it killed all the germs. Can I smoke tobacco pretty soon, Anne?"

"No, Davy, I hope you'll never use tobacco," said Anne absently.

"What'll you feel like if the germs kill me then?" demanded Davy.

Chapter XV
A Dream Turned Upside Down

"Just one more week and we go back to Redmond," said Anne. She was happy at the thought of returning to work, classes and Redmond friends. Pleasing visions were also being woven around Patty's Place. There was a warm pleasant sense of home in the thought of it, even though she had never lived there.

But the summer had been a very happy one, too—a time of glad living with summer suns and skies, a time of keen delight in wholesome things; a time of renewing and deepening of old friendships; a time in which she had learned to live more nobly, to work more patiently, to play more heartily.

"All life lessons are not learned at college," she thought. "Life teaches them everywhere."

But alas, the final week of that pleasant vacation was spoiled for Anne, by one of those impish happenings which are like a dream turned upside down.

"Been writing any more stories lately?" inquired Mr. Harrison genially one evening when Anne was taking tea with him and Mrs. Harrison.

"No," answered Anne, rather crisply.

"Well, no offense meant. Mrs. Hiram Sloane told me the other day that a big envelope addressed to the Rollings Reliable

Baking Powder Company of Montreal had been dropped into the post office box a month ago, and she suspicioned that somebody was trying for the prize they'd offered for the best story that introduced the name of their baking powder. She said it wasn't addressed in your writing, but I thought maybe it was you."

"Indeed, no! I saw the prize offer, but I'd never dream of competing for it. I think it would be perfectly disgraceful to write a story to advertise a baking powder. It would be almost as bad as Judson Parker's patent medicine fence."

So spake Anne loftily, little dreaming of the valley of humiliation awaiting her. That very evening Diana popped into the porch gable, bright-eyed and rosy cheeked, carrying a letter.

"Oh, Anne, here's a letter for you. I was at the office, so I thought I'd bring it along. Do open it quick. If it is what I believe it is I shall just be wild with delight." Anne, puzzled, opened the letter and glanced over the typewritten contents.

> Miss Anne Shirley,
> Green Gables,
> Avonlea, P.E. Island.
>
> "Dear Madam: We have much pleasure in informing you that your charming story 'Averil's Atonement' has won the prize of twenty-five dollars offered in our recent competition. We enclose the check herewith. We are arranging for the publication of the story in several prominent Canadian newspapers, and we also intend to have it printed in pamphlet form for distribution among our patrons. Thanking you for the interest you have shown in our enterprise,
>
> "We remain,
> "Yours very truly,
> "The Rollings Reliable Baking Powder Co."

"I don't understand," said Anne, blankly.

Diana clapped her hands.

"Oh, I *knew* it would win the prize—I was sure of it. *I* sent your story into the competition, Anne."

"Diana—Barry!"

"Yes, I did," said Diana gleefully, perching herself on the bed. "When I saw the offer I thought of your story in a minute, and at first I thought I'd ask you to send it in. But then I was afraid you wouldn't—you had so little faith left in it. So I just decided I'd send the copy you gave me, and say nothing about it. Then, if it didn't win the prize, you'd never know and you wouldn't feel badly over it, because the stories that failed were not to be returned, and if it did you'd have such a delightful surprise."

Diana was not the most discerning of mortals, but just at this moment it struck her that Anne was not looking exactly overjoyed. The surprise was there, beyond doubt—but where was the delight?

"Why, Anne, you don't seem a bit pleased!" she exclaimed.

Anne instantly manufactured a smile and put it on.

"Of course I couldn't be anything but pleased over your unselfish wish to give me pleasure," she said slowly. "But you know—I'm so amazed—I can't realize it—and I don't understand. There wasn't a word in my story about—about—" Anne choked a little over the word—"baking powder."

"Oh, *I* put that in," said Diana, reassured. "It was as easy as wink—and of course my experience in our old Story Club helped me. You know the scene where Averil makes the cake? Well, I just stated that she used the Rollings Reliable in it, and that was why it turned out so well; and then, in the last paragraph, where *Perceval* clasps *Averil* in his arms and says, 'Sweetheart, the beautiful coming years will bring us the fulfilment of our home of dreams,' I added, 'in which we will never use any baking powder except Rollings Reliable.'"

"Oh," gasped poor Anne, as if some one had dashed cold water on her.

"And you've won the twenty-five dollars," continued Diana jubilantly. "Why, I heard Priscilla say once that the *Canadian Woman* only pays five dollars for a story!"

Anne held out the hateful pink slip in shaking fingers.

"I can't take it—it's yours by right, Diana. You sent the story in and made the alterations. I—I would certainly never have sent it. So you must take the check."

"I'd like to see myself," said Diana scornfully. "Why, what I did wasn't any trouble. The honor of being a friend of the prize-winner is enough for me. Well, I must go. I should have gone straight home from the post office for we have company. But I simply had to come and hear the news. I'm so glad for your sake, Anne."

Anne suddenly bent forward, put her arms about Diana, and kissed her cheek.

"I think you are the sweetest and truest friend in the world, Diana," she said, with a little tremble in her voice, "and I assure you I appreciate the motive of what you've done."

Diana, pleased and embarrassed, got herself away, and poor Anne, after flinging the innocent check into her bureau drawer as if it were blood-money, cast herself on her bed and wept tears of shame and outraged sensibility. Oh, she could never live this down—never!

Gilbert arrived at dusk, brimming over with congratulations, for he had called at Orchard Slope and heard the news. But his congratulations died on his lips at sight of Anne's face.

"Why, Anne, what is the matter? I expected to find you radiant over winning Rollings Reliable prize. Good for you!"

"Oh, Gilbert, not you," implored Anne, in an *et-tu Brute* tone. "I thought *you* would understand. Can't you see how awful it is?"

"I must confess I can't. *What* is wrong?"

"Everything," moaned Anne. "I feel as if I were disgraced forever. What do you think a mother would feel like if she found her child tattooed over with a baking powder advertisement? I feel just the same. I loved my poor little story, and I wrote it out of the best that was in me. And it is *sacrilege* to have it degraded to the level of a baking powder advertisement. Don't you remember what Professor Hamilton used to tell us in the literature class at Queen's? He said we were never to write a word for a low or unworthy motive, but always to cling to the very highest ideals. What will he think when he hears I've written a story to advertise Rollings Reliable? And, oh, when it gets out at Redmond! Think how I'll be teased and laughed at!"

"That you won't," said Gilbert, wondering uneasily if it were that confounded Junior's opinion in particular over which Anne was worried. "The Reds will think just as I thought—that you, being like nine out of ten of us, not overburdened with worldly wealth, had taken this way of earning an honest penny to help yourself through the year. I don't see that there's anything low or unworthy about that, or anything ridiculous either. One would rather write masterpieces of literature no doubt—but meanwhile board and tuition fees have to be paid."

This commonsense, matter-of-fact view of the case cheered Anne a little. At least it removed her dread of being laughed at, though the deeper hurt of an outraged ideal remained.

Chapter XVI
Adjusted Relationships

"It's the homiest spot I ever saw—it's homier than home," avowed Philippa Gordon, looking about her with delighted eyes. They were all assembled at twilight in the big living-room at Patty's Place—Anne and Priscilla, Phil and Stella, Aunt Jamesina, Rusty, Joseph, the Sarah-Cat, and Gog and Magog. The firelight shadows were dancing over the walls; the cats were purring; and a huge bowl of hothouse chrysanthemums, sent to Phil by one of the victims, shone through the golden gloom like creamy moons.

It was three weeks since they had considered themselves settled, and already all believed the experiment would be a success. The first fortnight after their return had been a pleasantly exciting one; they had been busy setting up their household goods, organizing their little establishment, and adjusting different opinions.

Anne was not over-sorry to leave Avonlea when the time came to return to college. The last few days of her vacation had not been pleasant. Her prize story had been published in the Island papers; and Mr. William Blair had, upon the counter of his store, a huge pile of pink, green and yellow pamphlets, containing it, one of which he gave to every customer. He sent a complimentary bundle to Anne, who promptly dropped them all in the kitchen stove. Her humiliation was the consequence of her own ideals only, for Avonlea folks thought it quite splendid that she should have won the prize. Her many friends regarded her with honest admiration; her few foes with scornful envy. Josie Pye said she believed Anne Shirley had just copied the story; she was sure she remembered reading it in a paper years before. The Sloanes, who had found out or guessed that Charlie had been "turned down," said they didn't think it was much to be proud of; almost any one could have done it, if she tried. Aunt Atossa told Anne she was very sorry to hear she had taken to writing novels; nobody born and bred in Avonlea would do it; that was what came of adopting orphans from goodness knew where, with goodness knew what kind of parents. Even Mrs. Rachel Lynde was darkly dubious about the propriety of writing fiction, though she was almost reconciled to it by that twenty-five dollar check.

"It is perfectly amazing, the price they pay for such lies, that's what," she said, half-proudly, half-severely.

All things considered, it was a relief when going-away time came. And it was very jolly to be back at Redmond, a wise, experienced Soph with hosts of friends to greet on the merry opening day. Pris and Stella and Gilbert were there, Charlie Sloane, looking more important than ever a Sophomore looked before, Phil, with the Alec-and-Alonzo question still unsettled, and Moody Spurgeon MacPherson. Moody Spurgeon had been teaching school ever since leaving Queen's, but his mother had concluded it was high time he gave it up and turned his attention to learning how to be a minister. Poor Moody Spurgeon fell on hard luck at the very beginning of his college career. Half a dozen ruthless Sophs, who were among his fellow-boarders, swooped down upon him one night and shaved half of his head. In this guise the luckless Moody Spurgeon had to go about until his hair grew again. He told Anne bitterly that there were times when he had his doubts as to whether he was really called to be a minister.

Aunt Jamesina did not come until the girls had Patty's Place ready for her. Miss Patty had sent the key to Anne, with a letter in which she said Gog and Magog were packed in a box under the spare-room bed, but might be taken out when wanted; in a postscript she added that she hoped the girls would be careful about putting up pictures. The living room had been newly papered five years before and she and Miss Maria did not want any more holes made in that new paper than was absolutely necessary. For the rest she trusted everything to Anne.

How those girls enjoyed putting their nest in order! As Phil said, it was almost as good as getting married. You had the fun of homemaking without the bother of a husband. All brought something with them to adorn or make comfortable the little house. Pris and Phil and Stella had knick-knacks and pictures galore, which latter they proceeded to hang according to taste, in reckless disregard of Miss Patty's new paper.

"We'll putty the holes up when we leave, dear—she'll never know," they said to protesting Anne.

Diana had given Anne a pine needle cushion and Miss Ada had given both her and Priscilla a fearfully and wonderfully embroidered one. Marilla had sent a big box of preserves, and darkly hinted at a hamper for Thanksgiving, and Mrs. Lynde gave Anne a patchwork quilt and loaned her five more.

"You take them," she said authoritatively. "They might as well be in use as packed away in that trunk in the garret for moths to gnaw."

No moths would ever have ventured near those quilts, for they reeked of mothballs to such an extent that they had to be hung in the orchard of Patty's Place a full fortnight before they could be endured indoors. Verily, aristocratic Spofford Avenue had rarely beheld such a display. The gruff old millionaire who lived "next door" came over and wanted to buy the gorgeous red and yellow "tulip-pattern" one which Mrs. Rachel had given

Anne. He said his mother used to make quilts like that, and by Jove, he wanted one to remind him of her. Anne would not sell it, much to his disappointment, but she wrote all about it to Mrs. Lynde. That highly-gratified lady sent word back that she had one just like it to spare, so the tobacco king got his quilt after all, and insisted on having it spread on his bed, to the disgust of his fashionable wife.

Mrs. Lynde's quilts served a very useful purpose that winter. Patty's Place for all its many virtues, had its faults also. It was really a rather cold house; and when the frosty nights came the girls were very glad to snuggle down under Mrs. Lynde's quilts, and hoped that the loan of them might be accounted unto her for righteousness. Anne had the blue room she had coveted at sight. Priscilla and Stella had the large one. Phil was blissfully content with the little one over the kitchen; and Aunt Jamesina was to have the downstairs one off the living-room. Rusty at first slept on the doorstep.

Anne, walking home from Redmond a few days after her return, became aware that the people that she met surveyed her with a covert, indulgent smile. Anne wondered uneasily what was the matter with her. Was her hat crooked? Was her belt loose? Craning her head to investigate, Anne, for the first time, saw Rusty.

Trotting along behind her, close to her heels, was quite the most forlorn specimen of the cat tribe she had ever beheld. The animal was well past kitten-hood, lank, thin, disreputable looking. Pieces of both ears were lacking, one eye was temporarily out of repair, and one jowl ludicrously swollen. As for color, if a once black cat had been well and thoroughly singed the result would have resembled the hue of this waif's thin, draggled, unsightly fur.

Anne "shooed," but the cat would not "shoo." As long as she stood he sat back on his haunches and gazed at her reproachfully out of his one good eye; when she resumed her walk he followed. Anne resigned herself to his company until she reached the gate of Patty's Place, which she coldly shut in his face, fondly supposing she had seen the last of him. But when, fifteen minutes later, Phil opened the door, there sat the rusty-brown cat on the step. More, he promptly darted in and sprang upon Anne's lap with a half-pleading, half-triumphant "miaow."

"Anne," said Stella severely, "do you own that animal?"

"No, I do *not*," protested disgusted Anne. "The creature followed me home from somewhere. I couldn't get rid of him. Ugh, get down. I like decent cats reasonably well; but I don't like beasties of your complexion."

Pussy, however, refused to get down. He coolly curled up in Anne's lap and began to purr.

"He has evidently adopted you," laughed Priscilla.

"I won't BE adopted," said Anne stubbornly.

"The poor creature is starving," said Phil pityingly. "Why, his bones are almost coming through his skin."

"Well, I'll give him a square meal and then he must return to whence he came," said Anne resolutely.

The cat was fed and put out. In the morning he was still on the doorstep. On the doorstep he continued to sit, bolting in whenever the door was opened. No coolness of welcome had the least effect on him; of nobody save Anne did he take the least notice. Out of compassion the girls fed him; but when a week had passed they decided that something must be done. The cat's appearance had improved. His eye and cheek had resumed their normal appearance; he was not quite so thin; and he had been seen washing his face.

"But for all that we can't keep him," said Stella. "Aunt Jimsie is coming next week and she will bring the Sarah-cat with her. We can't keep two cats; and if we did this Rusty Coat would fight all the time with the Sarah-cat. He's a fighter by nature. He had a pitched battle last evening with the tobacco-king's cat and routed him, horse, foot and artillery."

"We must get rid of him," agreed Anne, looking darkly at the subject of their discussion, who was purring on the hearth rug with an air of lamb-like meekness. "But the question is—how? How can four unprotected females get rid of a cat who won't be got rid of?"

"We must chloroform him," said Phil briskly. "That is the most humane way."

"Who of us knows anything about chloroforming a cat?" demanded Anne gloomily.

"I do, honey. It's one of my few—sadly few—useful accomplishments. I've disposed of several at home. You take the cat in the morning and give him a good breakfast. Then you take an old burlap bag—there's one in the back porch—put the cat on it and turn over him a wooden box. Then take a two-ounce bottle of chloroform, uncork it, and slip it under the edge of the box. Put a heavy weight on top of the box and leave it till evening. The cat will be dead, curled up peacefully as if he were asleep. No pain—no struggle."

"It sounds easy," said Anne dubiously.

"It *is* easy. Just leave it to me. I'll see to it," said Phil reassuringly.

Accordingly the chloroform was procured, and the next morning Rusty was lured to his doom. He ate his breakfast, licked his chops, and climbed into Anne's lap. Anne's heart misgave her. This poor creature loved her—trusted her. How could she be a party to this destruction?

"Here, take him," she said hastily to Phil. "I feel like a murderess."

"He won't suffer, you know," comforted Phil, but Anne had fled.

The fatal deed was done in the back porch. Nobody went near it that day. But at dusk Phil declared that Rusty must be buried.

"Pris and Stella must dig his grave in the orchard," declared Phil, "and Anne must come with me to lift the box off. That's the part I always hate."

The two conspirators tip-toed reluctantly to the back porch. Phil gingerly lifted the stone she had put on the box. Suddenly, faint but distinct, sounded an unmistakable mew under the box.

"He—he isn't dead," gasped Anne, sitting blankly down on the kitchen doorstep.

"He must be," said Phil incredulously.

Another tiny mew proved that he wasn't. The two girls stared at each other.

"What will we do?" questioned Anne.

"Why in the world don't you come?" demanded Stella, appearing in the doorway. "We've got the grave ready. 'What silent still and silent all?'" she quoted teasingly.

"'Oh, no, the voices of the dead Sound like the distant torrent's fall,'" promptly counter-quoted Anne, pointing solemnly to the box.

A burst of laughter broke the tension.

"We must leave him here till morning," said Phil, replacing the stone. "He hasn't mewed for five minutes. Perhaps the mews we heard were his dying groan. Or perhaps we merely imagined them, under the strain of our guilty consciences."

But, when the box was lifted in the morning, Rusty bounded at one gay leap to Anne's shoulder where he began to lick her face affectionately. Never was there a cat more decidedly alive.

"Here's a knot hole in the box," groaned Phil. "I never saw it. That's why he didn't die. Now, we've got to do it all over again."

"No, we haven't," declared Anne suddenly. "Rusty isn't going to be killed again. He's my cat—and you've just got to make the best of it."

"Oh, well, if you'll settle with Aunt Jimsie and the Sarah-cat," said Stella, with the air of one washing her hands of the whole affair.

From that time Rusty was one of the family. He slept o'nights on the scrubbing cushion in the back porch and lived on the fat of the land. By the time Aunt Jamesina came he was plump and glossy and tolerably respectable. But, like Kipling's cat, he "walked by himself." His paw was against every cat, and every cat's paw against him. One by one he vanquished the aristocratic felines of Spofford Avenue. As for human beings, he loved Anne and Anne alone. Nobody else even dared stroke him. An angry spit and something that sounded much like very improper language greeted any one who did.

"The airs that cat puts on are perfectly intolerable," declared Stella.

"Him was a nice old pussens, him was," vowed Anne, cuddling her pet defiantly.

"Well, I don't know how he and the Sarah-cat will ever make out to live together," said Stella pesimistically. "Cat-fights in the orchard o'nights are bad enough. But cat-fights here in the livingroom are unthinkable." In due time Aunt Jamesina arrived. Anne and Priscilla and Phil had awaited her advent rather dubiously; but when Aunt Jamesina was enthroned in the rocking chair before the open fire they figuratively bowed down and worshipped her.

Aunt Jamesina was a tiny old woman with a little, softly-triangular face, and large, soft blue eyes that were alight with unquenchable youth, and as full of hopes as a girl's. She had pink cheeks and snow-white hair which she wore in quaint little puffs over her ears.

"It's a very old-fashioned way," she said, knitting industriously at something as dainty and pink as a sunset cloud. "But *I* am old-fashioned. My clothes are, and it stands to reason my opinions are, too. I don't say they're any the better of that, mind you. In fact, I daresay they're a good deal the worse. But they've worn nice and easy. New shoes are smarter than old ones, but the old ones are more comfortable. I'm old enough to indulge myself in the matter of shoes and opinions. I mean to take it real easy here. I know you expect me to look after you and keep you proper, but I'm not going to do it. You're old enough to know how to behave if you're ever going to be. So, as far as I am concerned," concluded Aunt Jamesina, with a twinkle in her young eyes, "you can all go to destruction in your own way."

"Oh, will somebody separate those cats?" pleaded Stella, shudderingly.

Aunt Jamesina had brought with her not only the Sarah-cat but Joseph. Joseph, she explained, had belonged to a dear friend of hers who had gone to live in Vancouver.

"She couldn't take Joseph with her so she begged me to take him. I really couldn't refuse. He's a beautiful cat—that is, his disposition is beautiful. She called him Joseph because his coat is of many colors."

It certainly was. Joseph, as the disgusted Stella said, looked like a walking rag-bag. It was impossible to say what his ground color was. His legs were white with black spots on them. His back was gray with a huge patch of yellow on one side and a black patch on the other. His tail was yellow with a gray tip. One ear was black and one yellow. A black patch over one eye gave him a fearfully rakish look. In reality he was meek and inoffensive, of a sociable disposition. In one respect, if in no other, Joseph was like a lily of the field. He toiled not neither did he spin or catch mice. Yet Solomon in all his glory slept not on softer cushions, or feasted more fully on fat things.

Joseph and the Sarah-cat arrived by express in separate boxes. After they had been released and fed, Joseph selected the cushion and corner which appealed to him, and the Sarah-cat gravely sat herself down before the fire and proceeded to wash her face. She was a large, sleek, gray-and-white cat, with an enormous dignity which was not at all impaired by any consciousness of her plebian origin. She had been given to Aunt Jamesina by her washerwoman.

"Her name was Sarah, so my husband always called puss the Sarah-cat," explained Aunt Jamesina. "She is eight years old, and a remarkable mouser. Don't worry, Stella. The Sarah-cat *never* fights and Joseph rarely."

"They'll have to fight here in self-defense," said Stella.

At this juncture Rusty arrived on the scene. He bounded joyously half way across the room before he saw the intruders. Then he stopped short; his tail expanded until it was as big as three tails. The fur on his back rose up in a defiant arch; Rusty lowered his head, uttered a fearful shriek of hatred and defiance, and launched himself at the Sarah-cat.

The stately animal had stopped washing her face and was looking at him curiously. She met his onslaught with one contemptuous sweep of her capable paw. Rusty went rolling helplessly over on the rug; he picked himself up dazedly. What sort of a cat was this who had boxed his ears? He looked dubiously at the Sarah-cat. Would he or would he not? The Sarah-cat deliberately turned her back on him and resumed her toilet operations. Rusty decided that he would not. He never did. From that time on the Sarah-cat ruled the roost. Rusty never again interfered with her.

But Joseph rashly sat up and yawned. Rusty, burning to avenge his disgrace, swooped down upon him. Joseph, pacific by nature, could fight upon occasion and fight well. The result was a series of drawn battles. Every day Rusty and Joseph fought at sight. Anne took Rusty's part and detested Joseph. Stella was in despair. But Aunt Jamesina only laughed

"Let them fight it out," she said tolerantly. "They'll make

friends after a bit. Joseph needs some exercise—he was getting too fat. And Rusty has to learn he isn't the only cat in the world."

Eventually Joseph and Rusty accepted the situation and from sworn enemies became sworn friends. They slept on the same cushion with their paws about each other, and gravely washed each other's faces.

"We've all got used to each other," said Phil. "And I've learned how to wash dishes and sweep a floor."

"But you needn't try to make us believe you can chloroform a cat," laughed Anne.

"It was all the fault of the knothole," protested Phil.

"It was a good thing the knothole was there," said Aunt Jamesina rather severely. "Kittens *have* to be drowned, I admit, or the world would be overrun. But no decent, grown-up cat should be done to death—unless he sucks eggs."

"You wouldn't have thought Rusty very decent if you'd seen him when he came here," said Stella. "He positively looked like the Old Nick."

"I don't believe Old Nick can be so very ugly," said Aunt Jamesina reflectively. "He wouldn't do so much harm if he was. *I* always think of him as a rather handsome gentleman."

Chapter XVII
A Letter from Davy

"It's beginning to snow, girls," said Phil, coming in one November evening, "and there are the loveliest little stars and crosses all over the garden walk. I never noticed before what exquisite things snowflakes really are. One has time to notice things like that in the simple life. Bless you all for permitting me to live it. It's really delightful to feel worried because butter has gone up five cents a pound."

"Has it?" demanded Stella, who kept the household accounts.

"It has—and here's your butter. I'm getting quite expert at marketing. It's better fun than flirting," concluded Phil gravely.

"Everything is going up scandalously," sighed Stella.

"Never mind. Thank goodness air and salvation are still free," said Aunt Jamesina.

"And so is laughter," added Anne. "There's no tax on it yet and that is well, because you're all going to laugh presently. I'm going to read you Davy's letter. His spelling has improved immensely this past year, though he is not strong on apostrophes, and he certainly possesses the gift of writing an interesting letter. Listen and laugh, before we settle down to the evening's study-grind."

"Dear Anne," ran Davy's letter, "I take my pen to tell you that we are all pretty well and hope this will find you the same. It's snowing some today and Marilla says the old woman in the sky is shaking her feather beds. Is the old woman in the sky God's wife, Anne? I want to know.

"Mrs. Lynde has been real sick but she is better now. She fell down the cellar stairs last week. When she fell she grabbed hold of the shelf with all the milk pails and stewpans on it, and it gave way and went down with her and made a splendid crash. Marilla thought it was an earthquake at first.

"One of the stewpans was all dinged up and Mrs. Lynde straned her ribs. The doctor came and gave her medicine to rub on her ribs but she didn't under stand him and took it all inside instead. The doctor said it was a wonder it dident kill her but it dident and it cured her ribs and Mrs. Lynde says doctors dont know much anyhow. But we couldent fix up the stewpan. Marilla had to throw it out. Thanksgiving was last week. There was no school and we had a great dinner. I et mince pie and rost turkey and frut cake and donuts and cheese and jam and choklut cake. Marilla said I'd die but I dident. Dora had earake after it, only it wasent in her ears it was in her stummick. I dident have earake anywhere.

"Our new teacher is a man. He does things for jokes. Last week he made all us third-class boys write a composishun on what kind of a wife we'd like to have and the girls on what kind of a husband. He laughed fit to kill when he read them. This was mine. I thought youd like to see it.

> "'The kind of a wife I'd like to Have.
>
> "'She must have good manners and get my meals on time and do what I tell her and always be very polite to me. She must be fifteen yers old. She must be good to the poor and keep her house tidy and be good tempered and go to church regularly. She must be very handsome and have curly hair. If I get a wife that is just what I like Ill be an awful good husband to her. I think a woman

ought to be awful good to her husband. Some poor women haven't any husbands.

"'THE END.'"

"I was at Mrs. Isaac Wrights funeral at White Sands last week. The husband of the corpse felt real sorry. Mrs. Lynde says Mrs. Wrights grandfather stole a sheep but Marilla says we mustent speak ill of the dead. Why mustent we, Anne? I want to know. It's pretty safe, ain't it?

"Mrs. Lynde was awful mad the other day because I asked her if she was alive in Noah's time. I dident mean to hurt her feelings. I just wanted to know. Was she, Anne?

"Mr. Harrison wanted to get rid of his dog. So he hunged him once but he come to life and scooted for the barn while Mr. Harrison was digging the grave, so he hunged him again and he stayed dead that time. Mr. Harrison has a new man working for him. He's awful okward. Mr. Harrison says he is left handed in both his feet. Mr. Barry's hired man is lazy. Mrs. Barry says that but Mr. Barry says he aint lazy exactly only he thinks it easier to pray for things than to work for them.

"Mrs. Harmon Andrews prize pig that she talked so much of died in a fit. Mrs. Lynde says it was a judgment on her for pride. But I think it was hard on the pig. Milty Boulter has been sick. The doctor gave him medicine and it tasted horrid. I offered to take it for him for a quarter but the Boulters are so mean. Milty says he'd rather take it himself and save his money. I asked Mrs. Boulter how a person would go about catching a man and she got awful mad and said she dident know, shed never chased men.

"The A.V.I.S. is going to paint the hall again. They're tired of having it blue.

"The new minister was here to tea last night. He took three pieces of pie. If I did that Mrs. Lynde would call me piggy. And he et fast and took big bites and Marilla is always telling me not to do that. Why can ministers do what boys can't? I want to know.

"I haven't any more news. Here are six kisses. xxxxxx. Dora sends one. Heres hers. x.

Your loving friend
DAVID KEITH"

"P.S. Anne, who was the devils father? I want to know."

Chapter XVIII
Miss Josephine Remembers the Anne-girl

When Christmas holidays came the girls of Patty's Place scattered to their respective homes, but Aunt Jamesina elected to stay where she was.

"I couldn't go to any of the places I've been invited and take those three cats," she said. "And I'm not going to leave the poor creatures here alone for nearly three weeks. If we had any decent neighbors who would feed them I might, but there's nothing except millionaires on this street. So I'll stay here and keep Patty's Place warm for you."

Anne went home with the usual joyous anticipations—which were not wholly fulfilled. She found Avonlea in the grip of such an early, cold, and stormy winter as even the "oldest inhabitant" could not recall. Green Gables was literally hemmed in by huge drifts. Almost every day of that ill-starred vacation it stormed fiercely; and even on fine days it drifted unceasingly. No sooner were the roads broken than they filled in again. It was almost impossible to stir out. The A.V.I.S. tried, on three evenings, to have a party in honor of the college students, and on each evening the storm was so wild that nobody could go, so they gave up the attempt in despair. Anne, despite her love of and loyalty to Green Gables, could not help thinking longingly of

Patty's Place, its cosy open fire, Aunt Jamesina's mirthful eyes, the three cats, the merry chatter of the girls, the pleasantness of Friday evenings when college friends dropped in to talk of grave and gay.

Anne was lonely; Diana, during the whole of the holidays, was imprisoned at home with a bad attack of bronchitis. She could not come to Green Gables and it was rarely Anne could get to Orchard Slope, for the old way through the Haunted Wood was impassable with drifts, and the long way over the frozen Lake of Shining Waters was almost as bad. Ruby Gillis was sleeping in the white-heaped graveyard; Jane Andrews was teaching a school on western prairies. Gilbert, to be sure, was still faithful, and waded up to Green Gables every possible evening. But Gilbert's visits were not what they once were. Anne almost dreaded them. It was very disconcerting to look up in the midst of a sudden silence and find Gilbert's hazel eyes fixed upon her with a quite unmistakable expression in their grave depths; and it was still more disconcerting to find herself blushing hotly and uncomfortably under his gaze, just as if—just as if—well, it was very embarrassing. Anne wished herself back at Patty's Place, where there was always somebody else about to take the edge off a delicate situation. At Green Gables Marilla went promptly to Mrs. Lynde's domain when Gilbert came and insisted on taking the twins with her. The significance of this was unmistakable and Anne was in a helpless fury over it.

Davy, however, was perfectly happy. He reveled in getting out in the morning and shoveling out the paths to the well and henhouse. He gloried in the Christmas-tide delicacies which Marilla and Mrs. Lynde vied with each other in preparing for Anne, and he was reading an enthralling tale, in a school library book, of a wonderful hero who seemed blessed with a miraculous faculty for getting into scrapes from which he was usually delivered by an earthquake or a volcanic explosion, which blew him high and dry out of his troubles, landed him in a fortune, and closed the story with proper *éclat*.

"I tell you it's a bully story, Anne," he said ecstatically. "I'd ever so much rather read it than the Bible."

"Would you?" smiled Anne.

Davy peered curiously at her.

"You don't seem a bit shocked, Anne. Mrs. Lynde was awful shocked when I said it to her."

"No, I'm not shocked, Davy. I think it's quite natural that a nine-year-old boy would sooner read an adventure story than the Bible. But when you are older I hope and think that you will realize what a wonderful book the Bible is."

"Oh, I think some parts of it are fine," conceded Davy. "That story about Joseph now—it's bully. But if I'd been Joseph *I* wouldn't have forgive the brothers. No, siree, Anne. I'd have cut all their heads off. Mrs. Lynde was awful mad when I said that and shut the Bible up and said she'd never read me any more of it if I talked like that. So I don't talk now when she reads it Sunday afternoons; I just think things and say them to Milty Boulter next day in school. I told Milty the story about Elisha and the bears and it scared him so he's never made fun of Mr. Harrison's bald head once. Are there any bears on P.E. Island, Anne? I want to know."

"Not nowadays," said Anne, absently, as the wind blew a scud of snow against the window. "Oh, dear, will it ever stop storming."

"God knows," said Davy airily, preparing to resume his reading.

Anne *was* shocked this time.

"Davy!" she exclaimed reproachfully.

"Mrs. Lynde says that," protested Davy. "One night last week Marilla said 'Will Ludovic Speed and Theodora Dix *ever* get married?" and Mrs. Lynde said, "'God knows'—just like that."

"Well, it wasn't right for her to say it," said Anne, promptly deciding upon which horn of this dilemma to empale herself. "It isn't right for anybody to take that name in vain or speak it lightly, Davy. Don't ever do it again."

"Not if I say it slow and solemn, like the minister?" queried Davy gravely.

"No, not even then."

"Well, I won't. Ludovic Speed and Theodora Dix live in Middle Grafton and Mrs. Rachel says he has been courting her for a hundred years. Won't they soon be too old to get married, Anne? I hope Gilbert won't court *you* that long. When are you going to be married, Anne? Mrs. Lynde says it's a sure thing."

"Mrs. Lynde is a—" began Anne hotly; then stopped. "Awful old gossip," completed Davy calmly. "That's what every one calls her. But is it a sure thing, Anne? I want to know."

"You're a very silly little boy, Davy," said Anne, stalking haughtily out of the room. The kitchen was deserted and she sat down by the window in the fast falling wintry twilight. The sun had set and the wind had died down. A pale chilly moon looked out behind a bank of purple clouds in the west. The sky faded out, but the strip of yellow along the western horizon grew brighter and fiercer, as if all the stray gleams of light were concentrating in one spot; the distant hills, rimmed with priest-like firs, stood out in dark distinctness against it. Anne looked across the still, white fields, cold and lifeless in the harsh light of that grim sunset, and sighed. She was very lonely; and she was sad at heart; for she was wondering if she would be able to return to Redmond next year. It did not seem likely. The only scholarship possible in the Sophomore year was a very small affair. She would not take Marilla's money; and there seemed little prospect of being able to earn enough in the summer vacation.

"I suppose I'll just have to drop out next year," she thought drearily, "and teach a district school again until I earn enough to finish my course. And by that time all my old class will have graduated and Patty's Place will be out of the question. But there! I'm not going to be a coward. I'm thankful I can earn my way through if necessary."

"Here's Mr. Harrison wading up the lane," announced Davy, running out. "I hope he's brought the mail. It's three days since we got it. I want to see what them pesky Grits are doing. I'm a Conservative, Anne. And I tell you, you have to keep your eye on them Grits."

Mr. Harrison had brought the mail, and merry letters from Stella and Priscilla and Phil soon dissipated Anne's blues. Aunt Jamesina, too, had written, saying that she was keeping the hearth-fire alight, and that the cats were all well, and the house plants doing fine.

"The weather has been real cold," she wrote, "so I let the cats sleep in the house—Rusty and Joseph on the sofa in the living-room, and the Sarah-cat on the foot of my bed. It's real company to hear her purring when I wake up in the night and think of my poor daughter in the foreign field. If it was anywhere but in India I wouldn't worry, but they say the snakes out there are terrible. It takes all the Sarah-cats's purring to drive away the thought of those snakes. I have enough faith for everything but the snakes. I can't think why Providence ever made them. Sometimes I don't think He did. I'm inclined to believe the Old Harry had a hand in making *them*."

Anne had left a thin, typewritten communication till the last, thinking it unimportant. When she had read it she sat very still, with tears in her eyes.

"What is the matter, Anne?" asked Marilla.

"Miss Josephine Barry is dead," said Anne, in a low tone.

"So she has gone at last," said Marilla. "Well, she has been sick for over a year, and the Barrys have been expecting to hear of her death any time. It is well she is at rest for she has suffered dreadfully, Anne. She was always kind to you."

"She has been kind to the last, Marilla. This letter is from her lawyer. She has left me a thousand dollars in her will."

"Gracious, ain't that an awful lot of money," exclaimed Davy. "She's the woman you and Diana lit on when you jumped into the spare room bed, ain't she? Diana told me that story. Is that why she left you so much?"

"Hush, Davy," said Anne gently. She slipped away to the porch gable with a full heart, leaving Marilla and Mrs. Lynde to talk over the news to their hearts' content.

"Do you s'pose Anne will ever get married now?" speculated Davy anxiously. "When Dorcas Sloane got married last summer she said if she'd had enough money to live on she'd never have been bothered with a man, but even a widower with eight children was better'n living with a sister-in-law."

"Davy Keith, do hold your tongue," said Mrs. Rachel severely. "The way you talk is scandalous for a small boy, that's what."

Chapter XIX
An Interlude

"To think that this is my twentieth birthday, and that I've left my teens behind me forever," said Anne, who was curled up on the hearth-rug with Rusty in her lap, to Aunt Jamesina who was reading in her pet chair. They were alone in the living room. Stella and Priscilla had gone to a committee meeting and Phil was upstairs adorning herself for a party.

"I suppose you feel kind of, sorry" said Aunt Jamesina. "The teens are such a nice part of life. I'm glad I've never gone out of them myself."

Anne laughed.

"You never will, Aunty. You'll be eighteen when you should be a hundred. Yes, I'm sorry, and a little dissatisfied as well. Miss Stacy told me long ago that by the time I was twenty my character would be formed, for good or evil. I don't feel that it's what it should be. It's full of flaws."

"So's everybody's," said Aunt Jamesina cheerfully. "Mine's cracked in a hundred places. Your Miss Stacy likely meant that when you are twenty your character would have got its permanent bent in one direction or 'tother, and would go on developing in that line. Don't worry over it, Anne. Do your duty by God and your neighbor and yourself, and have a good time. That's my philosophy and it's always worked pretty well. Where's Phil off to tonight?"

"She's going to a dance, and she's got the sweetest dress for it—creamy yellow silk and cobwebby lace. It just suits those brown tints of hers."

"There's magic in the words 'silk' and 'lace,' isn't there?" said Aunt Jamesina. "The very sound of them makes me feel like skipping off to a dance. And *yellow* silk. It makes one think of a dress of sunshine. I always wanted a yellow silk dress, but first my mother and then my husband wouldn't hear of it. The very first thing I'm going to do when I get to heaven is to get a yellow silk dress."

Amid Anne's peal of laughter Phil came downstairs, trailing clouds of glory, and surveyed herself in the long oval mirror on the wall.

"A flattering looking glass is a promoter of amiability," she said. "The one in my room does certainly make me green. Do I look pretty nice, Anne?"

"Do you really know how pretty you are, Phil?" asked Anne, in honest admiration.

"Of course I do. What are looking glasses and men for? That wasn't what I meant. Are all my ends tucked in? Is my skirt straight? And would this rose look better lower down? I'm afraid it's too high—it will make me look lop-sided. But I hate things tickling my ears."

"Everything is just right, and that southwest dimple of yours is lovely."

"Anne, there's one thing in particular I like about you—you're so ungrudging. There isn't a particle of envy in you."

"Why should she be envious?" demanded Aunt Jamesina. "She's not quite as goodlooking as you, maybe, but she's got a far handsomer nose."

"I know it," conceded Phil.

"My nose always has been a great comfort to me," confessed Anne.

"And I love the way your hair grows on your forehead, Anne. And that one wee curl, always looking as if it were going to drop, but never dropping, is delicious. But as for noses, mine is a dreadful worry to me. I know by the time I'm forty it will be Byrney. What do you think I'll look like when I'm forty, Anne?"

"Like an old, matronly, married woman," teased Anne.

"I won't," said Phil, sitting down comfortably to wait for her escort. "Joseph, you calico beastie, don't you dare jump on my lap. I won't go to a dance all over cat hairs. No, Anne, I *won't* look matronly. But no doubt I'll be married."

"To Alec or Alonzo?" asked Anne.

"To one of them, I suppose," sighed Phil, "if I can ever decide which."

"It shouldn't be hard to decide," scolded Aunt Jamesina.

"I was born a see-saw Aunty, and nothing can ever prevent me from teetering."

"You ought to be more levelheaded, Philippa."

"It's best to be levelheaded, of course," agreed Philippa, "but you miss lots of fun. As for Alec and Alonzo, if you knew them you'd understand why it's difficult to choose between them. They're equally nice."

"Then take somebody who is nicer" suggested Aunt Jamesina. "There's that Senior who is so devoted to you—Will Leslie. He has such nice, large, mild eyes."

"They're a little bit too large and too mild—like a cow's," said Phil cruelly.

"What do you say about George Parker?"

"There's nothing to say about him except that he always looks as if he had just been starched and ironed."

"Marr Holworthy then. You can't find a fault with him."

"No, he would do if he wasn't poor. I must marry a rich man, Aunt Jamesina. That—and good looks—is an indispensable qualification. I'd marry Gilbert Blythe if he were rich."

"Oh, would you?" said Anne, rather viciously.

"We don't like that idea a little bit, although we don't want Gilbert ourselves, oh, no," mocked Phil. "But don't let's talk of disagreeable subjects. I'll have to marry sometime, I suppose, but I shall put off the evil day as long as I can."

"You mustn't marry anybody you don't love, Phil, when all's said and done," said Aunt Jamesina.

> *"'Oh, hearts that loved in the good old way*
> *Have been out o' the fashion this many a day.'"*

trilled Phil mockingly. "There's the carriage. I fly—Bi-bi, you two old-fashioned darlings."

When Phil had gone Aunt Jamesina looked solemnly at Anne.

"That girl is pretty and sweet and goodhearted, but do you think she is quite right in her mind, by spells, Anne?"

"Oh, I don't think there's anything the matter with Phil's mind," said Anne, hiding a smile. "It's just her way of talking."

Aunt Jamesina shook her head.

"Well, I hope so, Anne. I do hope so, because I love her. But *I* can't understand her—she beats me. She isn't like any of the girls I ever knew, or any of the girls I was myself."

"How many girls were you, Aunt Jimsie?"

"About half a dozen, my dear."

Chapter XX
Gilbert Speaks

"This has been a dull, prosy day," yawned Phil, stretching herself idly on the sofa, having previously dispossessed two exceedingly indignant cats.

Anne looked up from *Pickwick Papers*. Now that spring examinations were over she was treating herself to Dickens.

"It has been a prosy day for us," she said thoughtfully, "but to some people it has been a wonderful day. Some one has been rapturously happy in it. Perhaps a great deed has been done somewhere today—or a great poem written—or a great man born. And some heart has been broken, Phil."

"Why did you spoil your pretty thought by tagging that last sentence on, honey?" grumbled Phil. "I don't like to think of broken hearts—or anything unpleasant."

"Do you think you'll be able to shirk unpleasant things all your life, Phil?"

"Dear me, no. Am I not up against them now? You don't call Alec and Alonzo pleasant things, do you, when they simply plague my life out?"

"You never take anything seriously, Phil."

"Why should I? There are enough folks who do. The world needs people like me, Anne, just to amuse it. It would be a terrible place if *everybody* were intellectual and serious and in deep, deadly earnest. MY mission is, as *Josiah Allen* says, 'to charm and allure.' Confess now. Hasn't life at Patty's Place been really much brighter and pleasanter this past winter because I've been here to leaven you?"

"Yes, it has," owned Anne.

"And you all love me—even Aunt Jamesina, who thinks I'm stark mad. So why should I try to be different? Oh, dear, I'm so sleepy. I was awake until one last night, reading a harrowing ghost story. I read it in bed, and after I had finished it do you suppose I could get out of bed to put the light out? No! And if Stella had not fortunately come in late that lamp would have burned good and bright till morning. When I heard Stella I called her in, explained my predicament, and got her to put out the light. If I had got out myself to do it I knew something would grab me by the feet when I was getting in again. By the way, Anne, has Aunt Jamesina decided what to do this summer?"

"Yes, she's going to stay here. I know she's doing it for the sake of those blessed cats, although she says it's too much trouble to open her own house, and she hates visiting."

"What are you reading?"

"*Pickwick.*"

"That's a book that always makes me hungry," said Phil. "There's so much good eating in it. The characters seem always to be reveling on ham and eggs and milk punch. I generally go on a cupboard rummage after reading *Pickwick*. The mere thought reminds me that I'm starving. Is there any tidbit in the pantry, Queen Anne?"

"I made a lemon pie this morning. You may have a piece of it."

Phil dashed out to the pantry and Anne betook herself to the orchard in company with Rusty. It was a moist, pleasantly-odorous night in early spring. The snow was not quite all gone from the park; a little dingy bank of it yet lay under the pines of the harbor road, screened from the influence of April suns. It kept the harbor road muddy, and chilled the evening air. But grass was growing green in sheltered spots and Gilbert had found some pale, sweet arbutus in a hidden corner. He came up from the park, his hands full of it.

Anne was sitting on the big gray boulder in the orchard looking at the poem of a bare, birchen bough hanging against the pale red sunset with the very perfection of grace. She was building a castle in air—a wondrous mansion whose sunlit courts and stately halls were steeped in Araby's perfume, and where she reigned queen and chatelaine. She frowned as she saw Gilbert coming through the orchard. Of late she had managed not to be left alone with Gilbert. But he had caught her fairly now; and even Rusty had deserted her.

Gilbert sat down beside her on the boulder and held out his Mayflowers.

"Don't these remind you of home and our old schoolday picnics, Anne?"

Anne took them and buried her face in them.

"I'm in Mr. Silas Sloane's barrens this very minute," she said rapturously.

"I suppose you will be there in reality in a few days?"

"No, not for a fortnight. I'm going to visit with Phil in Bolingbroke before I go home. You'll be in Avonlea before I will."

"No, I shall not be in Avonlea at all this summer, Anne. I've been offered a job in the Daily News office and I'm going to take it."

"Oh," said Anne vaguely. She wondered what a whole Avonlea summer would be like without Gilbert. Somehow she did not like the prospect. "Well," she concluded flatly, "it is a good thing for you, of course."

"Yes, I've been hoping I would get it. It will help me out next year."

"You mustn't work *too* hard," said Anne, without any very clear idea of what she was saying. She wished desperately that Phil would come out. "You've studied very constantly this winter. Isn't this a delightful evening? Do you know, I found a cluster of white violets under that old twisted tree over there today? I felt as if I had discovered a gold mine."

"You are always discovering gold mines," said Gilbert—also absently.

"Let us go and see if we can find some more," suggested Anne eagerly. "I'll call Phil and—"

"Never mind Phil and the violets just now, Anne," said Gilbert quietly, taking her hand in a clasp from which she could not free it. "There is something I want to say to you."

"Oh, don't say it," cried Anne, pleadingly. "Don't—*please*, Gilbert."

"I must. Things can't go on like this any longer. Anne, I love you. You know I do. I—I can't tell you how much. Will you promise me that some day you'll be my wife?"

"I—I can't," said Anne miserably. "Oh, Gilbert—you—you've spoiled everything."

"Don't you care for me at all?" Gilbert asked after a very dreadful pause, during which Anne had not dared to look up.

"Not—not in that way. I do care a great deal for you as a friend. But I don't love you, Gilbert."

"But can't you give me some hope that you will—yet?"

"No, I can't," exclaimed Anne desperately. "I never, never can love you—in that way—Gilbert. You must never speak of this to me again."

There was another pause—so long and so dreadful that Anne was driven at last to look up. Gilbert's face was white to the lips. And his eyes—but Anne shuddered and looked away. There was nothing romantic about this. Must proposals be either grotesque or—horrible? Could she ever forget Gilbert's face?

"Is there anybody else?" he asked at last in a low voice.

"No—no," said Anne eagerly. "I don't care for any one like *that*—and I *like* you better than anybody else in the world, Gilbert. And we must—we must go on being friends, Gilbert."

Gilbert gave a bitter little laugh.

"Friends! Your friendship can't satisfy me, Anne. I want your love—and you tell me I can never have that."

"I'm sorry. Forgive me, Gilbert," was all Anne could say. Where, oh, where were all the gracious and graceful speeches wherewith, in imagination, she had been wont to dismiss rejected suitors?

Gilbert released her hand gently.

"There isn't anything to forgive. There have been times when I thought you did care. I've deceived myself, that's all. Goodbye, Anne."

Anne got herself to her room, sat down on her window seat behind the pines, and cried bitterly. She felt as if something incalculably precious had gone out of her life. It was Gilbert's friendship, of course. Oh, why must she lose it after this fashion?

"What is the matter, honey?" asked Phil, coming in through the moonlit gloom.

Anne did not answer. At that moment she wished Phil were a thousand miles away.

"I suppose you've gone and refused Gilbert Blythe. You are an idiot, Anne Shirley!"

"Do you call it idiotic to refuse to marry a man I don't love?" said Anne coldly, goaded to reply.

"You don't know love when you see it. You've tricked something out with your imagination that you think love, and you expect the real thing to look like that. There, that's the first sensible thing I've ever said in my life. I wonder how I managed it?"

"Phil," pleaded Anne, "please go away and leave me alone for a little while. My world has tumbled into pieces. I want to reconstruct it."

"Without any Gilbert in it?" said Phil, going.

A world without any Gilbert in it! Anne repeated the words drearily. Would it not be a very lonely, forlorn place? Well, it was all Gilbert's fault. He had spoiled their beautiful comradeship. She must just learn to live without it.

Chapter XXI
Roses of Yesterday

The fortnight Anne spent in Bolingbroke was a very pleasant one, with a little under current of vague pain and dissatisfaction running through it whenever she thought about Gilbert. There was not, however, much time to think about him. "Mount Holly," the beautiful old Gordon homestead, was a very gay place, overrun by Phil's friends of both sexes. There was quite a bewildering succession of drives, dances, picnics and boating parties, all expressively lumped together by Phil under the head of "jamborees"; Alec and Alonzo were so constantly on hand that Anne wondered if they ever did anything but dance attendance on that will-o'-the-wisp of a Phil. They were both nice, manly fellows, but Anne would not be drawn into any opinion as to which was the nicer.

"And I depended so on you to help me make up my mind which of them I should promise to marry," mourned Phil.

"You must do that for yourself. You are quite expert at making up your mind as to whom other people should marry," retorted Anne, rather caustically.

"Oh, that's a very different thing," said Phil, truly.

But the sweetest incident of Anne's sojourn in Bolingbroke was the visit to her birthplace—the little shabby yellow house in an out-of-the-way street she had so often dreamed about. She looked at it with delighted eyes, as she and Phil turned in at the gate.

"It's almost exactly as I've pictured it," she said. "There is no honeysuckle over the windows, but there is a lilac tree by the gate, and—yes, there are the muslin curtains in the windows. How glad I am it is still painted yellow."

A very tall, very thin woman opened the door.

"Yes, the Shirleys lived here twenty years ago," she said, in answer to Anne's question. "They had it rented. I remember 'em. They both died of fever at onct. It was turrible sad. They left a baby. I guess it's dead long ago. It was a sickly thing. Old Thomas and his wife took it—as if they hadn't enough of their own."

"It didn't die," said Anne, smiling. "I was that baby."

"You don't say so! Why, you have grown," exclaimed the woman, as if she were much surprised that Anne was not still a baby. "Come to look at you, I see the resemblance. You're complected like your pa. He had red hair. But you favor your ma in your eyes and mouth. She was a nice little thing. My darter went to school to her and was nigh crazy about her. They was buried in the one grave and the School Board put up a tombstone to them as a reward for faithful service. Will you come in?"

"Will you let me go all over the house?" asked Anne eagerly.

"Laws, yes, you can if you like. 'Twon't take you long—there ain't much of it. I keep at my man to build a new kitchen, but he ain't one of your hustlers. The parlor's in there and there's two rooms upstairs. Just prowl about yourselves. I've got to see to the baby. The east room was the one you were born in. I remember your ma saying she loved to see the sunrise; and I mind hearing that you was born just as the sun was rising and its light on your face was the first thing your ma saw."

Anne went up the narrow stairs and into that little east room with a full heart. It was as a shrine to her. Here her mother had dreamed the exquisite, happy dreams of anticipated motherhood; here that red sunrise light had fallen over them both in the sacred hour of birth; here her mother had died. Anne looked about her reverently, her eyes with tears. It was for her one of the jeweled hours of life that gleam out radiantly forever in memory.

"Just to think of it—mother was younger than I am now when I was born," she whispered.

When Anne went downstairs the lady of the house met her in the hall. She held out a dusty little packet tied with faded blue ribbon.

"Here's a bundle of old letters I found in that closet upstairs when I came here," she said. "I dunno what they are—I never bothered to look in 'em, but the address on the top one is 'Miss Bertha Willis,' and that was your ma's maiden name. You can take 'em if you'd keer to have 'em."

"Oh, thank you—thank you," cried Anne, clasping the packet rapturously.

"That was all that was in the house," said her hostess. "The furniture was all sold to pay the doctor bills, and Mrs. Thomas got your ma's clothes and little things. I reckon they didn't last long among that drove of Thomas youngsters. They was destructive young animals, as I mind 'em."

"I haven't one thing that belonged to my mother," said Anne, chokily. "I—I can never thank you enough for these letters."

"You're quite welcome. Laws, but your eyes is like your ma's. She could just about talk with hers. Your father was sorter homely but awful nice. I mind hearing folks say when they was married that there never was two people more in love with each other—Pore creatures, they didn't live much longer; but they was awful happy while they was alive, and I s'pose that counts for a good deal."

Anne longed to get home to read her precious letters; but she made one little pilgrimage first. She went alone to the green corner of the "old" Bolingbroke cemetery where her father and mother were buried, and left on their grave the white flowers she carried. Then she hastened back to Mount Holly, shut herself up in her room, and read the letters. Some were written by her father, some by her mother. There were not many—only a dozen in all—for Walter and Bertha Shirley had not been often separated during their courtship. The letters were yellow and faded and dim, blurred with the touch of passing years. No profound words of wisdom were traced on the stained and wrinkled pages, but only lines of love and trust. The sweetness of forgotten things clung to them—the far-off, fond imaginings of those long-dead lovers. Bertha Shirley had possessed the gift of writing letters which embodied the charming personality of the writer in words and thoughts that retained their beauty and fragrance after the lapse of time. The letters were tender, intimate, sacred. To Anne, the sweetest of all was the one written after her birth to the father on a brief absence. It was full of a proud young mother's accounts of "baby"—her cleverness, her brightness, her thousand sweetnesses.

"I love her best when she is asleep and better still when she is awake," Bertha Shirley had written in the postscript. Probably it was the last sentence she had ever penned. The end was very near for her.

"This has been the most beautiful day of my life," Anne said to Phil that night. "I've FOUND my father and mother. Those letters have made them REAL to me. I'm not an orphan any longer. I feel as if I had opened a book and found roses of yesterday, sweet and beloved, between its leaves."

Chapter XXII
Spring and Anne Return to Green Gables

The firelight shadows were dancing over the kitchen walls at Green Gables, for the spring evening was chilly; through the open east window drifted in the subtly sweet voices of the night. Marilla was sitting by the fire—at least, in body. In spirit she was roaming olden ways, with feet grown young. Of late Marilla had thus spent many an hour, when she thought she should have been knitting for the twins.

"I suppose I'm growing old," she said.

Yet Marilla had changed but little in the past nine years, save to grow something thinner, and even more angular; there was a little more gray in the hair that was still twisted up in the same hard knot, with two hairpins—*were* they the same hairpins?—still stuck through it. But her expression was very different; the something about the mouth which had hinted at a sense of humor had developed wonderfully; her eyes were gentler and milder, her smile more frequent and tender.

Marilla was thinking of her whole past life, her cramped but not unhappy childhood, the jealously hidden dreams and the blighted hopes of her girlhood, the long, gray, narrow, monotonous years of dull middle life that followed. And the coming of Anne—the vivid, imaginative, impetuous child with her heart of love, and her world of fancy, bringing with her color and warmth and radiance, until the wilderness of existence had blossomed like the rose. Marilla felt that out of her sixty years she had lived only the nine that had followed the advent of Anne. And Anne would be home tomorrow night.

The kitchen door opened. Marilla looked up expecting to see Mrs. Lynde. Anne stood before her, tall and starry-eyed, with her hands full of Mayflowers and violets.

"Anne Shirley!" exclaimed Marilla. For once in her life she was surprised out of her reserve; she caught her girl in her arms and crushed her and her flowers against her heart, kissing the bright hair and sweet face warmly. "I never looked for you till tomorrow night. How did you get from Carmody?"

"Walked, dearest of Marillas. Haven't I done it a score of times in the Queen's days? The mailman is to bring my trunk tomorrow; I just got homesick all at once, and came a day earlier. And oh! I've had such a lovely walk in the May twilight; I stopped by the barrens and picked these Mayflowers; I came through Violet-Vale; it's just a big bowlful of violets now—the dear, sky-tinted things. Smell them, Marilla—drink them in."

Marilla sniffed obligingly, but she was more interested in Anne than in drinking violets.

"Sit down, child. You must be real tired. I'm going to get you some supper."

"There's a darling moonrise behind the hills tonight, Marilla, and oh, how the frogs sang me home from Carmody! I do love the music of the frogs. It seems bound up with all my happiest recollections of old spring evenings. And it always reminds me of the night I came here first. Do you remember it, Marilla?"

"Well, yes," said Marilla with emphasis. "I'm not likely to forget it ever."

"They used to sing so madly in the marsh and brook that year. I would listen to them at my window in the dusk, and wonder how they could seem so glad and so sad at the same time. Oh, but it's good to be home again! Redmond was splendid and Bolingbroke delightful—but Green Gables is *home*."

"Gilbert isn't coming home this summer, I hear," said Marilla.

"No." Something in Anne's tone made Marilla glance at her sharply, but Anne was apparently absorbed in arranging her violets in a bowl. "See, aren't they sweet?" she went on hurriedly. "The year is a book, isn't it, Marilla? Spring's pages are written in Mayflowers and violets, summer's in roses, autumn's in red maple leaves, and winter in holly and evergreen."

"Did Gilbert do well in his examinations?" persisted Marilla.

"Excellently well. He led his class. But where are the twins and Mrs. Lynde?"

"Rachel and Dora are over at Mr. Harrison's. Davy is down at Boulters'. I think I hear him coming now."

Davy burst in, saw Anne, stopped, and then hurled himself upon her with a joyful yell.

"Oh, Anne, ain't I glad to see you! Say, Anne, I've grown two inches since last fall. Mrs. Lynde measured me with her tape today, and say, Anne, see my front tooth. It's gone. Mrs. Lynde tied one end of a string to it and the other end to the door, and then shut the door. I sold it to Milty for two cents. Milty's collecting teeth."

"What in the world does he want teeth for?" asked Marilla.

"To make a necklace for playing Indian Chief," explained Davy, climbing upon Anne's lap. "He's got fifteen already, and everybody's else's promised, so there's no use in the rest of us starting to collect, too. I tell you the Boulters are great business people."

"Were you a good boy at Mrs. Boulter's?" asked Marilla severely.

"Yes; but say, Marilla, I'm tired of being good."

"You'd get tired of being bad much sooner, Davy-boy," said Anne.

"Well, it'd be fun while it lasted, wouldn't it?" persisted Davy. "I could be sorry for it afterwards, couldn't I?"

"Being sorry wouldn't do away with the consequences of being bad, Davy. Don't you remember the Sunday last summer when you ran away from Sunday School? You told me then that being bad wasn't worth while. What were you and Milty doing today?"

"Oh, we fished and chased the cat, and hunted for eggs, and yelled at the echo. There's a great echo in the bush behind the Boulter barn. Say, what is echo, Anne; I want to know."

"Echo is a beautiful nymph, Davy, living far away in the woods, and laughing at the world from among the hills."

"What does she look like?"

"Her hair and eyes are dark, but her neck and arms are white as snow. No mortal can ever see how fair she is. She is fleeter than a deer, and that mocking voice of hers is all we can know of her. You can hear her calling at night; you can hear her laughing under the stars. But you can never see her. She flies afar if you follow her, and laughs at you always just over the next hill."

"Is that true, Anne? Or is it a whopper?" demanded Davy staring.

"Davy," said Anne despairingly, "haven't you sense enough to distinguish between a fairytale and a falsehood?"

"Then what is it that sasses back from the Boulter bush? I want to know," insisted Davy.

"When you are a little older, Davy, I'll explain it all to you."

The mention of age evidently gave a new turn to Davy's thoughts for after a few moments of reflection, he whispered solemnly:

"Anne, I'm going to be married."

"When?" asked Anne with equal solemnity.

"Oh, not until I'm grown-up, of course."

"Well, that's a relief, Davy. Who is the lady?"

"Stella Fletcher; she's in my class at school. And say, Anne, she's the prettiest girl you ever saw. If I die before I grow up you'll keep an eye on her, won't you?"

"Davy Keith, do stop talking such nonsense," said Marilla severely.

"'Tisn't nonsense," protested Davy in an injured tone. "She's my promised wife, and if I was to die she'd be my promised widow, wouldn't she? And she hasn't got a soul to look after her except her old grandmother."

"Come and have your supper, Anne," said Marilla, "and don't encourage that child in his absurd talk."

Chapter XXIII
Paul Cannot Find the Rock People

Life was very pleasant in Avonlea that summer, although Anne, amid all her vacation joys, was haunted by a sense of "something gone which should be there." She would not admit, even in her inmost reflections, that this was caused by Gilbert's absence. But when she had to walk home alone from prayer meetings and A.V.I.S. pow-wows, while Diana and Fred, and many other gay couples, loitered along the dusky, starlit country roads, there was a queer, lonely ache in her heart which she could not explain away. Gilbert did not even write to her, as she thought he might have done. She knew he wrote to Diana occasionally, but she would not inquire about him; and Diana, supposing that Anne heard from him, volunteered no information. Gilbert's mother, who was a gay, frank, light-hearted lady, but not overburdened with tact, had a very embarrassing habit of asking Anne, always in a painfully distinct voice and always in the presence of a crowd, if she had heard from Gilbert lately. Poor Anne could only blush horribly and murmur, "not very lately," which was taken by all, Mrs. Blythe included, to be merely a maidenly evasion.

Apart from this, Anne enjoyed her summer. Priscilla came for a merry visit in June; and, when she had gone, Mr. and Mrs.

Irving, Paul and Charlotta the Fourth came "home" for July and August.

Echo Lodge was the scene of gaieties once more, and the echoes over the river were kept busy mimicking the laughter that rang in the old garden behind the spruces.

"Miss Lavendar" had not changed, except to grow even sweeter and prettier. Paul adored her, and the companionship between them was beautiful to see.

"But I don't call her 'mother' just by itself," he explained to Anne. "You see, *that* name belongs just to my own little mother, and I can't give it to any one else. You know, teacher. But I call her 'Mother Lavendar' and I love her next best to father. I—I even love her a *little* better than you, teacher."

"Which is just as it ought to be," answered Anne.

Paul was thirteen now and very tall for his years. His face and eyes were as beautiful as ever, and his fancy was still like a prism, separating everything that fell upon it into rainbows. He and Anne had delightful rambles to wood and field and shore. Never were there two more thoroughly "kindred spirits."

Charlotta the Fourth had blossomed out into young ladyhood. She wore her hair now in an enormous pompador and had discarded the blue ribbon bows of auld lang syne, but her face was as freckled, her nose as snubbed, and her mouth and smiles as wide as ever.

"You don't think I talk with a Yankee accent, do you, Miss Shirley, ma'am?" she demanded anxiously.

"I don't notice it, Charlotta."

"I'm real glad of that. They said I did at home, but I thought likely they just wanted to aggravate me. I don't want no Yankee accent. Not that I've a word to say against the Yankees, Miss Shirley, ma'am. They're real civilized. But give me old P.E. Island every time."

Paul spent his first fortnight with his grandmother Irving

in Avonlea. Anne was there to meet him when he came, and found him wild with eagerness to get to the shore—Nora and the Golden Lady and the Twin Sailors would be there. He could hardly wait to eat his supper. Could he not see Nora's elfin face peering around the point, watching for him wistfully? But it was a very sober Paul who came back from the shore in the twilight.

"Didn't you find your Rock People?" asked Anne.

Paul shook his chestnut curls sorrowfully.

"The Twin Sailors and the Golden Lady never came at all," he said. "Nora was there—but Nora is not the same, teacher. She is changed."

"Oh, Paul, it is you who are changed," said Anne. "You have grown too old for the Rock People. They like only children for playfellows. I am afraid the Twin Sailors will never again come to you in the pearly, enchanted boat with the sail of moonshine; and the Golden Lady will play no more for you on her golden harp. Even Nora will not meet you much longer. You must pay the penalty of growing-up, Paul. You must leave fairyland behind you."

"You two talk as much foolishness as ever you did," said old Mrs. Irving, half-indulgently, half-reprovingly.

"Oh, no, we don't," said Anne, shaking her head gravely. "We are getting very, very wise, and it is such a pity. We are never half so interesting when we have learned that language is given us to enable us to conceal our thoughts."

"But it isn't—it is given us to exchange our thoughts," said Mrs. Irving seriously. She had never heard of Tallyrand and did not understand epigrams.

Anne spent a fortnight of halcyon days at Echo Lodge in the golden prime of August. While there she incidentally contrived to hurry Ludovic Speed in his leisurely courting of Theodora Dix, as related duly in another chronicle of her history.(1) Arnold

Sherman, an elderly friend of the Irvings, was there at the same time, and added not a little to the general pleasantness of life.

(1 Chronicles of Avonlea.)

"What a nice play-time this has been," said Anne. "I feel like a giant refreshed. And it's only a fortnight more till I go back to Kingsport, and Redmond and Patty's Place. Patty's Place is the dearest spot, Miss Lavendar. I feel as if I had two homes—one at Green Gables and one at Patty's Place. But where has the summer gone? It doesn't seem a day since I came home that spring evening with the Mayflowers. When I was little I couldn't see from one end of the summer to the other. It stretched before me like an unending season. Now, "tis a handbreadth, 'tis a tale.'"

"Anne, are you and Gilbert Blythe as good friends as you used to be?" asked Miss Lavendar quietly.

"I am just as much Gilbert's friend as ever I was, Miss Lavendar."

Miss Lavendar shook her head.

"I see something's gone wrong, Anne. I'm going to be impertinent and ask what. Have you quarrelled?"

"No; it's only that Gilbert wants more than friendship and I can't give him more."

"Are you sure of that, Anne?"

"Perfectly sure."

"I'm very, very sorry."

"I wonder why everybody seems to think I ought to marry Gilbert Blythe," said Anne petulantly.

"Because you were made and meant for each other, Anne—that is why. You needn't toss that young head of yours. It's a fact."

Chapter XXIV
Enter Jonas

"PROSPECT POINT,
"August 20th.

"Dear Anne—spelled—with—an—E," wrote Phil, "I must prop my eyelids open long enough to write you. I've neglected you shamefully this summer, honey, but all my other correspondents have been neglected, too. I have a huge pile of letters to answer, so I must gird up the loins of my mind and hoe in. Excuse my mixed metaphors. I'm fearfully sleepy. Last night Cousin Emily and I were calling at a neighbor's. There were several other callers there, and as soon as those unfortunate creatures left, our hostess and her three daughters picked them all to pieces. I knew they would begin on Cousin Emily and me as soon as the door shut behind us. When we came home Mrs. Lilly informed us that the aforesaid neighbor's hired boy was supposed to be down with scarlet fever. You can always trust Mrs. Lilly to tell you cheerful things like that. I have a horror of scarlet fever. I couldn't sleep when I went to bed for thinking of it. I tossed and tumbled about, dreaming fearful dreams when I did snooze for a minute; and at three I wakened up with a high fever, a sore throat, and a raging headache. I knew I had scarlet fever; I got up in a panic and hunted up Cousin Emily's 'doctor book' to read up the symptoms. Anne, I had them all. So I went back to bed, and knowing the worst, slept like a top the rest of the night. Though why a top should sleep sounder than anything else I never could understand. But this morning I was quite well, so it couldn't have been the fever. I suppose if I did catch it last night it couldn't have developed so soon. I can remember that in daytime, but at three o'clock at night I never can be logical.

"I suppose you wonder what I'm doing at Prospect Point. Well, I always like to spend a month of summer at the shore, and father insists that I come to his second-cousin Emily's 'select boardinghouse' at Prospect Point. So a fortnight ago I came as usual. And as usual old 'Uncle Mark Miller' brought me from the station with his ancient buggy and what he calls his 'generous purpose' horse. He is a nice old man and gave me a handful of pink peppermints. Peppermints always seem to me such a religious sort of candy—I suppose because when I was a little girl Grandmother Gordon always gave them to me in church. Once I asked, referring to the smell of peppermints, 'Is that the odor of sanctity?' I didn't like to eat Uncle Mark's peppermints because he just fished them loose out of his pocket, and had to pick some rusty nails and other things from among them before he gave them to me. But I wouldn't hurt his dear old feelings for anything, so I carefully sowed them along the road at intervals. When the last one was gone, Uncle Mark said, a little rebukingly, 'Ye shouldn't a'et all them candies to onct, Miss Phil. You'll likely have the stummick-ache.'

"Cousin Emily has only five boarders besides myself—four old ladies and one young man. My right-hand neighbor is Mrs. Lilly. She is one of those people who seem to take a gruesome pleasure in detailing all their many aches and pains and sicknesses. You cannot mention any ailment but she says, shaking her head, 'Ah, I know too well what that is'—and then you get all the details. Jonas declares he once spoke of locomotor ataxia in hearing and she said she knew too well what that was. She suffered from it for ten years and was finally cured by a traveling doctor.

"Who is Jonas? Just wait, Anne Shirley. You'll hear all about Jonas in the proper time and place. He is not to be mixed up with estimable old ladies.

"My left-hand neighbor at the table is Mrs. Phinney. She always speaks with a wailing, dolorous voice—you are nervously expecting her to burst into tears every moment. She gives you the impression that life to her is indeed a vale of tears, and that a smile, never to speak of a laugh, is a frivolity truly reprehensible. She has a worse opinion of me than Aunt Jamesina, and she doesn't love me hard to atone for it, as Aunty J. does, either.

"Miss Maria Grimsby sits cati-corner from me. The first day I came I remarked to Miss Maria that it looked a little like rain—and Miss Maria laughed. I said the road from the station was very pretty—and Miss Maria laughed. I said there seemed to be a few mosquitoes left yet—and Miss Maria laughed. I said that Prospect Point was as beautiful as ever—and Miss Maria laughed. If I were to say to Miss Maria, 'My father has hanged himself, my mother has taken poison, my brother is in the penitentiary, and I am in the last stages of consumption,' Miss Maria would laugh. She can't help it—she was born so; but is very sad and awful.

"The fifth old lady is Mrs. Grant. She is a sweet old thing; but she never says anything but good of anybody and so she is a very uninteresting conversationalist.

"And now for Jonas, Anne.

"That first day I came I saw a young man sitting opposite me at the table, smiling at me as if he had known me from my cradle. I knew, for Uncle Mark had told me, that his name was Jonas Blake, that he was a Theological Student from St. Columbia, and that he had taken charge of the Point Prospect Mission Church for the summer.

"He is a very ugly young man—really, the ugliest young man

I've ever seen. He has a big, loose-jointed figure with absurdly long legs. His hair is tow-color and lank, his eyes are green, and his mouth is big, and his ears—but I never think about his ears if I can help it.

"He has a lovely voice—if you shut your eyes he is adorable—and he certainly has a beautiful soul and disposition.

"We were good chums right way. Of course he is a graduate of Redmond, and that is a link between us. We fished and boated together; and we walked on the sands by moonlight. He didn't look so homely by moonlight and oh, he was nice. Niceness fairly exhaled from him. The old ladies—except Mrs. Grant—don't approve of Jonas, because he laughs and jokes—and because he evidently likes the society of frivolous me better than theirs.

"Somehow, Anne, I don't want him to think me frivolous. This is ridiculous. Why should I care what a tow-haired person called Jonas, whom I never saw before thinks of me?

"Last Sunday Jonas preached in the village church. I went, of course, but I couldn't realize that Jonas was going to preach. The fact that he was a minister—or going to be one—persisted in seeming a huge joke to me.

"Well, Jonas preached. And, by the time he had preached ten minutes, I felt so small and insignificant that I thought I must be invisible to the naked eye. Jonas never said a word about women and he never looked at me. But I realized then and there what a pitiful, frivolous, small-souled little butterfly I was, and how horribly different I must be from Jonas' ideal woman. *She* would be grand and strong and noble. He was so earnest and tender and true. He was everything a minister ought to be. I wondered how I could ever have thought him ugly—but he really is!—with those inspired eyes and that intellectual brow which the roughly-falling hair hid on week days.

"It was a splendid sermon and I could have listened to it

forever, and it made me feel utterly wretched. Oh, I wish I was like *you*, Anne.

"He caught up with me on the road home, and grinned as cheerfully as usual. But his grin could never deceive me again. I had seen the *real* Jonas. I wondered if he could ever see the *real Phil*—whom *nobody*, not even you, Anne, has ever seen yet.

"'Jonas,' I said—I forgot to call him Mr. Blake. Wasn't it dreadful? But there are times when things like that don't matter—'Jonas, you were born to be a minister. You *couldn't* be anything else.'

"'No, I couldn't,' he said soberly. 'I tried to be something else for a long time—I didn't want to be a minister. But I came to see at last that it was the work given me to do—and God helping me, I shall try to do it.'

"His voice was low and reverent. I thought that he would do his work and do it well and nobly; and happy the woman fitted by nature and training to help him do it. *She* would be no feather, blown about by every fickle wind of fancy. *She* would always know what hat to put on. Probably she would have only one. Ministers never have much money. But she wouldn't mind having one hat or none at all, because she would have Jonas.

"Anne Shirley, don't you dare to say or hint or think that I've fallen in love with Mr. Blake. Could *I* care for a lank, poor, ugly theologue—named Jonas? As Uncle Mark says, 'It's impossible, and what's more it's improbable.'

"Good night,
PHIL."

"P.S. It is impossible—but I am horribly afraid it's true. I'm happy and wretched and scared. *He* can *never* care for me, I know. Do you think I could ever develop into a passable minister's wife, Anne? And *would* they expect me to lead in prayer? P G."

Chapter XXV
Enter Prince Charming

"I'm contrasting the claims of indoors and out," said Anne, looking from the window of Patty's Place to the distant pines of the park.

"I've an afternoon to spend in sweet doing nothing, Aunt Jimsie. Shall I spend it here where there is a cosy fire, a plateful of delicious russets, three purring and harmonious cats, and two impeccable china dogs with green noses? Or shall I go to the park, where there is the lure of gray woods and of gray water lapping on the harbor rocks?"

"If I was as young as you, I'd decide in favor of the park," said Aunt Jamesina, tickling Joseph's yellow ear with a knitting needle.

"I thought that you claimed to be as young as any of us, Aunty," teased Anne.

"Yes, in my soul. But I'll admit my legs aren't as young as yours. You go and get some fresh air, Anne. You look pale lately."

"I think I'll go to the park," said Anne restlessly. "I don't feel like tame domestic joys today. I want to feel alone and free and wild. The park will be empty, for every one will be at the football match."

"Why didn't you go to it?"

"'Nobody axed me, sir, she said'—at least, nobody but that

horrid little Dan Ranger. I wouldn't go anywhere with him; but rather than hurt his poor little tender feelings I said I wasn't going to the game at all. I don't mind. I'm not in the mood for football today somehow."

"You go and get some fresh air," repeated Aunt Jamesina, "but take your umbrella, for I believe it's going to rain. I've rheumatism in my leg."

"Only old people should have rheumatism, Aunty."

"Anybody is liable to rheumatism in her legs, Anne. It's only old people who should have rheumatism in their souls, though. Thank goodness, I never have. When you get rheumatism in your soul you might as well go and pick out your coffin."

It was November—the month of crimson sunsets, parting birds, deep, sad hymns of the sea, passionate wind-songs in the pines. Anne roamed through the pineland alleys in the park and, as she said, let that great sweeping wind blow the fogs out of her soul. Anne was not wont to be troubled with soul fog. But, somehow, since her return to Redmond for this third year, life had not mirrored her spirit back to her with its old, perfect, sparkling clearness.

Outwardly, existence at Patty's Place was the same pleasant round of work and study and recreation that it had always been. On Friday evenings the big, fire-lighted livingroom was crowded by callers and echoed to endless jest and laughter, while Aunt Jamesina smiled beamingly on them all. The "Jonas" of Phil's letter came often, running up from St. Columbia on the early train and departing on the late. He was a general favorite at Patty's Place, though Aunt Jamesina shook her head and opined that divinity students were not what they used to be.

"He's *very* nice, my dear," she told Phil, "but ministers ought to be graver and more dignified."

"Can't a man laugh and laugh and be a Christian still?"

demanded Phil.

"Oh, *men*—yes. But I was speaking of *ministers*, my dear," said Aunt Jamesina rebukingly. "And you shouldn't flirt so with Mr. Blake—you really shouldn't."

"I'm not flirting with him," protested Phil.

Nobody believed her, except Anne. The others thought she was amusing herself as usual, and told her roundly that she was behaving very badly.

"Mr. Blake isn't of the Alec-and-Alonzo type, Phil," said Stella severely. "He takes things seriously. You may break his heart."

"Do you really think I could?" asked Phil. "I'd love to think so."

"Philippa Gordon! I never thought you were utterly unfeeling. The idea of you saying you'd love to break a man's heart!"

"I didn't say so, honey. Quote me correctly. I said I'd like to think I *could* break it. I would like to know I had the *power* to do it."

"I don't understand you, Phil. You are leading that man on deliberately—and you know you don't mean anything by it."

"I mean to make him ask me to marry him if I can," said Phil calmly.

"I give you up," said Stella hopelessly.

Gilbert came occasionally on Friday evenings. He seemed always in good spirits, and held his own in the jests and repartee that flew about. He neither sought nor avoided Anne. When circumstances brought them in contact he talked to her pleasantly and courteously, as to any newly-made acquaintance. The old camaraderie was gone entirely. Anne felt it keenly; but she told herself she was very glad and thankful that Gilbert had got so completely over his disappointment in regard to her. She had really been afraid, that April evening in the orchard, that she had hurt him terribly and that the wound would be long in healing. Now she saw that she need not have worried. Men have died and the worms have eaten them but not for love. Gilbert evidently was in no danger of immediate dissolution. He was enjoying life, and he was full of ambition and zest. For him there was to be no wasting in despair because a woman was fair and cold. Anne, as she listened to the ceaseless badinage that went on between him and Phil, wondered if she had only imagined that look in his eyes when she had told him she could never care for him.

There were not lacking those who would gladly have stepped into Gilbert's vacant place. But Anne snubbed them without fear and without reproach. If the real Prince Charming was never to come she would have none of a substitute. So she sternly told herself that gray day in the windy park.

Suddenly the rain of Aunt Jamesina's prophecy came with a swish and rush. Anne put up her umbrella and hurried down the slope. As she turned out on the harbor road a savage gust of wind tore along it. Instantly her umbrella turned wrong side out. Anne clutched at it in despair. And then—there came a voice close to her.

"Pardon me—may I offer you the shelter of my umbrella?"

Anne looked up. Tall and handsome and distinguished-looking—dark, melancholy, inscrutable eyes—melting, musical, sympathetic voice—yes, the very hero of her dreams stood before her in the flesh. He could not have more closely resembled her ideal if he had been made to order.

"Thank you," she said confusedly.

"We'd better hurry over to that little pavillion on the point," suggested the unknown. "We can wait there until this shower is over. It is not likely to rain so heavily very long."

The words were very commonplace, but oh, the tone! And

the smile which accompanied them! Anne felt her heart beating strangely.

Together they scurried to the pavilion and sat breathlessly down under its friendly roof. Anne laughingly held up her false umbrella.

"It is when my umbrella turns inside out that I am convinced of the total depravity of inanimate things," she said gaily.

The raindrops sparkled on her shining hair; its loosened rings curled around her neck and forehead. Her cheeks were flushed, her eyes big and starry. Her companion looked down at her admiringly. She felt herself blushing under his gaze. Who could he be? Why, there was a bit of the Redmond white and scarlet pinned to his coat lapel. Yet she had thought she knew, by sight at least, all the Redmond students except the Freshmen. And this courtly youth surely was no Freshman.

"We are schoolmates, I see," he said, smiling at Anne's colors. "That ought to be sufficient introduction. My name is Royal Gardner. And you are the Miss Shirley who read the Tennyson paper at the Philomathic the other evening, aren't you?"

"Yes; but I cannot place you at all," said Anne, frankly. "Please, where *do* you belong?"

"I feel as if I didn't belong anywhere yet. I put in my Freshman and Sophomore years at Redmond two years ago. I've been in Europe ever since. Now I've come back to finish my Arts course."

"This is my Junior year, too," said Anne.

"So we are classmates as well as collegemates. I am reconciled to the loss of the years that the locust has eaten," said her companion, with a world of meaning in those wonderful eyes of his.

The rain came steadily down for the best part of an hour. But the time seemed really very short. When the clouds parted and a burst of pale November sunshine fell athwart the harbor and the pines Anne and her companion walked home together. By the time they had reached the gate of Patty's Place he had asked permission to call, and had received it. Anne went in with cheeks of flame and her heart beating to her fingertips. Rusty, who climbed into her lap and tried to kiss her, found a very absent welcome. Anne, with her soul full of romantic thrills, had no attention to spare just then for a crop-eared pussy cat.

That evening a parcel was left at Patty's Place for Miss Shirley. It was a box containing a dozen magnificent roses. Phil pounced impertinently on the card that fell from it, read the name and the poetical quotation written on the back.

"Royal Gardner!" she exclaimed. "Why, Anne, I didn't know you were acquainted with Roy Gardner!"

"I met him in the park this afternoon in the rain," explained Anne hurriedly. "My umbrella turned inside out and he came to my rescue with his."

"Oh!" Phil peered curiously at Anne. "And is that exceedingly commonplace incident any reason why he should send us long-stemmed roses by the dozen, with a very sentimental rhyme? Or why we should blush divinest rosy-red when we look at his card? Anne, thy face betrayeth thee."

"Don't talk nonsense, Phil. Do you know Mr. Gardner?"

"I've met his two sisters, and I know of him. So does everybody worthwhile in Kingsport. The Gardners are among the richest, bluest, of Bluenoses. Roy is adorably handsome and clever. Two years ago his mother's health failed and he had to leave college and go abroad with her—his father is dead. He must have been greatly disappointed to have to give up his class, but they say he was perfectly sweet about it. Fee—fi—fo—fum, Anne. I smell romance. Almost do I envy you, but not quite. After all, Roy Gardner isn't Jonas."

"You goose!" said Anne loftily. But she lay long awake that night, nor did she wish for sleep. Her waking fancies were more alluring than any vision of dreamland. Had the real Prince come at last? Recalling those glorious dark eyes which had gazed so deeply into her own, Anne was very strongly inclined to think he had.

Chapter XXVI
Enter Christine

The girls at Patty's Place were dressing for the reception which the Juniors were giving for the Seniors in February. Anne surveyed herself in the mirror of the blue room with girlish satisfaction. She had a particularly pretty gown on. Originally it had been only a simple little slip of cream silk with a chiffon overdress. But Phil had insisted on taking it home with her in the Christmas holidays and embroidering tiny rosebuds all over the chiffon. Phil's fingers were deft, and the result was a dress which was the envy of every Redmond girl. Even Allie Boone, whose frocks came from Paris, was wont to look with longing eyes on that rosebud concoction as Anne trailed up the main staircase at Redmond in it.

Anne was trying the effect of a white orchid in her hair. Roy Gardner had sent her white orchids for the reception, and she knew no other Redmond girl would have them that night—when Phil came in with admiring gaze.

"Anne, this is certainly your night for looking handsome. Nine nights out of ten I can easily outshine you. The tenth you blossom out suddenly into something that eclipses me altogether. How do you manage it?"

"It's the dress, dear. Fine feathers."

"'Tisn't. The last evening you flamed out into beauty you wore your old blue flannel shirtwaist that Mrs. Lynde made you. If Roy hadn't already lost head and heart about you he certainly would tonight. But I don't like orchids on you, Anne. No; it isn't jealousy. Orchids don't seem to *belong* to you. They're too exotic—too tropical—too insolent. Don't put them in your hair, anyway."

"Well, I won't. I admit I'm not fond of orchids myself. I don't think they're related to me. Roy doesn't often send them—he knows I like flowers I can live with. Orchids are only things you can visit with."

"Jonas sent me some dear pink rosebuds for the evening—but—he isn't coming himself. He said he had to lead a prayer-meeting in the slums! I don't believe he wanted to come. Anne, I'm horribly afraid Jonas doesn't really care anything about me. And I'm trying to decide whether I'll pine away and die, or go on and get my B.A. and be sensible and useful."

"You couldn't possibly be sensible and useful, Phil, so you'd better pine away and die," said Anne cruelly.

"Heartless Anne!"

"Silly Phil! You know quite well that Jonas loves you."

"But—he won't *tell* me so. And I can't *make* him. He *looks* it, I'll admit. But speak-to-me-only-with-thine-eyes isn't a really reliable reason for embroidering doilies and hemstitching tablecloths. I don't want to begin such work until I'm really engaged. It would be tempting Fate."

"Mr. Blake is afraid to ask you to marry him, Phil. He is poor and can't offer you a home such as you've always had. You know that is the only reason he hasn't spoken long ago."

"I suppose so," agreed Phil dolefully. "Well"—brightening up—"if he *won't* ask me to marry him I'll ask him, that's all. So it's bound to come right. I won't worry. By the way, Gilbert Blythe is going about constantly with Christine Stuart. Did you know?"

Anne was trying to fasten a little gold chain about her throat. She suddenly found the clasp difficult to manage. *What* was the matter with it—or with her fingers?

"No," she said carelessly. "Who is Christine Stuart?"

"Ronald Stuart's sister. She's in Kingsport this winter studying music. I haven't seen her, but they say she's very pretty and that Gilbert is quite crazy over her. How angry I was when you refused Gilbert, Anne. But Roy Gardner was foreordained for you. I can see that now. You were right, after all."

Anne did not blush, as she usually did when the girls assumed that her eventual marriage to Roy Gardner was a settled thing. All at once she felt rather dull. Phil's chatter seemed trivial and the reception a bore. She boxed poor Rusty's ears.

"Get off that cushion instantly, you cat, you! Why don't you stay down where you belong?"

Anne picked up her orchids and went downstairs, where Aunt Jamesina was presiding over a row of coats hung before the fire to warm. Roy Gardner was waiting for Anne and teasing the Sarah-cat while he waited. The Sarah-cat did not approve of him. She always turned her back on him. But everybody else at Patty's Place liked him very much. Aunt Jamesina, carried away by his unfailing and deferential courtesy, and the pleading tones of his delightful voice, declared he was the nicest young man she ever knew, and that Anne was a very fortunate girl. Such remarks made Anne restive. Roy's wooing had certainly been as romantic as girlish heart could desire, but—she wished Aunt Jamesina and the girls would not take things so for granted. When Roy murmured a poetical compliment as he helped her on with her coat, she did not blush and thrill as usual; and he found her rather silent in their brief walk to Redmond. He thought she looked a little pale when she came out of the coeds' dressing room; but as they entered the reception room her color and sparkle suddenly returned to her. She turned to Roy with her gayest expression. He smiled back at her with what Phil called "his deep, black, velvety smile." Yet she really did not see Roy at all. She was acutely conscious that Gilbert was standing under the palms just across the room talking to a girl who must be Christine Stuart.

She was very handsome, in the stately style destined to become rather massive in middle life. A tall girl, with large dark-blue eyes, ivory outlines, and a gloss of darkness on her smooth hair.

"She looks just as I've always wanted to look," thought Anne miserably. "Rose-leaf complexion—starry violet eyes—raven hair—yes, she has them all. It's a wonder her name isn't Cordelia Fitzgerald into the bargain! But I don't believe her figure is as good as mine, and her nose certainly isn't."

Anne felt a little comforted by this conclusion.

Chapter XXVII
Mutual Confidences

March came in that winter like the meekest and mildest of lambs, bringing days that were crisp and golden and tingling, each followed by a frosty pink twilight which gradually lost itself in an elfland of moonshine.

Over the girls at Patty's Place was falling the shadow of April examinations. They were studying hard; even Phil had settled down to text and notebooks with a doggedness not to be expected of her.

"I'm going to take the Johnson Scholarship in Mathematics," she announced calmly. "I could take the one in Greek easily, but I'd rather take the mathematical one because I want to prove to Jonas that I'm really enormously clever."

"Jonas likes you better for your big brown eyes and your crooked smile than for all the brains you carry under your curls," said Anne.

"When I was a girl it wasn't considered lady-like to know anything about Mathematics," said Aunt Jamesina. "But times have changed. I don't know that it's all for the better. Can you cook, Phil?"

"No, I never cooked anything in my life except a gingerbread and it was a failure—flat in the middle and hilly round the edges. You know the kind. But, Aunty, when I begin in good earnest to learn to cook don't you think the brains that enable me to win a mathematical scholarship will also enable me to learn cooking just as well?"

"Maybe," said Aunt Jamesina cautiously. "I am not decrying the higher education of women. My daughter is an M.A. She can cook, too. But I taught her to cook *before* I let a college professor teach her Mathematics."

In mid-March came a letter from Miss Patty Spofford, saying that she and Miss Maria had decided to remain abroad for another year.

"So you may have Patty's Place next winter, too," she wrote. "Maria and I are going to run over Egypt. I want to see the Sphinx once before I die."

"Fancy those two dames 'running over Egypt'! I wonder if they'll look up at the Sphinx and knit," laughed Priscilla.

"I'm so glad we can keep Patty's Place for another year," said Stella. "I was afraid they'd come back. And then our jolly little nest here would be broken up—and we poor callow nestlings thrown out on the cruel world of boardinghouses again."

"I'm off for a tramp in the park," announced Phil, tossing her book aside. "I think when I am eighty I'll be glad I went for a walk in the park tonight."

"What do you mean?" asked Anne.

"Come with me and I'll tell you, honey."

They captured in their ramble all the mysteries and magics of a March evening. Very still and mild it was, wrapped in a great, white, brooding silence—a silence which was yet threaded through with many little silvery sounds which you could hear if you hearkened as much with your soul as your ears. The girls wandered down a long pineland aisle that seemed to lead right out into the heart of a deep-red, overflowing winter sunset.

"I'd go home and write a poem this blessed minute if I only knew how," declared Phil, pausing in an open space where a rosy light was staining the green tips of the pines. "It's all so wonderful here—this great, white stillness, and those dark trees that always seem to be thinking."

"'The woods were God's first temples,'" quoted Anne softly. "One can't help feeling reverent and adoring in such a place. I always feel so near Him when I walk among the pines."

"Anne, I'm the happiest girl in the world," confessed Phil suddenly.

"So Mr. Blake has asked you to marry him at last?" said Anne calmly.

"Yes. And I sneezed three times while he was asking me. Wasn't that horrid? But I said 'yes' almost before he finished—I was so afraid he might change his mind and stop. I'm besottedly happy. I couldn't really believe before that Jonas would ever care for frivolous me."

"Phil, you're not really frivolous," said Anne gravely. "'Way down underneath that frivolous exterior of yours you've got a dear, loyal, womanly little soul. Why do you hide it so?"

"I can't help it, Queen Anne. You are right—I'm not frivolous at heart. But there's a sort of frivolous skin over my soul and I can't take it off. As Mrs. Poyser says, I'd have to be hatched over again and hatched different before I could change it. But Jonas knows the real me and loves me, frivolity and all. And I love him. I never was so surprised in my life as I was when I found out I loved him. I'd never thought it possible to fall in love with an ugly man. Fancy me coming down to one solitary beau. And one named Jonas! But I mean to call him Jo. That's such a nice, crisp little name. I couldn't nickname Alonzo."

"What about Alec and Alonzo?"

"Oh, I told them at Christmas that I never could marry either of them. It seems so funny now to remember that I ever thought it possible that I might. They felt so badly I just cried over both of them—howled. But I knew there was only one man in the world I could ever marry. I had made up my own mind for once and it was real easy, too. It's very delightful to feel so sure, and know it's your own sureness and not somebody else's."

"Do you suppose you'll be able to keep it up?"

"Making up my mind, you mean? I don't know, but Jo has given me a splendid rule. He says, when I'm perplexed, just to do what I would wish I had done when I shall be eighty. Anyhow, Jo can make up his mind quickly enough, and it would be uncomfortable to have too much mind in the same house."

"What will your father and mother say?"

"Father won't say much. He thinks everything I do right. But mother *will* talk. Oh, her tongue will be as Byrney as her nose. But in the end it will be all right."

"You'll have to give up a good many things you've always had, when you marry Mr. Blake, Phil."

"But I'll have *him*. I won't miss the other things. We're to be married a year from next June. Jo graduates from St. Columbia this spring, you know. Then he's going to take a little mission church down on Patterson Street in the slums. Fancy me in the slums! But I'd go there or to Greenland's icy mountains with him."

"And this is the girl who would *never* marry a man who wasn't rich," commented Anne to a young pine tree.

"Oh, don't cast up the follies of my youth to me. I shall be poor as gaily as I've been rich. You'll see. I'm going to learn how to cook and make over dresses. I've learned how to market since I've lived at Patty's Place; and once I taught a Sunday School class for a whole summer. Aunt Jamesina says I'll ruin Jo's career if I marry him. But I won't. I know I haven't much sense or sobriety, but I've got what is ever so much better—the knack of making people like me. There is a man in Bolingbroke who lisps and always testifies in prayer-meeting. He says, 'If you can't thine like an electric thtar thine like a candlethtick.' I'll be Jo's little candlestick."

"Phil, you're incorrigible. Well, I love you so much that I can't make nice, light, congratulatory little speeches. But I'm heart-glad of your happiness."

"I know. Those big gray eyes of yours are brimming over with real friendship, Anne. Some day I'll look the same way at you. You're going to marry Roy, aren't you, Anne?"

"My dear Philippa, did you ever hear of the famous Betty Baxter, who 'refused a man before he'd axed her'? I am not going to emulate that celebrated lady by either refusing or accepting any one before he 'axes' me."

"All Redmond knows that Roy is crazy about you," said Phil candidly. "And you *do* love him, don't you, Anne?"

"I—I suppose so," said Anne reluctantly. She felt that she ought to be blushing while making such a confession; but she was not; on the other hand, she always blushed hotly when any one said anything about Gilbert Blythe or Christine Stuart in her hearing. Gilbert Blythe and Christine Stuart were nothing to her—absolutely nothing. But Anne had given up trying to analyze the reason of her blushes. As for Roy, of course she was in love with him—madly so. How could she help it? Was he not her ideal? Who could resist those glorious dark eyes, and that pleading voice? Were not half the Redmond girls wildly envious? And what a charming sonnet he had sent her, with a box of violets, on her birthday! Anne knew every word of it by heart. It was very good stuff of its kind, too. Not exactly up to the level of Keats or Shakespeare—even Anne was not so deeply in love as to think that. But it was very tolerable magazine verse. And it was addressed to *her*—not to Laura or Beatrice or the Maid of Athens, but to her, Anne Shirley. To be told in rhythmical cadences that her eyes were stars of the morning—that her cheek had the flush it stole from the sunrise—that her lips were redder than the roses of Paradise, was thrillingly romantic. Gilbert would never have dreamed of writing a sonnet to her eyebrows.

But then, Gilbert could see a joke. She had once told Roy a funny story—and he had not seen the point of it. She recalled the chummy laugh she and Gilbert had had together over it, and wondered uneasily if life with a man who had no sense of humor might not be somewhat uninteresting in the long run. But who could expect a melancholy, inscrutable hero to see the humorous side of things? It would be flatly unreasonable.

Chapter XXVIII
A June Evening

"I wonder what it would be like to live in a world where it was always June," said Anne, as she came through the spice and bloom of the twilit orchard to the front door steps, where Marilla and Mrs. Rachel were sitting, talking over Mrs. Samson Coates' funeral, which they had attended that day. Dora sat between them, diligently studying her lessons; but Davy was sitting tailor-fashion on the grass, looking as gloomy and depressed as his single dimple would let him.

"You'd get tired of it," said Marilla, with a sigh.

"I daresay; but just now I feel that it would take me a long time to get tired of it, if it were all as charming as today. Everything loves June. Davy-boy, why this melancholy November face in blossom-time?"

"I'm just sick and tired of living," said the youthful pessimist.

"At ten years? Dear me, how sad!"

"I'm not making fun," said Davy with dignity. "I'm dis—dis—discouraged"—bringing out the big word with a valiant effort.

"Why and wherefore?" asked Anne, sitting down beside him.

"'Cause the new teacher that come when Mr. Holmes got sick give me ten sums to do for Monday. It'll take me all day tomorrow to do them. It isn't fair to have to work Saturdays. Milty Boulter said he wouldn't do them, but Marilla says I've got to. I don't like Miss Carson a bit."

"Don't talk like that about your teacher, Davy Keith," said Mrs. Rachel severely. "Miss Carson is a very fine girl. There is no nonsense about her."

"That doesn't sound very attractive," laughed Anne. "I like people to have a little nonsense about them. But I'm inclined to have a better opinion of Miss Carson than you have. I saw her in prayer-meeting last night, and she has a pair of eyes that can't always look sensible. Now, Davy-boy, take heart of grace. 'Tomorrow will bring another day' and I'll help you with the sums as far as in me lies. Don't waste this lovely hour 'twixt light and dark worrying over arithmetic."

"Well, I won't," said Davy, brightening up. "If you help me with the sums I'll have 'em done in time to go fishing with Milty. I wish old Aunt Atossa's funeral was tomorrow instead of today. I wanted to go to it 'cause Milty said his mother said Aunt Atossa would be sure to rise up in her coffin and say sarcastic things to the folks that come to see her buried. But Marilla said she didn't."

"Poor Atossa laid in her coffin peaceful enough," said Mrs. Lynde solemnly. "I never saw her look so pleasant before, that's what. Well, there weren't many tears shed over her, poor old soul. The Elisha Wrights are thankful to be rid of her, and I can't say I blame them a mite."

"It seems to me a most dreadful thing to go out of the world and not leave one person behind you who is sorry you are gone," said Anne, shuddering.

"Nobody except her parents ever loved poor Atossa, that's certain, not even her husband," averred Mrs. Lynde. "She was his fourth wife. He'd sort of got into the habit of marrying. He only lived a few years after he married her. The doctor said he died of dyspepsia, but I shall always maintain that he died of Atossa's tongue, that's what. Poor soul, she always knew everything about her neighbors, but she never was very well acquainted with herself. Well, she's gone anyhow; and I suppose the next excitement will be Diana's wedding."

"It seems funny and horrible to think of Diana's being married," sighed Anne, hugging her knees and looking through the gap in the Haunted Wood to the light that was shining in Diana's room.

"I don't see what's horrible about it, when she's doing so well," said Mrs. Lynde emphatically. "Fred Wright has a fine farm and he is a model young man."

"He certainly isn't the wild, dashing, wicked, young man Diana once wanted to marry," smiled Anne. "Fred is extremely good."

"That's just what he ought to be. Would you want Diana to marry a wicked man? Or marry one yourself?"

"Oh, no. I wouldn't want to marry anybody who was wicked, but I think I'd like it if he *could* be wicked and *wouldn't*. Now, Fred is *hopelessly* good."

"You'll have more sense some day, I hope," said Marilla.

Marilla spoke rather bitterly. She was grievously disappointed. She knew Anne had refused Gilbert Blythe. Avonlea gossip buzzed over the fact, which had leaked out, nobody knew how. Perhaps Charlie Sloane had guessed and told his guesses for truth. Perhaps Diana had betrayed it to Fred and Fred had been indiscreet. At all events it was known; Mrs. Blythe no longer asked Anne, in public or private, if she had heard lately from Gilbert, but passed her by with a frosty bow. Anne, who had always liked Gilbert's merry, young-hearted mother, was grieved in secret over this. Marilla said nothing; but Mrs. Lynde gave Anne many exasperated digs about it, until fresh gossip reached that worthy lady, through the medium of Moody Spurgeon MacPherson's mother, that Anne had another "beau" at college, who was rich and handsome and good all in one. After that Mrs. Rachel held her tongue, though she still wished in her inmost heart that Anne had accepted Gilbert. Riches were all very well; but even Mrs. Rachel, practical soul though she was, did not consider them the one essential. If Anne "liked" the Handsome Unknown better than Gilbert there was nothing more to be said; but Mrs. Rachel was dreadfully afraid that Anne was going to make the mistake of marrying for money. Marilla knew Anne too well to fear this; but she felt that something in the universal scheme of things had gone sadly awry.

"What is to be, will be," said Mrs. Rachel gloomily, "and what isn't to be happens sometimes. I can't help believing it's going to happen in Anne's case, if Providence doesn't interfere, that's what." Mrs. Rachel sighed. She was afraid Providence wouldn't interfere; and she didn't dare to.

Anne had wandered down to the Dryad's Bubble and was curled up among the ferns at the root of the big white birch where she and Gilbert had so often sat in summers gone by. He had gone into the newspaper office again when college closed, and Avonlea seemed very dull without him. He never wrote to her, and Anne missed the letters that never came. To be sure, Roy wrote twice a week; his letters were exquisite compositions which would have read beautifully in a memoir or biography. Anne felt herself more deeply in love with him than ever when she read them; but her heart never gave the queer, quick, painful bound at sight of his letters which it had given one day when Mrs. Hiram Sloane had handed her out an envelope addressed in Gilbert's black, upright handwriting. Anne had hurried home to the east gable and opened it eagerly—to find a typewritten copy of some college society report—"only that and nothing more." Anne flung the harmless screed across her room and sat down to write an especially nice epistle to Roy.

Diana was to be married in five more days. The gray house at Orchard Slope was in a turmoil of baking and brewing and boiling and stewing, for there was to be a big, old-timey wedding.

Anne, of course, was to be bridesmaid, as had been arranged when they were twelve years old, and Gilbert was coming from Kingsport to be best man. Anne was enjoying the excitement of the various preparations, but under it all she carried a little heartache. She was, in a sense, losing her dear old chum; Diana's new home would be two miles from Green Gables, and the old constant companionship could never be theirs again. Anne looked up at Diana's light and thought how it had beaconed to her for many years; but soon it would shine through the summer twilights no more. Two big, painful tears welled up in her gray eyes.

"Oh," she thought, "how horrible it is that people have to grow up—and marry—and *change!*"

Chapter XXIX
Diana's Wedding

"After all, the only real roses are the pink ones," said Anne, as she tied white ribbon around Diana's bouquet in the westward-looking gable at Orchard Slope. "They are the flowers of love and faith."

Diana was standing nervously in the middle of the room, arrayed in her bridal white, her black curls frosted over with the film of her wedding veil. Anne had draped that veil, in accordance with the sentimental compact of years before.

"It's all pretty much as I used to imagine it long ago, when I wept over your inevitable marriage and our consequent parting," she laughed. "You are the bride of my dreams, Diana, with the 'lovely misty veil'; and I am *your* bridesmaid. But, alas! I haven't the puffed sleeves—though these short lace ones are even prettier. Neither is my heart wholly breaking nor do I exactly hate Fred."

"We are not really parting, Anne," protested Diana. "I'm not going far away. We'll love each other just as much as ever. We've always kept that 'oath' of friendship we swore long ago, haven't we?"

"Yes. We've kept it faithfully. We've had a beautiful friendship, Diana. We've never marred it by one quarrel or coolness or unkind word; and I hope it will always be so. But things can't be quite the same after this. You'll have other interests. I'll just be on the outside. But 'such is life' as Mrs. Rachel says. Mrs.

Rachel has given you one of her beloved knitted quilts of the 'tobacco stripe' pattern, and she says when I am married she'll give me one, too."

"The mean thing about your getting married is that I won't be able to be your bridesmaid," lamented Diana.

"I'm to be Phil's bridesmaid next June, when she marries Mr. Blake, and then I must stop, for you know the proverb 'three times a bridesmaid, never a bride,'" said Anne, peeping through the window over the pink and snow of the blossoming orchard beneath. "Here comes the minister, Diana."

"Oh, Anne," gasped Diana, suddenly turning very pale and beginning to tremble. "Oh, Anne—I'm so nervous—I can't go through with it—Anne, I know I'm going to faint."

"If you do I'll drag you down to the rainwater hogshed and drop you in," said Anne unsympathetically. "Cheer up, dearest. Getting married can't be so very terrible when so many people survive the ceremony. See how cool and composed I am, and take courage."

"Wait till your turn comes, Miss Anne. Oh, Anne, I hear father coming upstairs. Give me my bouquet. Is my veil right? Am I very pale?"

"You look just lovely. Di, darling, kiss me good-bye for the last time. Diana Barry will never kiss me again."

"Diana Wright will, though. There, mother's calling. Come."

Following the simple, old-fashioned way in vogue then, Anne went down to the parlor on Gilbert's arm. They met at the top of the stairs for the first time since they had left Kingsport, for Gilbert had arrived only that day. Gilbert shook hands courteously. He was looking very well, though, as Anne instantly noted, rather thin. He was not pale; there was a flush on his cheek that had burned into it as Anne came along the hall towards him, in her soft, white dress with lilies-of-the-valley in the shining masses of her hair. As they entered the crowded parlor together a little murmur of admiration ran around the room. "What a fine-looking pair they are," whispered the impressible Mrs. Rachel to Marilla.

Fred ambled in alone, with a very red face, and then Diana swept in on her father's arm. She did not faint, and nothing untoward occurred to interrupt the ceremony. Feasting and merry-making followed; then, as the evening waned, Fred and Diana drove away through the moonlight to their new home, and Gilbert walked with Anne to Green Gables.

Something of their old comradeship had returned during the informal mirth of the evening. Oh, it was nice to be walking over that well-known road with Gilbert again!

The night was so very still that one should have been able to hear the whisper of roses in blossom—the laughter of daisies—the piping of grasses—many sweet sounds, all tangled up together. The beauty of moonlight on familiar fields irradiated the world.

"Can't we take a ramble up Lovers' Lane before you go in?" asked Gilbert as they crossed the bridge over the Lake of Shining Waters, in which the moon lay like a great, drowned blossom of gold.

Anne assented readily. Lovers' Lane was a veritable path in a fairyland that night—a shimmering, mysterious place, full of wizardry in the white-woven enchantment of moonlight. There had been a time when such a walk with Gilbert through Lovers' Lane would have been far too dangerous. But Roy and Christine had made it very safe now. Anne found herself thinking a good deal about Christine as she chatted lightly to Gilbert. She had met her several times before leaving Kingsport, and had been charmingly sweet to her. Christine had also been charmingly sweet. Indeed, they were a most cordial pair. But for all that, their acquaintance had not ripened into friendship. Evidently Christine was not a kindred spirit.

"Are you going to be in Avonlea all summer?" asked Gilbert.

"No. I'm going down east to Valley Road next week. Esther Haythorne wants me to teach for her through July and August. They have a summer term in that school, and Esther isn't feeling well. So I'm going to substitute for her. In one way I don't mind. Do you know, I'm beginning to feel a little bit like a stranger in Avonlea now? It makes me sorry—but it's true. It's quite appalling to see the number of children who have shot up into big boys and girls—really young men and women—these past two years. Half of my pupils are grown up. It makes me feel awfully old to see them in the places you and I and our mates used to fill."

Anne laughed and sighed. She felt very old and mature and wise—which showed how young she was. She told herself that she longed greatly to go back to those dear merry days when life was seen through a rosy mist of hope and illusion, and possessed an indefinable something that had passed away forever. Where was it now—the glory and the dream?

"'So wags the world away,'" quoted Gilbert practically, and a trifle absently. Anne wondered if he were thinking of Christine. Oh, Avonlea was going to be so lonely now—with Diana gone!

Chapter XXX
Mrs. Skinner's Romance

Anne stepped off the train at Valley Road station and looked about to see if any one had come to meet her. She was to board with a certain Miss Janet Sweet, but she saw no one who answered in the least to her preconception of that lady, as formed from Esther's letter. The only person in sight was an elderly woman, sitting in a wagon with mail bags piled around her. Two hundred would have been a charitable guess at her weight; her face was as round and red as a harvest-moon and almost as featureless. She wore a tight, black, cashmere dress, made in the fashion of ten years ago, a little dusty black straw hat trimmed with bows of yellow ribbon, and faded black lace mits.

"Here, you," she called, waving her whip at Anne. "Are you the new Valley Road schoolma'am?"

"Yes."

"Well, I thought so. Valley Road is noted for its good-looking schoolma'ams, just as Millersville is noted for its humly ones. Janet Sweet asked me this morning if I could bring you out. I said, 'Sartin I kin, if she don't mind being scrunched up some. This rig of mine's kinder small for the mail bags and I'm some heftier than Thomas!' Just wait, miss, till I shift these bags a bit and I'll tuck you in somehow. It's only two miles to Janet's. Her next-door neighbor's hired boy is coming for your trunk tonight. My name is Skinner—Amelia Skinner."

Anne was eventually tucked in, exchanging amused smiles with herself during the process.

"Jog along, black mare," commanded Mrs. Skinner, gathering up the reins in her pudgy hands. "This is my first trip on the mail rowte. Thomas wanted to hoe his turnips today so he asked me to come. So I jest sot down and took a standing-up snack and started. I sorter like it. O' course it's rather tejus. Part of the time I sits and thinks and the rest I jest sits. Jog along, black mare. I want to git home airly. Thomas is terrible lonesome when I'm away. You see, we haven't been married very long."

"Oh!" said Anne politely.

"Just a month. Thomas courted me for quite a spell, though. It was real romantic." Anne tried to picture Mrs. Skinner on speaking terms with romance and failed.

"Oh?" she said again.

"Yes. Y'see, there was another man after me. Jog along, black mare. I'd been a widder so long folks had given up expecting me to marry again. But when my darter—she's a schoolma'am like you—went out West to teach I felt real lonesome and wasn't nowise sot against the idea. Bime-by Thomas began to come up and so did the other feller—William Obadiah Seaman, his name was. For a long time I couldn't make up my mind which of them to take, and they kep' coming and coming, and I kep' worrying. Y'see, W.O. was rich—he had a fine place and carried considerable style. He was by far the best match. Jog along, black mare."

"Why didn't you marry him?" asked Anne.

"Well, y'see, he didn't love me," answered Mrs. Skinner, solemnly.

Anne opened her eyes widely and looked at Mrs. Skinner. But there was not a glint of humor on that lady's face. Evidently Mrs. Skinner saw nothing amusing in her own case.

"He'd been a widder-man for three yers, and his sister kept house for him. Then she got married and he just wanted some one to look after his house. It was worth looking after, too, mind you that. It's a handsome house. Jog along, black mare. As for Thomas, he was poor, and if his house didn't leak in dry weather it was about all that could be said for it, though it looks kind of pictureaskew. But, y'see, I loved Thomas, and I didn't care one red cent for W.O. So I argued it out with myself. 'Sarah Crowe,' say I—my first was a Crowe—'you can marry your rich man if you like but you won't be happy. Folks can't get along together in this world without a little bit of love. You'd just better tie up to Thomas, for he loves you and you love him and nothing else ain't going to do you.' Jog along, black mare. So I told Thomas I'd take him. All the time I was getting ready I never dared drive past W.O.'s place for fear the sight of that fine house of his would put me in the swithers again. But now I never think of it at all, and I'm just that comfortable and happy with Thomas. Jog along, black mare."

"How did William Obadiah take it?" queried Anne.

"Oh, he rumpussed a bit. But he's going to see a skinny old maid in Millersville now, and I guess she'll take him fast enough. She'll make him a better wife than his first did. W.O. never wanted to marry her. He just asked her to marry him 'cause his father wanted him to, never dreaming but that she'd say 'no.' But mind you, she said 'yes.' There was a predicament for you. Jog along, black mare. She was a great housekeeper, but most awful mean. She wore the same bonnet for eighteen years. Then she got a new one and W.O. met her on the road and didn't know her. Jog along, black mare. I feel that I'd a narrer escape. I might have married him and been most awful miserable, like my poor cousin, Jane Ann. Jane Ann married a rich man she didn't care anything about, and she hasn't the life of a dog. She come to see me last week and says, says she, 'Sarah Skinner, I envy you. I'd rather live in a little hut on the side of the road with a man I was fond of than in my big house with the one I've got.' Jane

Ann's man ain't such a bad sort, nuther, though he's so contrary that he wears his fur coat when the thermometer's at ninety. The only way to git him to do anything is to coax him to do the opposite. But there ain't any love to smooth things down and it's a poor way of living. Jog along, black mare. There's Janet's place in the hollow—'Wayside,' she calls it. Quite pictureaskew, ain't it? I guess you'll be glad to git out of this, with all them mail bags jamming round you."

"Yes, but I have enjoyed my drive with you very much," said Anne sincerely.

"Git away now!" said Mrs. Skinner, highly flattered. "Wait till I tell Thomas that. He always feels dretful tickled when I git a compliment. Jog along, black mare. Well, here we are. I hope you'll git on well in the school, miss. There's a short cut to it through the ma'sh back of Janet's. If you take that way be awful keerful. If you once got stuck in that black mud you'd be sucked right down and never seen or heard tell of again till the day of judgment, like Adam Palmer's cow. Jog along, black mare."

Chapter XXXI
Anne to Philippa

"Anne Shirley to Philippa Gordon, greeting.

"Well-beloved, it's high time I was writing you. Here am I, installed once more as a country 'schoolma'am' at Valley Road, boarding at 'Wayside,' the home of Miss Janet Sweet. Janet is a dear soul and very nicelooking; tall, but not over-tall; stoutish, yet with a certain restraint of outline suggestive of a thrifty soul who is not going to be overlavish even in the matter of avoirdupois. She has a knot of soft, crimpy, brown hair with a thread of gray in it, a sunny face with rosy cheeks, and big, kind eyes as blue as forget-me-nots. Moreover, she is one of those delightful, old-fashioned cooks who don't care a bit if they ruin your digestion as long as they can give you feasts of fat things.

"I like her; and she likes me—principally, it seems, because she had a sister named Anne who died young.

"'I'm real glad to see you,' she said briskly, when I landed in her yard. 'My, you don't look a mite like I expected. I was sure you'd be dark—my sister Anne was dark. And here you're redheaded!'

"For a few minutes I thought I wasn't going to like Janet as much as I had expected at first sight. Then I reminded myself that I really must be more sensible than to be prejudiced against any one simply because she called my hair red. Probably the word 'auburn' was not in Janet's vocabulary at all.

"'Wayside' is a dear sort of little spot. The house is small and white, set down in a delightful little hollow that drops away from the road. Between road and house is an orchard and flower-garden all mixed up together. The front door walk is bordered with quahog clam-shells—'cow-hawks,' Janet calls them; there is Virginia Creeper over the porch and moss on the roof. My room is a neat little spot 'off the parlor'—just big enough for the bed and me. Over the head of my bed there is a picture of Robby Burns standing at Highland Mary's grave, shadowed by an enormous weeping willow tree. Robby's face is so lugubrious that it is no wonder I have bad dreams. Why, the first night I was here I dreamed I *couldn't laugh*.

"The parlor is tiny and neat. Its one window is so shaded by a huge willow that the room has a grotto-like effect of emerald gloom. There are wonderful tidies on the chairs, and gay mats on the floor, and books and cards carefully arranged on a round table, and vases of dried grass on the mantel-piece. Between the vases is a cheerful decoration of preserved coffin plates—five in all, pertaining respectively to Janet's father and mother, a brother, her sister Anne, and a hired man who died here once! If I go suddenly insane some of these days 'know all men by these presents' that those coffin-plates have caused it.

"But it's all delightful and I said so. Janet loved me for it, just as she detested poor Esther because Esther had said so much shade was unhygienic and had objected to sleeping on a feather bed. Now, I glory in feather-beds, and the more unhygienic and feathery they are the more I glory. Janet says it is such a comfort to see me eat; she had been so afraid I would be like Miss Haythorne, who wouldn't eat anything but fruit and hot water for breakfast and tried to make Janet give up frying things. Esther is really a dear girl, but she is rather given to fads. The trouble is that she hasn't enough imagination and HAS a tendency to indigestion.

"Janet told me I could have the use of the parlor when any young men called! I don't think there are many to call. I haven't seen a young man in Valley Road yet, except the next-door hired boy—Sam Toliver, a very tall, lank, tow-haired youth. He came over one evening recently and sat for an hour on the garden fence, near the front porch where Janet and I were doing fancy-work. The only remarks he volunteered in all that time were, 'Hev a peppermint, miss! Dew now-fine thing for ca*rarrh*, peppermints,' and, 'Powerful lot o' jump-grasses round here ternight. Yep.'

"But there is a love affair going on here. It seems to be my fortune to be mixed up, more or less actively, with elderly love affairs. Mr. and Mrs. Irving always say that I brought about their marriage. Mrs. Stephen Clark of Carmody persists in being most grateful to me for a suggestion which somebody else would probably have made if I hadn't. I do really think, though, that Ludovic Speed would never have got any further along than placid courtship if I had not helped him and Theodora Dix out.

"In the present affair I am only a passive spectator. I've tried once to help things along and made an awful mess of it. So I shall not meddle again. I'll tell you all about it when we meet."

Chapter XXXII
Tea with Mrs. Douglas

On the first Thursday night of Anne's sojourn in Valley Road Janet asked her to go to prayer-meeting. Janet blossomed out like a rose to attend that prayer-meeting. She wore a pale-blue, pansy-sprinkled muslin dress with more ruffles than one would ever have supposed economical Janet could be guilty of, and a white leghorn hat with pink roses and three ostrich feathers on it. Anne felt quite amazed. Later on, she found out Janet's motive in so arraying herself—a motive as old as Eden.

Valley Road prayer-meetings seemed to be essentially feminine. There were thirty-two women present, two half-grown boys, and one solitary man, beside the minister. Anne found herself studying this man. He was not handsome or young or graceful; he had remarkably long legs—so long that he had to keep them coiled up under his chair to dispose of them—and he was stoop-shouldered. His hands were big, his hair wanted barbering, and his moustache was unkempt. But Anne thought she liked his face; it was kind and honest and tender; there was something else in it, too—just what, Anne found it hard to define. She finally concluded that this man had suffered and been strong, and it had been made manifest in his face. There was a sort of patient, humorous endurance in his expression which indicated that he would go to the stake if need be, but would keep on looking pleasant until he really had to begin squirming.

When prayer-meeting was over this man came up to Janet and said,

"May I see you home, Janet?"

Janet took his arm—"as primly and shyly as if she were no more than sixteen, having her first escort home," Anne told the girls at Patty's Place later on.

"Miss Shirley, permit me to introduce Mr. Douglas," she said stiffly.

Mr. Douglas nodded and said, "I was looking at you in prayer-meeting, miss, and thinking what a nice little girl you were."

Such a speech from ninety-nine people out of a hundred would have annoyed Anne bitterly; but the way in which Mr. Douglas said it made her feel that she had received a very real and pleasing compliment. She smiled appreciatively at him and dropped obligingly behind on the moonlit road.

So Janet had a beau! Anne was delighted. Janet would make a paragon of a wife—cheery, economical, tolerant, and a very queen of cooks. It would be a flagrant waste on Nature's part to keep her a permanent old maid.

"John Douglas asked me to take you up to see his mother," said Janet the next day. "She's bed-rid a lot of the time and never goes out of the house. But she's powerful fond of company and always wants to see my boarders. Can you go up this evening?"

Anne assented; but later in the day Mr. Douglas called on his mother's behalf to invite them up to tea on Saturday evening.

"Oh, why didn't you put on your pretty pansy dress?" asked Anne, when they left home. It was a hot day, and poor Janet, between her excitement and her heavy black cashmere dress, looked as if she were being broiled alive.

"Old Mrs. Douglas would think it terrible frivolous and unsuitable, I'm afraid. John likes that dress, though," she added wistfully.

The old Douglas homestead was half a mile from "Wayside" cresting a windy hill. The house itself was large and comfortable, old enough to be dignified, and girdled with maple groves and orchards. There were big, trim barns behind it, and everything bespoke prosperity. Whatever the patient endurance in Mr. Douglas' face had meant it hadn't, so Anne reflected, meant debts and duns.

John Douglas met them at the door and took them into the sitting-room, where his mother was enthroned in an armchair.

Anne had expected old Mrs. Douglas to be tall and thin, because Mr. Douglas was. Instead, she was a tiny scrap of a woman, with soft pink cheeks, mild blue eyes, and a mouth like a baby's. Dressed in a beautiful, fashionably-made black silk dress, with a fluffy white shawl over her shoulders, and her snowy hair surmounted by a dainty lace cap, she might have posed as a grandmother doll.

"How do you do, Janet dear?" she said sweetly. "I am so glad to see you again, dear." She put up her pretty old face to be kissed. "And this is our new teacher. I'm delighted to meet you. My son has been singing your praises until I'm half jealous, and I'm sure Janet ought to be wholly so."

Poor Janet blushed, Anne said something polite and conventional, and then everybody sat down and made talk. It was hard work, even for Anne, for nobody seemed at ease except old Mrs. Douglas, who certainly did not find any difficulty in talking. She made Janet sit by her and stroked her hand occasionally. Janet sat and smiled, looking horribly uncomfortable in her hideous dress, and John Douglas sat without smiling.

At the tea table Mrs. Douglas gracefully asked Janet to pour the tea. Janet turned redder than ever but did it. Anne wrote a description of that meal to Stella.

"We had cold tongue and chicken and strawberry preserves, lemon pie and tarts and chocolate cake and raisin cookies and pound cake and fruit cake—and a few other things, including more pie—caramel pie, I think it was. After I had eaten twice as much as was good for me, Mrs. Douglas sighed and said she feared she had nothing to tempt my appetite.

"'I'm afraid dear Janet's cooking has spoiled you for any other,' she said sweetly. 'Of course nobody in Valley Road aspires to rival *her*. *Won't* you have another piece of pie, Miss Shirley? You haven't eaten *anything*.'

"Stella, I had eaten a helping of tongue and one of chicken, three biscuits, a generous allowance of preserves, a piece of pie, a tart, and a square of chocolate cake!"

After tea Mrs. Douglas smiled benevolently and told John to take "dear Janet" out into the garden and get her some roses. "Miss Shirley will keep me company while you are out—won't you?" she said plaintively. She settled down in her armchair with a sigh.

"I am a very frail old woman, Miss Shirley. For over twenty years I've been a great sufferer. For twenty long, weary years I've been dying by inches."

"How painful!" said Anne, trying to be sympathetic and succeeding only in feeling idiotic.

"There have been scores of nights when they've thought I could never live to see the dawn," went on Mrs. Douglas solemnly. "Nobody knows what I've gone through—nobody can know but myself. Well, it can't last very much longer now. My weary pilgrimage will soon be over, Miss Shirley. It is a great comfort to me that John will have such a good wife to look after him when his mother is gone—a great comfort, Miss Shirley."

"Janet is a lovely woman," said Anne warmly.

"Lovely! A beautiful character," assented Mrs. Douglas. "And a perfect housekeeper—something I never was. My health would not permit it, Miss Shirley. I am indeed thankful that John has made such a wise choice. I hope and believe that he will be happy. He is my only son, Miss Shirley, and his happiness lies very near my heart."

"Of course," said Anne stupidly. For the first time in her life she was stupid. Yet she could not imagine why. She seemed to have absolutely nothing to say to this sweet, smiling, angelic old lady who was patting her hand so kindly.

"Come and see me soon again, dear Janet," said Mrs. Douglas lovingly, when they left. "You don't come half often enough. But then I suppose John will be bringing you here to stay all the time one of these days." Anne, happening to glance at John Douglas, as his mother spoke, gave a positive start of dismay. He looked as a tortured man might look when his tormentors gave the rack the last turn of possible endurance. She felt sure he must be ill and hurried poor blushing Janet away.

"Isn't old Mrs. Douglas a sweet woman?" asked Janet, as they went down the road.

"M—m," answered Anne absently. She was wondering why John Douglas had looked so.

"She's been a terrible sufferer," said Janet feelingly. "She takes terrible spells. It keeps John all worried up. He's scared to leave home for fear his mother will take a spell and nobody there but the hired girl."

Chapter XXXIII
"He Just Kept Coming and Coming"

Three days later Anne came home from school and found Janet crying. Tears and Janet seemed so incongruous that Anne was honestly alarmed.

"Oh, what is the matter?" she cried anxiously.

"I'm—I'm forty today," sobbed Janet.

"Well, you were nearly that yesterday and it didn't hurt," comforted Anne, trying not to smile.

"But—but," went on Janet with a big gulp, "John Douglas won't ask me to marry him."

"Oh, but he will," said Anne lamely. "You must give him time, Janet

"Time!" said Janet with indescribable scorn. "He has had twenty years. How much time does he want?"

"Do you mean that John Douglas has been coming to see you for twenty years?"

"He has. And he has never so much as mentioned marriage to me. And I don't believe he ever will now. I've never said a word to a mortal about it, but it seems to me I've just got to talk it out with some one at last or go crazy. John Douglas begun to go with me twenty years ago, before mother died. Well, he kept coming and coming, and after a spell I begun making quilts and things; but he never said anything about getting married, only just kept coming and coming. There wasn't anything I could do. Mother died when we'd been going together for eight years. I thought he maybe would speak out then, seeing as I was left alone in the world. He was real kind and feeling, and did everything he could for me, but he never said marry. And that's the way it has been going on ever since. People blame *me* for it. They say I won't marry him because his mother is so sickly and I don't want the bother of waiting on her. Why, I'd *love* to wait on John's mother! But I let them think so. I'd rather they'd blame me than pity me! It's so dreadful humiliating that John won't ask me. And *why* won't he? Seems to me if I only knew his reason I wouldn't mind it so much."

"Perhaps his mother doesn't want him to marry anybody," suggested Anne.

"Oh, she does. She's told me time and again that she'd love to see John settled before her time comes. She's always giving him hints—you heard her yourself the other day. I thought I'd ha' gone through the floor."

"It's beyond me," said Anne helplessly. She thought of Ludovic Speed. But the cases were not parallel. John Douglas was not a man of Ludovic's type.

"You should show more spirit, Janet," she went on resolutely. "Why didn't you send him about his business long ago?"

"I couldn't," said poor Janet pathetically. "You see, Anne, I've always been awful fond of John. He might just as well keep coming as not, for there was never anybody else I'd want, so it didn't matter."

"But it might have made him speak out like a man," urged Anne.

Janet shook her head.

"No, I guess not. I was afraid to try, anyway, for fear he'd think I meant it and just go. I suppose I'm a poor-spirited creature, but that is how I feel. And I can't help it."

"Oh, you *could* help it, Janet. It isn't too late yet. Take a firm stand. Let that man know you are not going to endure his shillyshallying any longer. *I'll* back you up."

"I dunno," said Janet hopelessly. "I dunno if I could ever get up enough spunk. Things have drifted so long. But I'll think it over."

Anne felt that she was disappointed in John Douglas. She had liked him so well, and she had not thought him the sort of man who would play fast and loose with a woman's feelings for twenty years. He certainly should be taught a lesson, and Anne felt vindictively that she would enjoy seeing the process. Therefore she was delighted when Janet told her, as they were going to prayer-meeting the next night, that she meant to show some "sperrit."

"I'll let John Douglas see I'm not going to be trodden on any longer."

"You are perfectly right," said Anne emphatically.

When prayer-meeting was over John Douglas came up with his usual request. Janet looked frightened but resolute.

"No, thank you," she said icily. "I know the road home pretty well alone. I ought to, seeing I've been traveling it for forty years. So you needn't trouble yourself, *Mr.* Douglas."

Anne was looking at John Douglas; and, in that brilliant moonlight, she saw the last twist of the rack again. Without a word he turned and strode down the road.

"Stop! Stop!" Anne called wildly after him, not caring in the least for the other dumbfounded onlookers. "Mr. Douglas, stop! Come back."

John Douglas stopped but he did not come back. Anne flew down the road, caught his arm and fairly dragged him back to Janet.

"You must come back," she said imploringly. "It's all a mistake, Mr. Douglas—all my fault. I made Janet do it. She didn't want to—but it's all right now, isn't it, Janet?"

Without a word Janet took his arm and walked away. Anne followed them meekly home and slipped in by the back door.

"Well, you are a nice person to back me up," said Janet sarcastically.

"I couldn't help it, Janet," said Anne repentantly. "I just felt as if I had stood by and seen murder done. I *had* to run after him."

"Oh, I'm just as glad you did. When I saw John Douglas making off down that road I just felt as if every little bit of joy and happiness that was left in my life was going with him. It was an awful feeling."

"Did he ask you why you did it?" asked Anne.

"No, he never said a word about it," replied Janet dully.

Chapter XXXIV
John Douglas Speaks at Last

Anne was not without a feeble hope that something might come of it after all. But nothing did. John Douglas came and took Janet driving, and walked home from prayer-meeting with her, as he had been doing for twenty years, and as he seemed likely to do for twenty years more. The summer waned. Anne taught her school and wrote letters and studied a little. Her walks to and from school were pleasant. She always went by way of the swamp; it was a lovely place—a boggy soil, green with the greenest of mossy hillocks; a silvery brook meandered through it and spruces stood erectly, their boughs a-trail with gray-green mosses, their roots overgrown with all sorts of woodland lovelinesses.

Nevertheless, Anne found life in Valley Road a little monotonous. To be sure, there was one diverting incident.

She had not seen the lank, tow-headed Samuel of the peppermints since the evening of his call, save for chance meetings on the road. But one warm August night he appeared, and solemnly seated himself on the rustic bench by the porch. He wore his usual working habiliments, consisting of varipatched trousers, a blue jean shirt, out at the elbows, and a ragged straw hat. He was chewing a straw and he kept on chewing it while he looked solemnly at Anne. Anne laid her book aside with a sigh and took up her doily. Conversation with Sam was really out of the question.

After a long silence Sam suddenly spoke.

"I'm leaving over there," he said abruptly, waving his straw in the direction of the neighboring house.

"Oh, are you?" said Anne politely.

"Yep."

"And where are you going now?"

"Wall, I've been thinking some of gitting a place of my own. There's one that'd suit me over at Millersville. But ef I rents it I'll want a woman."

"I suppose so," said Anne vaguely.

"Yep."

There was another long silence. Finally Sam removed his straw again and said,

"Will yeh hev me?"

"Wh—a—t!" gasped Anne.

"Will yeh hev me?"

"Do you mean—MARRY you?" queried poor Anne feebly.

"Yep."

"Why, I'm hardly acquainted with you," cried Anne indignantly.

"But yeh'd git acquainted with me after we was married," said Sam.

Anne gathered up her poor dignity.

"Certainly I won't marry you," she said haughtily.

"Wall, yeh might do worse," expostulated Sam. "I'm a good worker and I've got some money in the bank."

"Don't speak of this to me again. Whatever put such an idea into your head?" said Anne, her sense of humor getting the better of her wrath. It was such an absurd situation.

"Yeh're a likely-looking girl and hev a right-smart way o' stepping," said Sam. "I don't want no lazy woman. Think it over. I won't change my mind yit awhile. Wall, I must be gitting. Gotter milk the cows."

Anne's illusions concerning proposals had suffered so much of late years that there were few of them left. So she could laugh wholeheartedly over this one, not feeling any secret sting. She mimicked poor Sam to Janet that night, and both of them laughed immoderately over his plunge into sentiment.

One afternoon, when Anne's sojourn in Valley Road was drawing to a close, Alec Ward came driving down to "Wayside" in hot haste for Janet.

"They want you at the Douglas place quick," he said. "I really believe old Mrs. Douglas is going to die at last, after pretending to do it for twenty years."

Janet ran to get her hat. Anne asked if Mrs. Douglas was worse than usual.

"She's not half as bad," said Alec solemnly, "and that's what makes me think it's serious. Other times she'd be screaming and throwing herself all over the place. This time she's lying still and mum. When Mrs. Douglas is mum she is pretty sick, you bet."

"You don't like old Mrs. Douglas?" said Anne curiously.

"I like cats as *is* cats. I don't like cats as is women," was Alec's cryptic reply.

Janet came home in the twilight.

"Mrs. Douglas is dead," she said wearily. "She died soon after I got there. She just spoke to me once—'I suppose you'll marry John now?' she said. It cut me to the heart, Anne. To think John's own mother thought I wouldn't marry him because of her! I couldn't say a word either—there were other women there. I was thankful John had gone out."

Janet began to cry drearily. But Anne brewed her a hot drink of ginger tea to her comforting. To be sure, Anne discovered later on that she had used white pepper instead of ginger; but Janet never knew the difference.

The evening after the funeral Janet and Anne were sitting on the front porch steps at sunset. The wind had fallen asleep in the pinelands and lurid sheets of heat-lightning flickered across the northern skies. Janet wore her ugly black dress and looked her very worst, her eyes and nose red from crying. They talked little, for Janet seemed faintly to resent Anne's efforts to cheer her up. She plainly preferred to be miserable.

Suddenly the gate-latch clicked and John Douglas strode into the garden. He walked towards them straight over the geranium bed. Janet stood up. So did Anne. Anne was a tall girl and wore a white dress; but John Douglas did not see her.

"Janet," he said, "will you marry me?"

The words burst out as if they had been wanting to be said for twenty years and *must* be uttered now, before anything else.

Janet's face was so red from crying that it couldn't turn any redder, so it turned a most unbecoming purple.

"Why didn't you ask me before?" she said slowly.

"I couldn't. She made me promise not to—mother made me promise not to. Nineteen years ago she took a terrible spell. We thought she couldn't live through it. She implored me to promise not to ask you to marry me while she was alive. I didn't want to promise such a thing, even though we all thought she couldn't live very long—the doctor only gave her six months. But she begged it on her knees, sick and suffering. I had to promise."

"What had your mother against me?" cried Janet.

"Nothing—nothing. She just didn't want another woman—*any* woman—there while she was living. She said if I didn't promise she'd die right there and I'd have killed her. So I promised. And she's held me to that promise ever since, though I've gone on my knees to her in my turn to beg her to let me off."

"Why didn't you tell me this?" asked Janet chokingly. "If I'd only *known!* Why didn't you just tell me?"

"She made me promise I wouldn't tell a soul," said John hoarsely. "She swore me to it on the Bible; Janet, I'd never have done it if I'd dreamed it was to be for so long. Janet, you'll never know what I've suffered these nineteen years. I know I've made you suffer, too, but you'll marry me for all, won't you, Janet? Oh, Janet, won't you? I've come as soon as I could to ask you."

At this moment the stupefied Anne came to her senses and realized that she had no business to be there. She slipped away and did not see Janet until the next morning, when the latter told her the rest of the story.

"That cruel, relentless, deceitful old woman!" cried Anne.

"Hush—she's dead," said Janet solemnly. "If she wasn't—but she *is*. So we mustn't speak evil of her. But I'm happy at last, Anne. And I wouldn't have minded waiting so long a bit if I'd only known why."

"When are you to be married?"

"Next month. Of course it will be very quiet. I suppose people will talk terrible. They'll say I made enough haste to snap John up as soon as his poor mother was out of the way. John wanted to let them know the truth but I said, 'No, John; after all she was your mother, and we'll keep the secret between us, and not cast any shadow on her memory. I don't mind what people say, now that I know the truth myself. It don't matter a mite. Let it all be buried with the dead' says I to him. So I coaxed him round to agree with me."

"You're much more forgiving than I could ever be," Anne said, rather crossly.

"You'll feel differently about a good many things when you get to be my age," said Janet tolerantly. "That's one of the things we learn as we grow older—how to forgive. It comes easier at forty than it did at twenty."

Chapter XXXV
The Last Redmond Year Opens

"Here we are, all back again, nicely sunburned and rejoicing as a strong man to run a race," said Phil, sitting down on a suitcase with a sigh of pleasure. "Isn't it jolly to see this dear old Patty's Place again—and Aunty—and the cats? Rusty has lost another piece of ear, hasn't he?"

"Rusty would be the nicest cat in the world if he had no ears at all," declared Anne loyally from her trunk, while Rusty writhed about her lap in a frenzy of welcome.

"Aren't you glad to see us back, Aunty?" demanded Phil.

"Yes. But I wish you'd tidy things up," said Aunt Jamesina plaintively, looking at the wilderness of trunks and suitcases by which the four laughing, chattering girls were surrounded. "You can talk just as well later on. Work first and then play used to be my motto when I was a girl."

"Oh, we've just reversed that in this generation, Aunty. *Our* motto is play your play and then dig in. You can do your work so much better if you've had a good bout of play first."

"If you are going to marry a minister," said Aunt Jamesina, picking up Joseph and her knitting and resigning herself to the inevitable with the charming grace that made her the queen of housemothers, "you will have to give up such expressions as 'dig in.'"

"Why?" moaned Phil. "Oh, why must a minister's wife be supposed to utter only prunes and prisms? I shan't. Everybody on Patterson Street uses slang—that is to say, metaphorical language—and if I didn't they would think me insufferably proud and stuck up."

"Have you broken the news to your family?" asked Priscilla, feeding the Sarah-cat bits from her lunchbasket.

Phil nodded.

"How did they take it?"

"Oh, mother rampaged. But I stood rockfirm—even I, Philippa Gordon, who never before could hold fast to anything. Father was calmer. Father's own daddy was a minister, so you see he has a soft spot in his heart for the cloth. I had Jo up to Mount Holly, after mother grew calm, and they both loved him. But mother gave him some frightful hints in every conversation regarding what she had hoped for me. Oh, my vacation pathway hasn't been exactly strewn with roses, girls dear. But—I've won out and I've got Jo. Nothing else matters."

"To you," said Aunt Jamesina darkly.

"Nor to Jo, either," retorted Phil. "You keep on pitying him. Why, pray? I think he's to be envied. He's getting brains, beauty, and a heart of gold in *me*."

"It's well we know how to take your speeches," said Aunt Jamesina patiently. "I hope you don't talk like that before strangers. What would they think?"

"Oh, I don't want to know what they think. I don't want to see myself as others see me. I'm sure it would be horribly uncomfortable most of the time. I don't believe Burns was really sincere in that prayer, either."

"Oh, I daresay we all pray for some things that we really don't want, if we were only honest enough to look into our hearts," owned Aunt Jamesina candidly. "I've a notion that such prayers don't rise very far. *I* used to pray that I might be enabled to forgive a certain person, but I know now I really didn't want to forgive her. When I finally got that I *did* want to I forgave her without having to pray about it."

"I can't picture you as being unforgiving for long," said Stella.

"Oh, I used to be. But holding spite doesn't seem worth while when you get along in years."

"That reminds me," said Anne, and told the tale of John and Janet.

"And now tell us about that romantic scene you hinted so darkly at in one of your letters," demanded Phil.

Anne acted out Samuel's proposal with great spirit. The girls shrieked with laughter and Aunt Jamesina smiled.

"It isn't in good taste to make fun of your beaux," she said severely; "but," she added calmly, "I always did it myself."

"Tell us about your beaux, Aunty," entreated Phil. "You must have had any number of them."

"They're not in the past tense," retorted Aunt Jamesina. "I've got them yet. There are three old widowers at home who have been casting sheep's eyes at me for some time. You children needn't think you own all the romance in the world."

"Widowers and sheep's eyes don't sound very romantic, Aunty."

"Well, no; but young folks aren't always romantic either. Some of my beaux certainly weren't. I used to laugh at them scandalous, poor boys. There was Jim Elwood—he was always in a sort of day-dream—never seemed to sense what was going on. He didn't wake up to the fact that I'd said 'no' till a year after I'd said it. When he did get married his wife fell out of the sleigh one night when they were driving home from church and he never missed her. Then there was Dan Winston. He knew too much. He knew everything in this world and most of what is in the next. He could give you an answer to any question, even if you asked him when the Judgment Day was to be. Milton Edwards was real nice and I liked him but I didn't marry him. For one thing, he took a week to get a joke through his head, and for another he never asked me. Horatio Reeve was the most interesting beau I ever had. But when he told a story he dressed it up so that you couldn't see it for frills. I never could decide whether he was lying or just letting his imagination run loose."

"And what about the others, Aunty?"

"Go away and unpack," said Aunt Jamesina, waving Joseph at them by mistake for a needle. "The others were too nice to make fun of. I shall respect their memory. There's a box of flowers in your room, Anne. They came about an hour ago."

After the first week the girls of Patty's Place settled down to a steady grind of study; for this was their last year at Redmond and graduation honors must be fought for persistently. Anne devoted herself to English, Priscilla pored over classics, and Philippa pounded away at Mathematics. Sometimes they grew tired, sometimes they felt discouraged, sometimes nothing seemed worth the struggle for it. In one such mood Stella wandered up to the blue room one rainy November evening. Anne sat on the floor in a little circle of light cast by the lamp beside her, amid a surrounding snow of crumpled manuscript.

"What in the world are you doing?"

"Just looking over some old Story Club yarns. I wanted something to cheer *and* inebriate. I'd studied until the world seemed azure. So I came up here and dug these out of my trunk. They are so drenched in tears and tragedy that they are excruciatingly funny."

"I'm blue and discouraged myself," said Stella, throwing herself on the couch. "Nothing seems worthwhile. My very thoughts are old. I've thought them all before. What is the use of living after all, Anne?"

"Honey, it's just brain fag that makes us feel that way, and the weather. A pouring rainy night like this, coming after a hard day's grind, would squelch any one but a Mark Tapley. You know it *is* worthwhile to live."

"Oh, I suppose so. But I can't prove it to myself just now."

"Just think of all the great and noble souls who have lived and worked in the world," said Anne dreamily. "Isn't it worthwhile to come after them and inherit what they won and taught? Isn't it worthwhile to think we can share their inspiration? And then, all the great souls that will come in the future? Isn't it worthwhile to work a little and prepare the way for them—make just one step in their path easier?"

"Oh, my mind agrees with you, Anne. But my soul remains doleful and uninspired. I'm always grubby and dingy on rainy nights."

"Some nights I like the rain—I like to lie in bed and hear it pattering on the roof and drifting through the pines."

"I like it when it stays on the roof," said Stella. "It doesn't always. I spent a gruesome night in an old country farmhouse last summer. The roof leaked and the rain came pattering down on my bed. There was no poetry in *that*. I had to get up in the 'mirk midnight' and chivy round to pull the bedstead out of the drip—and it was one of those solid, old-fashioned beds that weigh a ton—more or less. And then that drip-drop, drip-drop kept up all night until my nerves just went to pieces. You've no idea what an eerie noise a great drop of rain falling with a mushy thud on a bare floor makes in the night. It sounds like ghostly footsteps and all that sort of thing. What are you laughing over, Anne?"

"These stories. As Phil would say they are killing—in more senses than one, for everybody died in them. What dazzlingly lovely heroines we had—and how we dressed them!

"Silks—satins—velvets—jewels—laces—they never wore anything else. Here is one of Jane Andrews' stories depicting her heroine as sleeping in a beautiful white satin nightdress trimmed with seed pearls."

"Go on," said Stella. "I begin to feel that life is worth living as long as there's a laugh in it."

"Here's one I wrote. My heroine is disporting herself at a ball 'glittering from head to foot with large diamonds of the first water.' But what booted beauty or rich attire? 'The paths of glory lead but to the grave.' They must either be murdered or die of a broken heart. There was no escape for them."

"Let me read some of your stories."

"Well, here's my masterpiece. Note its cheerful title—'My Graves.' I shed quarts of tears while writing it, and the other girls shed gallons while I read it. Jane Andrews' mother scolded her frightfully because she had so many handkerchiefs in the wash that week. It's a harrowing tale of the wanderings of a Methodist minister's wife. I made her a Methodist because it was necessary that she should wander. She buried a child every place she lived in. There were nine of them and their graves were severed far apart, ranging from Newfoundland to Vancouver. I described the children, pictured their several death beds, and detailed their tombstones and epitaphs. I had intended to bury the whole nine but when I had disposed of eight my invention of horrors gave out and I permitted the ninth to live as a hopeless cripple."

While Stella read My Graves, punctuating its tragic paragraphs with chuckles, and Rusty slept the sleep of a just cat who has been out all night curled up on a Jane Andrews tale of a beautiful maiden of fifteen who went to nurse in a leper colony—of course dying of the loathsome disease finally—Anne glanced over the other manuscripts and recalled the old days at Avonlea school when the members of the Story Club, sitting under the spruce trees or down among the ferns by the brook, had written them. What fun they had had! How the sunshine and mirth of those olden summers returned as she read. Not all the glory that was Greece or the grandeur that was Rome could weave such wizardry as those funny, tearful tales of the Story Club. Among the manuscripts Anne found one written on sheets of wrapping paper. A wave of laughter filled her gray eyes as she recalled the time and place of its genesis. It was the sketch she had written the day she fell through the roof of the Cobb duckhouse on the Tory Road.

Anne glanced over it, then fell to reading it intently. It was a little dialogue between asters and sweet-peas, wild canaries in the lilac bush, and the guardian spirit of the garden. After she had read it, she sat, staring into space; and when Stella had gone she smoothed out the crumpled manuscript.

"I believe I will," she said resolutely.

Chapter XXXVI
The Gardners' Call

"Here is a letter with an Indian stamp for you, Aunt Jimsie," said Phil. "Here are three for Stella, and two for Pris, and a glorious fat one for me from Jo. There's nothing for you, Anne, except a circular."

Nobody noticed Anne's flush as she took the thin letter Phil tossed her carelessly. But a few minutes later Phil looked up to see a transfigured Anne.

"Honey, what good thing has happened?"

"The Youth's Friend has accepted a little sketch I sent them a fortnight ago," said Anne, trying hard to speak as if she were accustomed to having sketches accepted every mail, but not quite succeeding.

"Anne Shirley! How glorious! What was it? When is it to be published? Did they pay you for it?"

"Yes; they've sent a check for ten dollars, and the editor writes that he would like to see more of my work. Dear man, he shall. It was an old sketch I found in my box. I re-wrote it and sent it in—but I never really thought it could be accepted because it had no plot," said Anne, recalling the bitter experience of Averil's Atonement.

"What are you going to do with that ten dollars, Anne? Let's all go up town and get drunk," suggested Phil.

"I *am* going to squander it in a wild soulless revel of some sort," declared Anne gaily. "At all events it isn't tainted money—like the check I got for that horrible Reliable Baking Powder story. I spent *it* usefully for clothes and hated them every time I put them on."

"Think of having a real live author at Patty's Place," said Priscilla.

"It's a great responsibility," said Aunt Jamesina solemnly.

"Indeed it is," agreed Pris with equal solemnity. "Authors are kittle cattle. You never know when or how they will break out. Anne may make copy of us."

"I meant that the ability to write for the Press was a great responsibility," said Aunt Jamesina severely, "and I hope Anne realizes, it. My daughter used to write stories before she went to the foreign field, but now she has turned her attention to higher things. She used to say her motto was 'Never write a line you would be ashamed to read at your own funeral.' You'd better take that for yours, Anne, if you are going to embark in literature. Though, to be sure," added Aunt Jamesina perplexedly, "Elizabeth always used to laugh when she said it. She always laughed so much that I don't know how she ever came to decide on being a missionary. I'm thankful she did—I prayed that she might—but—I wish she hadn't."

Then Aunt Jamesina wondered why those giddy girls all laughed.

Anne's eyes shone all that day; literary ambitions sprouted and budded in her brain; their exhilaration accompanied her to Jennie Cooper's walking party, and not even the sight of Gilbert and Christine, walking just ahead of her and Roy, could quite subdue the sparkle of her starry hopes. Nevertheless, she was not so rapt from things of earth as to be unable to notice that Christine's walk was decidedly ungraceful.

"But I suppose Gilbert looks only at her face. So like a man," thought Anne scornfully.

"Shall you be home Saturday afternoon?" asked Roy.

"Yes."

"My mother and sisters are coming to call on you," said Roy quietly.

Something went over Anne which might be described as a thrill, but it was hardly a pleasant one. She had never met any of Roy's family; she realized the significance of his statement; and it had, somehow, an irrevocableness about it that chilled her.

"I shall be glad to see them," she said flatly; and then wondered if she really would be glad. She ought to be, of course. But would it not be something of an ordeal? Gossip had filtered to Anne regarding the light in which the Gardners viewed the "infatuation" of son and brother. Roy must have brought pressure to bear in the matter of this call. Anne knew she would be weighed in the balance. From the fact that they had consented to call she understood that, willingly or unwillingly, they regarded her as a possible member of their clan.

"I shall just be myself. I shall not *try* to make a good impression," thought Anne loftily. But she was wondering what dress she would better wear Saturday afternoon, and if the new style of high hair-dressing would suit her better than the old; and the walking party was rather spoiled for her. By night she had decided that she would wear her brown chiffon on Saturday, but would do her hair low.

Friday afternoon none of the girls had classes at Redmond. Stella took the opportunity to write a paper for the Philomathic Society, and was sitting at the table in the corner of the living-room with an untidy litter of notes and manuscript on the floor around her. Stella always vowed she never could write anything unless she threw each sheet down as she completed it. Anne, in her flannel blouse and serge skirt, with her hair rather blown from her windy walk home, was sitting squarely in the middle of the floor, teasing the Sarah-cat with a wishbone. Joseph and Rusty were both curled up in her lap. A warm plummy odor filled the whole house, for Priscilla was cooking in the kitchen. Presently she came in, enshrouded in a huge work-apron, with a smudge of flour on her nose, to show Aunt Jamesina the chocolate cake she had just iced.

At this auspicious moment the knocker sounded. Nobody paid any attention to it save Phil, who sprang up and opened it, expecting a boy with the hat she had bought that morning. On the doorstep stood Mrs. Gardner and her daughters.

Anne scrambled to her feet somehow, emptying two indignant cats out of her lap as she did so, and mechanically shifting her wishbone from her right hand to her left. Priscilla, who would have had to cross the room to reach the kitchen door, lost her head, wildly plunged the chocolate cake under a cushion on the inglenook sofa, and dashed upstairs. Stella began feverishly gathering up her manuscript. Only Aunt Jamesina and Phil remained normal. Thanks to them, everybody was soon sitting at ease, even Anne. Priscilla came down, apronless and smudgeless, Stella reduced her corner to decency, and Phil saved the situation by a stream of ready small talk.

Mrs. Gardner was tall and thin and handsome, exquisitely gowned, cordial with a cordiality that seemed a trifle forced. Aline Gardner was a younger edition of her mother, lacking the cordiality. She endeavored to be nice, but succeeded only in being haughty and patronizing. Dorothy Gardner was slim and jolly and rather tomboyish. Anne knew she was Roy's favorite sister and warmed to her. She would have looked very much like Roy if she had had dreamy dark eyes instead of roguish hazel ones. Thanks to her and Phil, the call really went off very well, except for a slight sense of strain in the atmosphere and two rather untoward incidents. Rusty and Joseph, left to themselves, began a game of chase, and sprang madly into Mrs. Gardner's silken lap and out of it in their wild career. Mrs. Gardner lifted her lorgnette and gazed after their flying forms as if she had never seen cats before, and Anne, choking back slightly nervous laughter, apologized as best she could.

"You are fond of cats?" said Mrs. Gardner, with a slight intonation of tolerant wonder.

Anne, despite her affection for Rusty, was not especially fond of cats, but Mrs. Gardner's tone annoyed her. Inconsequently she remembered that Mrs. John Blythe was so fond of cats that she kept as many as her husband would allow.

"They *are* adorable animals, aren't they?" she said wickedly.

"I have never liked cats," said Mrs. Gardner remotely.

"I love them," said Dorothy. "They are so nice and selfish. Dogs are *too* good and unselfish. They make me feel uncomfortable. But cats are gloriously human."

"You have two delightful old china dogs there. May I look at them closely?" said Aline, crossing the room towards the fireplace and thereby becoming the unconscious cause of the other accident. Picking up Magog, she sat down on the cushion under which was secreted Priscilla's chocolate cake. Priscilla and Anne exchanged agonized glances but could do nothing. The stately Aline continued to sit on the cushion and discuss china dogs until the time of departure.

Dorothy lingered behind a moment to squeeze Anne's hand and whisper impulsively.

"I *know* you and I are going to be chums. Oh, Roy has told me all about you. I'm the only one of the family he tells things to, poor boy—nobody *could* confide in mamma and Aline, you know. What glorious times you girls must have here! Won't you let me come often and have a share in them?"

"Come as often as you like," Anne responded heartily, thankful that one of Roy's sisters was likable. She would never like Aline, so much was certain; and Aline would never like her, though Mrs. Gardner might be won. Altogether, Anne sighed with relief when the ordeal was over.

> *"'Of all sad words of tongue or pen*
> *The saddest are it might have been,'"*

quoted Priscilla tragically, lifting the cushion. "This cake is now what you might call a flat failure. And the cushion is likewise ruined. Never tell me that Friday isn't unlucky."

"People who send word they are coming on Saturday shouldn't come on Friday," said Aunt Jamesina.

"I fancy it was Roy's mistake," said Phil. "That boy isn't really responsible for what he says when he talks to Anne. Where *is* Anne?"

Anne had gone upstairs. She felt oddly like crying. But she made herself laugh instead. Rusty and Joseph had been *too* awful! And Dorothy *was* a dear.

Chapter XXXVII
Full-fledged B.A.'s

"I wish I were dead, or that it were tomorrow night," groaned Phil.

"If you live long enough both wishes will come true," said Anne calmly.

"It's easy for you to be serene. You're at home in Philosophy. I'm not—and when I think of that horrible paper tomorrow I quail. If I should fail in it what would Jo say?"

"You won't fail. How did you get on in Greek today?"

"I don't know. Perhaps it was a good paper and perhaps it was bad enough to make Homer turn over in his grave. I've studied and mulled over notebooks until I'm incapable of forming an opinion of anything. How thankful little Phil will be when all this examinating is over."

"Examinating? I never heard such a word."

"Well, haven't I as good a right to make a word as any one else?" demanded Phil.

"Words aren't made—they grow," said Anne.

"Never mind—I begin faintly to discern clear water ahead where no examination breakers loom. Girls, do you—can you realize that our Redmond Life is almost over?"

"I can't," said Anne, sorrowfully. "It seems just yesterday that Pris and I were alone in that crowd of Freshmen at Redmond. And now we are Seniors in our final examinations."

"'Potent, wise, and reverend Seniors,'" quoted Phil. "Do you suppose we really are any wiser than when we came to Redmond?"

"You don't act as if you were by times," said Aunt Jamesina severely.

"Oh, Aunt Jimsie, haven't we been pretty good girls, take us by and large, these three winters you've mothered us?" pleaded Phil.

"You've been four of the dearest, sweetest, goodest girls that ever went together through college," averred Aunt Jamesina, who never spoiled a compliment by misplaced economy.

"But I mistrust you haven't any too much sense yet. It's not to be expected, of course. Experience teaches sense. You can't learn it in a college course. You've been to college four years and I never was, but I know heaps more than you do, young ladies."

"'There are lots of things that never go by rule,
There's a powerful pile o' knowledge
That you never get at college,
There are heaps of things you never learn at school,'"

quoted Stella.

"Have you learned anything at Redmond except dead languages and geometry and such trash?" queried Aunt Jamesina.

"Oh, yes. I think we have, Aunty," protested Anne.

"We've learned the truth of what Professor Woodleigh told us last Philomathic," said Phil. "He said, 'Humor is the spiciest condiment in the feast of existence. Laugh at your mistakes but learn from them, joke over your troubles but gather strength from them, make a jest of your difficulties but overcome them.' Isn't that worth learning, Aunt Jimsie?"

"Yes, it is, dearie. When you've learned to laugh at the things that should be laughed at, and not to laugh at those that shouldn't, you've got wisdom and understanding."

"What have you got out of your Redmond course, Anne?" murmured Priscilla aside.

"I think," said Anne slowly, "that I really have learned to look upon each little hindrance as a jest and each great one as the foreshadowing of victory. Summing up, I think that is what Redmond has given me."

"I shall have to fall back on another Professor Woodleigh quotation to express what it has done for me," said Priscilla. "You remember that he said in his address, 'There is so much in the world for us all if we only have the eyes to see it, and the heart to love it, and the hand to gather it to ourselves—so much in men and women, so much in art and literature, so much everywhere in which to delight, and for which to be thankful.' I think Redmond has taught me that in some measure, Anne."

"Judging from what you all, say" remarked Aunt Jamesina, "the sum and substance is that you can learn—if you've got natural gumption enough—in four years at college what it would take about twenty years of living to teach you. Well, that justifies higher education in my opinion. It's a matter I was always dubious about before."

"But what about people who haven't natural gumption, Aunt Jimsie?"

"People who haven't natural gumption never learn," retorted Aunt Jamesina, "neither in college nor life. If they live to be a hundred they really don't know anything more than when they were born. It's their misfortune not their fault, poor souls. But those of us who have some gumption should duly thank the Lord for it."

"Will you please define what gumption is, Aunt Jimsie?" asked Phil.

"No, I won't, young woman. Any one who has gumption knows what it is, and any one who hasn't can never know what it is. So there is no need of defining it."

The busy days flew by and examinations were over. Anne took High Honors in English. Priscilla took Honors in Classics, and Phil in Mathematics. Stella obtained a good all-round showing. Then came Convocation.

"This is what I would once have called an epoch in my life," said Anne, as she took Roy's violets out of their box and gazed at them thoughtfully. She meant to carry them, of course, but her eyes wandered to another box on her table. It was filled with lilies-of-the-valley, as fresh and fragrant as those which bloomed in the Green Gables yard when June came to Avonlea. Gilbert Blythe's card lay beside it.

Anne wondered why Gilbert should have sent her flowers for Convocation. She had seen very little of him during the past winter. He had come to Patty's Place only one Friday evening since the Christmas holidays, and they rarely met elsewhere. She knew he was studying very hard, aiming at High Honors and the Cooper Prize, and he took little part in the social doings of Redmond. Anne's own winter had been quite gay socially. She had seen a good deal of the Gardners; she and Dorothy were very intimate; college circles expected the announcement of her engagement to Roy any day. Anne expected it herself. Yet just before she left Patty's Place for Convocation she flung Roy's violets aside and put Gilbert's lilies-of-the-valley in their place. She could not have told why she did it. Somehow, old Avonlea days and dreams and friendships seemed very close to her in this attainment of her long-cherished ambitions. She and Gilbert had once picturedout merrily the day on which they should be capped and gowned graduates in Arts. The wonderful day had come and Roy's violets had no place in it. Only her old friend's flowers seemed to belong to this fruition of old-blossoming hopes which he had once shared.

For years this day had beckoned and allured to her; but when it came the one single, keen, abiding memory it left with her was not that of the breathless moment when the stately president of Redmond gave her cap and diploma and hailed her B.A.; it was not of the flash in Gilbert's eyes when he saw her lilies, nor the puzzled pained glance Roy gave her as he passed her on the platform. It was not of Aline Gardner's condescending congratulations, or Dorothy's ardent, impulsive good wishes. It was of one strange, unaccountable pang that spoiled this long-expected day for her and left in it a certain faint but enduring flavor of bitterness.

The Arts graduates gave a graduation dance that night. When Anne dressed for it she tossed aside the pearl beads she usually wore and took from her trunk the small box that had come to Green Gables on Christmas day. In it was a thread-like gold chain with a tiny pink enamel heart as a pendant. On the accompanying card was written, "With all good wishes from your old chum, Gilbert." Anne, laughing over the memory the enamel heart conjured up the fatal day when Gilbert had called her "Carrots" and vainly tried to make his peace with a pink candy heart, had written him a nice little note of thanks. But she had never worn the trinket. Tonight she fastened it about her white throat with a dreamy smile.

She and Phil walked to Redmond together. Anne walked in silence; Phil chattered of many things. Suddenly she said,

"I heard today that Gilbert Blythe's engagement to Christine Stuart was to be announced as soon as Convocation was over. Did you hear anything of it?"

"No," said Anne.

"I think it's true," said Phil lightly.

Anne did not speak. In the darkness she felt her face burning. She slipped her hand inside her collar and caught at the gold chain. One energetic twist and it gave way. Anne thrust the broken trinket into her pocket. Her hands were trembling and her eyes were smarting.

But she was the gayest of all the gay revellers that night, and told Gilbert unregretfully that her card was full when he came to ask her for a dance. Afterwards, when she sat with the girls before the dying embers at Patty's Place, removing the spring chilliness from their satin skins, none chatted more blithely than she of the day's events.

"Moody Spurgeon MacPherson called here tonight after you left," said Aunt Jamesina, who had sat up to keep the fire on. "He didn't know about the graduation dance. That boy ought to sleep with a rubber band around his head to train his ears not to stick out. I had a beau once who did that and it improved him immensely. It was I who suggested it to him and he took my advice, but he never forgave me for it."

"Moody Spurgeon is a very serious young man," yawned Priscilla. "He is concerned with graver matters than his ears. He is going to be a minister, you know."

"Well, I suppose the Lord doesn't regard the ears of a man," said Aunt Jamesina gravely, dropping all further criticism of Moody Spurgeon. Aunt Jamesina had a proper respect for the cloth even in the case of an unfledged parson.

Chapter XXXVIII
False Dawn

"Just imagine—this night week I'll be in Avonlea—delightful thought!" said Anne, bending over the box in which she was packing Mrs. Rachel Lynde's quilts. "But just imagine—this night week I'll be gone forever from Patty's Place—horrible thought!"

"I wonder if the ghost of all our laughter will echo through the maiden dreams of Miss Patty and Miss Maria," speculated Phil.

Miss Patty and Miss Maria were coming home, after having trotted over most of the habitable globe.

"We'll be back the second week in May" wrote Miss Patty. "I expect Patty's Place will seem rather small after the Hall of the Kings at Karnak, but I never did like big places to live in. And I'll be glad enough to be home again. When you start traveling late in life you're apt to do too much of it because you know you haven't much time left, and it's a thing that grows on you. I'm afraid Maria will never be contented again."

"I shall leave here my fancies and dreams to bless the next comer," said Anne, looking around the blue room wistfully—her pretty blue room where she had spent three such happy years. She had knelt at its window to pray and had bent from it to watch the sunset behind the pines. She had heard the autumn raindrops beating against it and had welcomed the spring robins at its sill. She wondered if old dreams could haunt rooms—if, when one left forever the room where she had joyed and suffered and laughed and wept, something of her, intangible and invisible, yet nonetheless real, did not remain behind like a voiceful memory.

"I think," said Phil, "that a room where one dreams and grieves and rejoices and lives becomes inseparably connected with those processes and acquires a personality of its own. I am sure if I came into this room fifty years from now it would say 'Anne, Anne' to me. What nice times we've had here, honey! What chats and jokes and good chummy jamborees! Oh, dear me! I'm to marry Jo in June and I know I will be rapturously happy. But just now I feel as if I wanted this lovely Redmond life to go on forever."

"I'm unreasonable enough just now to wish that, too," admitted Anne. "No matter what deeper joys may come to us later on we'll never again have just the same delightful, irresponsible existence we've had here. It's over forever, Phil."

"What are you going to do with Rusty?" asked Phil, as that privileged pussy padded into the room.

"I am going to take him home with me and Joseph and the Sarah-cat," announced Aunt Jamesina, following Rusty. "It would be a shame to separate those cats now that they have learned to live together. It's a hard lesson for cats and humans to learn."

"I'm sorry to part with Rusty," said Anne regretfully, "but it would be no use to take him to Green Gables. Marilla detests cats, and Davy would tease his life out. Besides, I don't suppose I'll be home very long. I've been offered the principalship of the Summerside High School."

"Are you going to accept it?" asked Phil.

"I—I haven't decided yet," answered Anne, with a confused flush.

Phil nodded understandingly. Naturally Anne's plans could not be settled until Roy had spoken. He would soon—there was no doubt of that. And there was no doubt that Anne would say "yes" when he said "Will you please?" Anne herself regarded the state of affairs with a seldom-ruffled complacency. She was deeply in love with Roy. True, it was not just what she had imagined love to be. But was anything in life, Anne asked herself wearily, like one's imagination of it? It was the old diamond disillusion of childhood repeated—the same disappointment she had felt when she had first seen the chill sparkle instead of the purple splendor she had anticipated. "That's not my idea of a diamond," she had said. But Roy was a dear fellow and they would be very happy together, even if some indefinable zest was missing out of life. When Roy came down that evening and asked Anne to walk in the park every one at Patty's Place knew what he had come to say; and every one knew, or thought they knew, what Anne's answer would be.

"Anne is a very fortunate girl," said Aunt Jamesina.

"I suppose so," said Stella, shrugging her shoulders. "Roy is a nice fellow and all that. But there's really nothing in him."

"That sounds very like a jealous remark, Stella Maynard," said Aunt Jamesina rebukingly.

"It does—but I am not jealous," said Stella calmly. "I love Anne and I like Roy. Everybody says she is making a brilliant match, and even Mrs. Gardner thinks her charming now. It all sounds as if it were made in heaven, but I have my doubts. Make the most of that, Aunt Jamesina."

Roy asked Anne to marry him in the little pavilion on the harbor shore where they had talked on the rainy day of their first meeting. Anne thought it very romantic that he should have chosen that spot. And his proposal was as beautifully worded as if he had copied it, as one of Ruby Gillis' lovers had done, out of a Deportment of Courtship and Marriage. The whole effect was quite flawless. And it was also sincere. There was no doubt that Roy meant what he said. There was no false note to jar the symphony. Anne felt that she ought to be thrilling from head to foot. But she wasn't; she was horribly cool. When Roy paused for his answer she opened her lips to say her fateful yes. And then—she found herself trembling as if she were reeling back from a precipice. To her came one of those moments when we realize, as by a blinding flash of illumination, more than all our previous years have taught us. She pulled her hand from Roy's.

"Oh, I can't marry you—I can't—I can't," she cried, wildly.

Roy turned pale—and also looked rather foolish. He had—small blame to him—felt very sure.

"What do you mean?" he stammered.

"I mean that I can't marry you," repeated Anne desperately. "I thought I could—but I can't."

"Why can't you?" Roy asked more calmly.

"Because—I don't care enough for you."

A crimson streak came into Roy's face.

"So you've just been amusing yourself these two years?" he said slowly.

"No, no, I haven't," gasped poor Anne. Oh, how could she explain? She *couldn't* explain. There are some things that cannot be explained. "I did think I cared—truly I did—but I know now I don't."

"You have ruined my life," said Roy bitterly.

"Forgive me," pleaded Anne miserably, with hot cheeks and stinging eyes.

Roy turned away and stood for a few minutes looking out seaward. When he came back to Anne, he was very pale again.

"You can give me no hope?" he said.

Anne shook her head mutely.

"Then—good-bye," said Roy. "I can't understand it—I can't believe you are not the woman I've believed you to be. But reproaches are idle between us. You are the only woman I can ever love. I thank you for your friendship, at least. Good-bye, Anne."

"Good-bye," faltered Anne. When Roy had gone she sat for a long time in the pavilion, watching a white mist creeping subtly and remorselessly landward up the harbor. It was her hour of humiliation and self-contempt and shame. Their waves went over her. And yet, underneath it all, was a queer sense of recovered freedom.

She slipped into Patty's Place in the dusk and escaped to her room. But Phil was there on the window seat.

"Wait," said Anne, flushing to anticipate the scene. "Wait til you hear what I have to say. Phil, Roy asked me to marry him-and I refused."

"You—you *refused* him?" said Phil blankly.

"Yes."

"Anne Shirley, are you in your senses?"

"I think so," said Anne wearily. "Oh, Phil, don't scold me. You don't understand."

"I certainly don't understand. You've encouraged Roy Gardner in every way for two years—and now you tell me you've refused him. Then you've just been flirting scandalously with him. Anne, I couldn't have believed it of *you*."

"I *wasn't* flirting with him—I honestly thought I cared up to the last minute—and then—well, I just knew I *never* could marry him."

"I suppose," said Phil cruelly, "that you intended to marry him for his money, and then your better self rose up and prevented you."

"I *didn't*. I never thought about his money. Oh, I can't explain it to you any more than I could to him."

"Well, I certainly think you have treated Roy shamefully," said Phil in exasperation. "He's handsome and clever and rich and good. What more do you want?"

"I want some one who *belongs* in my life. He doesn't. I was swept off my feet at first by his good looks and knack of paying romantic compliments; and later on I thought I *must* be in love because he was my dark-eyed ideal."

"I am bad enough for not knowing my own mind, but you are worse," said Phil.

"*I do* know my own mind," protested Anne. "The trouble is, my mind changes and then I have to get acquainted with it all over again."

"Well, I suppose there is no use in saying anything to you."

"There is no need, Phil. I'm in the dust. This has spoiled everything backwards. I can never think of Redmond days without recalling the humiliation of this evening. Roy despises me—and you despise me—and I despise myself."

"You poor darling," said Phil, melting. "Just come here and let me comfort you. I've no right to scold you. I'd have married Alec or Alonzo if I hadn't met Jo. Oh, Anne, things are so mixed-up in real life. They aren't clear-cut and trimmed off, as they are in novels."

"I hope that *no* one will ever again ask me to marry him as long as I live," sobbed poor Anne, devoutly believing that she meant it.

Chapter XXXIX
Deals with Weddings

Anne felt that life partook of the nature of an anticlimax during the first few weeks after her return to Green Gables. She missed the merry comradeship of Patty's Place. She had dreamed some brilliant dreams during the past winter and now they lay in the dust around her. In her present mood of self-disgust, she could not immediately begin dreaming again. And she discovered that, while solitude with dreams is glorious, solitude without them has few charms.

She had not seen Roy again after their painful parting in the park pavilion; but Dorothy came to see her before she left Kingsport.

"I'm awfully sorry you won't marry Roy," she said. "I did want you for a sister. But you are quite right. He would bore you to death. I love him, and he is a dear sweet boy, but really he isn't a bit interesting. He looks as if he ought to be, but he isn't."

"This won't spoil *our* friendship, will it, Dorothy?" Anne had asked wistfully.

"No, indeed. You're too good to lose. If I can't have you for a sister I mean to keep you as a chum anyway. And don't fret over Roy. He is feeling terribly just now—I have to listen to his outpourings every day—but he'll get over it. He always does."

"Oh—*always?*" said Anne with a slight change of voice. "So he has 'got over it' before?"

"Dear me, yes," said Dorothy frankly. "Twice before. And he raved to me just the same both times. Not that the others actually refused him—they simply announced their engagements to some one else. Of course, when he met you he vowed to me that he had never really loved before—that the previous affairs had been merely boyish fancies. But I don't think you need worry."

Anne decided not to worry. Her feelings were a mixture of relief and resentment. Roy had certainly told her she was the only one he had ever loved. No doubt he believed it. But it was a comfort to feel that she had not, in all likelihood, ruined his life. There were other goddesses, and Roy, according to Dorothy, must needs be worshipping at some shrine. Nevertheless, life was stripped of several more illusions, and Anne began to think drearily that it seemed rather bare.

She came down from the porch gable on the evening of her return with a sorrowful face.

"What has happened to the old Snow Queen, Marilla?"

"Oh, I knew you'd feel bad over that," said Marilla. "I felt bad myself. That tree was there ever since I was a young girl. It blew down in the big gale we had in March. It was rotten at the core."

"I'll miss it so," grieved Anne. "The porch gable doesn't seem the same room without it. I'll never look from its window again without a sense of loss. And oh, I never came home to Green Gables before that Diana wasn't here to welcome me."

"Diana has something else to think of just now," said Mrs. Lynde significantly.

"Well, tell me all the Avonlea news," said Anne, sitting down on the porch steps, where the evening sunshine fell over her hair in a fine golden rain.

"There isn't much news except what we've wrote you," said Mrs. Lynde. "I suppose you haven't heard that Simon Fletcher broke his leg last week. It's a great thing for his family. They're getting a hundred things done that they've always wanted to do but couldn't as long as he was about, the old crank."

"He came of an aggravating family," remarked Marilla.

"Aggravating? Well, rather! His mother used to get up in prayer-meeting and tell all her children's shortcomings and ask prayers for them. 'Course it made them mad, and worse than ever."

"You haven't told Anne the news about Jane," suggested Marilla.

"Oh, Jane," sniffed Mrs. Lynde. "Well," she conceded grudgingly, "Jane Andrews is home from the West—came last week—and she's going to be married to a Winnipeg millionaire. You may be sure Mrs. Harmon lost no time in telling it far and wide."

"Dear old Jane—I'm so glad," said Anne heartily. "She deserves the good things of life."

"Oh, I ain't saying anything against Jane. She's a nice enough girl. But she isn't in the millionaire class, and you'll find there's not much to recommend that man but his money, that's what. Mrs. Harmon says he's an Englishman who has made money in mines but *I* believe he'll turn out to be a Yankee. He certainly must have money, for he has just showered Jane with jewelry. Her engagement ring is a diamond cluster so big that it looks like a plaster on Jane's fat paw."

Mrs. Lynde could not keep some bitterness out of her tone. Here was Jane Andrews, that plain little plodder, engaged to a millionaire, while Anne, it seemed, was not yet bespoken by any one, rich or poor. And Mrs. Harmon Andrews did brag insufferably.

"What has Gilbert Blythe been doing to at college?" asked Marilla. "I saw him when he came home last week, and he is so pale and thin I hardly knew him."

"He studied very hard last winter," said Anne. "You know he took High Honors in Classics and the Cooper Prize. It hasn't been taken for five years! So I think he's rather run down. We're all a little tired."

"Anyhow, you're a B.A. and Jane Andrews isn't and never will be," said Mrs. Lynde, with gloomy satisfaction.

A few evenings later Anne went down to see Jane, but the latter was away in Charlottetown—"getting sewing done," Mrs. Harmon informed Anne proudly. "Of course an Avonlea dress-maker wouldn't do for Jane under the circumstances."

"I've heard something very nice about Jane," said Anne.

"Yes, Jane has done pretty well, even if she isn't a B.A.," said Mrs. Harmon, with a slight toss of her head. "Mr. Inglis is worth millions, and they're going to Europe on their wedding tour. When they come back they'll live in a perfect mansion of marble in Winnipeg. Jane has only one trouble—she can cook so well and her husband won't let her cook. He is so rich he hires his cooking done. They're going to keep a cook and two other maids and a coachman and a man-of-all-work. But what about *you*, Anne? I don't hear anything of your being married, after all your college-going."

"Oh," laughed Anne, "I am going to be an old maid. I really can't find any one to suit me." It was rather wicked of her. She deliberately meant to remind Mrs. Andrews that if she became an old maid it was not because she had not had at least one chance of marriage. But Mrs. Harmon took swift revenge.

"Well, the over-particular girls generally get left, I notice. And what's this I hear about Gilbert Blythe being engaged to a Miss Stuart? Charlie Sloane tells me she is perfectly beautiful. Is it true?"

"I don't know if it is true that he is engaged to Miss Stuart," replied Anne, with Spartan composure, "but it is certainly true that she is very lovely."

"I once thought you and Gilbert would have made a match of it," said Mrs. Harmon. "If you don't take care, Anne, all of your beaux will slip through your fingers."

Anne decided not to continue her duel with Mrs. Harmon. You could not fence with an antagonist who met rapier thrust with blow of battle axe.

"Since Jane is away," she said, rising haughtily, "I don't think I can stay longer this morning. I'll come down when she comes home."

"Do," said Mrs. Harmon effusively. "Jane isn't a bit proud. She just means to associate with her old friends the same as ever. She'll be real glad to see you."

Jane's millionaire arrived the last of May and carried her off in a blaze of splendor. Mrs. Lynde was spitefully gratified to find that Mr. Inglis was every day of forty, and short and thin and grayish. Mrs. Lynde did not spare him in her enumeration of his shortcomings, you may be sure.

"It will take all his gold to gild a pill like him, that's what," said Mrs. Rachel solemnly.

"He looks kind and good-hearted," said Anne loyally, "and I'm sure he thinks the world of Jane."

"Humph!" said Mrs. Rachel.

Phil Gordon was married the next week and Anne went over to Bolingbroke to be her bridesmaid. Phil made a dainty fairy of a bride, and the Rev. Jo was so radiant in his happiness that nobody thought him plain.

"We're going for a lovers' saunter through the land of Evangeline," said Phil, "and then we'll settle down on Patterson Street. Mother thinks it is terrible—she thinks Jo might at least take a church in a decent place. But the wilderness of the Patterson slums will blossom like the rose for me if Jo is there. Oh, Anne, I'm so happy my heart aches with it."

Anne was always glad in the happiness of her friends; but it is sometimes a little lonely to be surrounded everywhere by a happiness that is not your own. And it was just the same when she went back to Avonlea. This time it was Diana who was bathed in the wonderful glory that comes to a woman when her first-born is laid beside her. Anne looked at the white young mother with a certain awe that had never entered into her feelings for Diana before. Could this pale woman with the rapture in her eyes be the little black-curled, rosy-cheeked Diana she had played with in vanished schooldays? It gave her a queer desolate feeling that she herself somehow belonged only in those past years and had no business in the present at all.

"Isn't he perfectly beautiful?" said Diana proudly.

The little fat fellow was absurdly like Fred—just as round, just as red. Anne really could not say conscientiously that she thought him beautiful, but she vowed sincerely that he was sweet and kissable and altogether delightful.

"Before he came I wanted a girl, so that I could call her ANNE," said Diana. "But now that little Fred is here I wouldn't exchange him for a million girls. He just *couldn't* have been anything but his own precious self."

"'Every little baby is the sweetest and the best,'" quoted Mrs. Allan gaily. "If little Anne *had* come you'd have felt just the same about her."

Mrs. Allan was visiting in Avonlea, for the first time since leaving it. She was as gay and sweet and sympathetic as ever. Her old girl friends had welcomed her back rapturously. The reigning minister's wife was an estimable lady, but she was not exactly a kindred spirit.

"I can hardly wait till he gets old enough to talk," sighed Diana. "I just long to hear him say 'mother.' And oh, I'm determined that his first memory of me shall be a nice one. The first memory I have of my mother is of her slapping me for something I had done. I am sure I deserved it, and mother was always a good mother and I love her dearly. But I do wish my first memory of her was nicer."

"I have just one memory of my mother and it is the sweetest of all my memories," said Mrs. Allan. "I was five years old, and I had been allowed to go to school one day with my two older sisters. When school came out my sisters went home in different groups, each supposing I was with the other. Instead I had run off with a little girl I had played with at recess. We went to her home, which was near the school, and began making mud pies. We were having a glorious time when my older sister arrived, breathless and angry.

"'You naughty girl" she cried, snatching my reluctant hand and dragging me along with her. 'Come home this minute. Oh, you're going to catch it! Mother is awful cross. She is going to give you a good whipping.'

"I had never been whipped. Dread and terror filled my poor little heart. I have never been so miserable in my life as I was on that walk home. I had not meant to be naughty. Phemy Cameron had asked me to go home with her and I had not known it was wrong to go. And now I was to be whipped for it. When we got home my sister dragged me into the kitchen where mother was sitting by the fire in the twilight. My poor wee legs were trembling so that I could hardly stand. And mother—mother just took me up in her arms, without one word of rebuke or harshness, kissed me and held me close to her heart. 'I was so frightened you were lost, darling,' she said tenderly. I could see the love shining in her eyes as she looked down on me. She never scolded or reproached me for what I had done—only told me I must never go away again without asking permission. She died very soon afterwards. That is the only memory I have of her. Isn't it a beautiful one?"

Anne felt lonelier than ever as she walked home, going by way of the Birch Path and Willowmere. She had not walked that way for many moons. It was a darkly-purple bloomy night. The air was heavy with blossom fragrance—almost too heavy. The cloyed senses recoiled from it as from an overfull cup. The birches of the path had grown from the fairy saplings of old to big trees. Everything had changed. Anne felt that she would be glad when the summer was over and she was away at work again. Perhaps life would not seem so empty then.

> *"'I've tried the world—it wears no more*
> *The coloring of romance it wore,'"*

sighed Anne—and was straightway much comforted by the romance in the idea of the world being denuded of romance!

Chapter XL

A Book of Revelation

The Irvings came back to Echo Lodge for the summer, and Anne spent a happy three weeks there in July. Miss Lavendar had not changed; Charlotta the Fourth was a very grown-up young lady now, but still adored Anne sincerely.

"When all's said and done, Miss Shirley, ma'am, I haven't seen any one in Boston that's equal to you," she said frankly.

Paul was almost grown up, too. He was sixteen, his chestnut curls had given place to close-cropped brown locks, and he was more interested in football than fairies. But the bond between him and his old teacher still held. Kindred spirits alone do not change with changing years.

It was a wet, bleak, cruel evening in July when Anne came back to Green Gables. One of the fierce summer storms which sometimes sweep over the gulf was ravaging the sea. As Anne came in the first raindrops dashed against the panes.

"Was that Paul who brought you home?" asked Marilla. "Why didn't you make him stay all night. It's going to be a wild evening."

"He'll reach Echo Lodge before the rain gets very heavy, I think. Anyway, he wanted to go back tonight. Well, I've had a splendid visit, but I'm glad to see you dear folks again. 'East, west, hame's best.' Davy, have you been growing again lately?"

"I've growed a whole inch since you left," said Davy proudly. "I'm as tall as Milty Boulter now. Ain't I glad. He'll have to stop crowing about being bigger. Say, Anne, did you know that Gilbert Blythe is dying?" Anne stood quite silent and motionless, looking at Davy. Her face had gone so white that Marilla thought she was going to faint.

"Davy, hold your tongue," said Mrs. Rachel angrily. "Anne, don't look like that—*don't look like that!* We didn't mean to tell you so suddenly."

"Is—it—true?" asked Anne in a voice that was not hers.

"Gilbert is very ill," said Mrs. Lynde gravely. "He took down with typhoid fever just after you left for Echo Lodge. Did you never hear of it?"

"No," said that unknown voice.

"It was a very bad case from the start. The doctor said he'd been terribly run down. They've a trained nurse and everything's been done. *don't* look like that, Anne. While there's life there's hope."

"Mr. Harrison was here this evening and he said they had no hope of him," reiterated Davy.

Marilla, looking old and worn and tired, got up and marched Davy grimly out of the kitchen.

"Oh, *don't* look so, dear," said Mrs. Rachel, putting her kind old arms about the pallid girl. "I haven't given up hope, indeed I haven't. He's got the Blythe constitution in his favor, that's what."

Anne gently put Mrs. Lynde's arms away from her, walked blindly across the kitchen, through the hall, up the stairs to her old room. At its window she knelt down, staring out unseeingly. It was very dark. The rain was beating down over the shivering fields. The Haunted Woods was full of the groans of mighty trees wrung in the tempest, and the air throbbed with the thunderous crash of billows on the distant shore. And Gilbert was dying!

There is a book of Revelation in every one's life, as there is in the Bible. Anne read hers that bitter night, as she kept her agonized vigil through the hours of storm and darkness. She loved Gilbert—had always loved him! She knew that now. She knew that she could no more cast him out of her life without agony than she could have cut off her right hand and cast it from her. And the knowledge had come too late—too late even for the bitter solace of being with him at the last. If she had not been so blind—so foolish—she would have had the right to go to him now. But he would never know that she loved him—he would go away from this life thinking that she did not care. Oh, the black years of emptiness stretching before her! She could not live through them—she could not! She cowered down by her window and wished, for the first time in her gay young life, that she could die, too. If Gilbert went away from her, without one word or sign or message, she could not live. Nothing was of any value without him. She belonged to him and he to her. In her hour of supreme agony she had no doubt of that. He did not love Christine Stuart—never had loved Christine Stuart. Oh, what a fool she had been not to realize what the bond was that had held her to Gilbert—to think that the flattered fancy she had felt for Roy Gardner had been love. And now she must pay for her folly as for a crime.

Mrs. Lynde and Marilla crept to her door before they went to bed, shook their heads doubtfully at each other over the silence, and went away. The storm raged all night, but when the dawn came it was spent. Anne saw a fairy fringe of light on the skirts of darkness. Soon the eastern hilltops had a fire-shot ruby rim. The clouds rolled themselves away into great, soft, white masses on the horizon; the sky gleamed blue and silvery. A hush fell over the world.

Anne rose from her knees and crept downstairs. The freshness of the rain-wind blew against her white face as she went out into the yard, and cooled her dry, burning eyes. A merry rollicking whistle was lilting up the lane. A moment later Pacifique Buote came in sight.

Anne's physical strength suddenly failed her. If she had not clutched at a low willow bough she would have fallen. Pacifique was George Fletcher's hired man, and George Fletcher lived next door to the Blythes. Mrs. Fletcher was Gilbert's aunt. Pacifique would know if—if—Pacifique would know what there was to be known.

Pacifique strode sturdily on along the red lane, whistling. He did not see Anne. She made three futile attempts to call him. He was almost past before she succeeded in making her quivering lips call, "Pacifique!"

Pacifique turned with a grin and a cheerful good morning.

"Pacifique," said Anne faintly, "did you come from George Fletcher's this morning?"

"Sure," said Pacifique amiably. "I got de word las' night dat my fader, he was seeck. It was so stormy dat I couldn't go den, so I start vair early dis mornin'. I'm goin' troo de woods for short cut."

"Did you hear how Gilbert Blythe was this morning?" Anne's desperation drove her to the question. Even the worst would be more endurable than this hideous suspense.

"He's better," said Pacifique. "He got de turn las' night. De doctor say he'll be all right now dis soon while. Had close shave, dough! Dat boy, he jus' keel himself at college. Well, I mus' hurry. De old man, he'll be in hurry to see me."

Pacifique resumed his walk and his whistle. Anne gazed after him with eyes where joy was driving out the strained anguish of the night. He was a very lank, very ragged, very homely youth. But in her sight he was as beautiful as those who bring good tidings on the mountains. Never, as long as she lived, would Anne see Pacifique's brown, round, black-eyed face without a warm remembrance of the moment when he had given to her the oil of joy for mourning.

Long after Pacifique's gay whistle had faded into the phantom of music and then into silence far up under the maples of Lover's Lane Anne stood under the willows, tasting the poignant sweetness of life when some great dread has been removed from it. The morning was a cup filled with mist and glamor. In the corner near her was a rich surprise of new-blown, crystal-dewed roses. The trills and trickles of song from the birds in the big tree above her seemed in perfect accord with her mood. A sentence from a very old, very true, very wonderful Book came to her lips,

"Weeping may endure for a night but joy cometh in the morning."

Chapter XLI
Love Takes Up the Glass of Time

"I've come up to ask you to go for one of our old-time rambles through September woods and 'over hills where spices grow,' this afternoon," said Gilbert, coming suddenly around the porch corner. "Suppose we visit Hester Gray's garden."

Anne, sitting on the stone step with her lap full of a pale, filmy, green stuff, looked up rather blankly.

"Oh, I wish I could," she said slowly, "but I really can't, Gilbert. I'm going to Alice Penhallow's wedding this evening, you know. I've got to do something to this dress, and by the time it's finished I'll have to get ready. I'm so sorry. I'd love to go."

"Well, can you go tomorrow afternoon, then?" asked Gilbert, apparently not much disappointed.

"Yes, I think so."

"In that case I shall hie me home at once to do something I should otherwise have to do tomorrow. So Alice Penhallow is to be married tonight. Three weddings for you in one summer, Anne—Phil's, Alice's, and Jane's. I'll never forgive Jane for not inviting me to her wedding."

"You really can't blame her when you think of the tremendous Andrews connection who had to be invited. The house could hardly hold them all. I was only bidden by grace of being

Jane's old chum—at least on Jane's part. I think Mrs. Harmon's motive for inviting me was to let me see Jane's surpassing gorgeousness."

"Is it true that she wore so many diamonds that you couldn't tell where the diamonds left off and Jane began?"

Anne laughed.

"She certainly wore a good many. What with all the diamonds and white satin and tulle and lace and roses and orange blossoms, prim little Jane was almost lost to sight. But she was *very* happy, and so was Mr. Inglis—and so was Mrs. Harmon."

"Is that the dress you're going to wear tonight?" asked Gilbert, looking down at the fluffs and frills.

"Yes. Isn't it pretty? And I shall wear starflowers in my hair. The Haunted Wood is full of them this summer."

Gilbert had a sudden vision of Anne, arrayed in a frilly green gown, with the virginal curves of arms and throat slipping out of it, and white stars shining against the coils of her ruddy hair. The vision made him catch his breath. But he turned lightly away.

"Well, I'll be up tomorrow. Hope you'll have a nice time tonight."

Anne looked after him as he strode away, and sighed. Gilbert was friendly—very friendly—far too friendly. He had come quite often to Green Gables after his recovery, and something of their old comradeship had returned. But Anne no longer found it satisfying. The rose of love made the blossom of friendship pale and scentless by contrast. And Anne had again begun to doubt if Gilbert now felt anything for her but friendship. In the common light of common day her radiant certainty of that rapt morning had faded. She was haunted by a miserable fear that her mistake could never be rectified. It was quite likely that it was Christine whom Gilbert loved after all. Perhaps he was even engaged to her. Anne tried to put all unsettling hopes out of her heart, and reconcile herself to a future where work and ambition must take the place of love. She could do good, if not noble, work as a teacher; and the success her little sketches were beginning to meet with in certain editorial sanctums augured well for her budding literary dreams. But—but—Anne picked up her green dress and sighed again.

When Gilbert came the next afternoon he found Anne waiting for him, fresh as the dawn and fair as a star, after all the gaiety of the preceding night. She wore a green dress—not the one she had worn to the wedding, but an old one which Gilbert had told her at a Redmond reception he liked especially. It was just the shade of green that brought out the rich tints of her hair, and the starry gray of her eyes and the iris-like delicacy of her skin. Gilbert, glancing at her sideways as they walked along a shadowy woodpath, thought she had never looked so lovely. Anne, glancing sideways at Gilbert, now and then, thought how much older he looked since his illness. It was as if he had put boyhood behind him forever.

The day was beautiful and the way was beautiful. Anne was almost sorry when they reached Hester Gray's garden, and sat down on the old bench. But it was beautiful there, too—as beautiful as it had been on the faraway day of the Golden Picnic, when Diana and Jane and Priscilla and she had found it. Then it had been lovely with narcissus and violets; now golden rod had kindled its fairy torches in the corners and asters dotted it bluely. The call of the brook came up through the woods from the valley of birches with all its old allurement; the mellow air was full of the purr of the sea; beyond were fields rimmed by fences bleached silvery gray in the suns of many summers, and long hills scarfed with the shadows of autumnal clouds; with the blowing of the west wind old dreams returned.

"I think," said Anne softly, "that 'the land where dreams come true' is in the blue haze yonder, over that little valley."

"Have you any unfulfilled dreams, Anne?" asked Gilbert.

Something in his tone—something she had not heard since that miserable evening in the orchard at Patty's Place—made Anne's heart beat wildly. But she made answer lightly.

"Of course. Everybody has. It wouldn't do for us to have all our dreams fulfilled. We would be as good as dead if we had nothing left to dream about. What a delicious aroma that low-descending sun is extracting from the asters and ferns. I wish we could see perfumes as well as smell them. I'm sure they would be very beautiful."

Gilbert was not to be thus sidetracked.

"I have a dream," he said slowly. "I persist in dreaming it, although it has often seemed to me that it could never come true. I dream of a home with a hearth-fire in it, a cat and dog, the footsteps of friends—and *you!*"

Anne wanted to speak but she could find no words. Happiness was breaking over her like a wave. It almost frightened her.

"I asked you a question over two years ago, Anne. If I ask it again today will you give me a different answer?"

Still Anne could not speak. But she lifted her eyes, shining with all the love-rapture of countless generations, and looked into his for a moment. He wanted no other answer.

They lingered in the old garden until twilight, sweet as dusk in Eden must have been, crept over it. There was so much to talk over and recall—things said and done and heard and thought and felt and misunderstood.

"I thought you loved Christine Stuart," Anne told him, as reproachfully as if she had not given him every reason to suppose that she loved Roy Gardner.

Gilbert laughed boyishly.

"Christine was engaged to somebody in her home town. I knew it and she knew I knew it. When her brother graduated he told me his sister was coming to Kingsport the next winter to take music, and asked me if I would look after her a bit, as she knew no one and would be very lonely. So I did. And then I liked Christine for her own sake. She is one of the nicest girls I've ever known. I knew college gossip credited us with being in love with each other. I didn't care. Nothing mattered much to me for a time there, after you told me you could never love me, Anne. There was nobody else—there never could be anybody else for me but you. I've loved you ever since that day you broke your slate over my head in school."

"I don't see how you could keep on loving me when I was such a little fool," said Anne.

"Well, I tried to stop," said Gilbert frankly, "not because I thought you what you call yourself, but because I felt sure there was no chance for me after Gardner came on the scene. But I couldn't—and I can't tell you, either, what it's meant to me these two years to believe you were going to marry him, and be told every week by some busybody that your engagement was on the point of being announced. I believed it until one blessed day when I was sitting up after the fever. I got a letter from Phil Gordon—Phil Blake, rather—in which she told me there was really nothing between you and Roy, and advised me to 'try again.' Well, the doctor was amazed at my rapid recovery after that."

Anne laughed—then shivered.

"I can never forget the night I thought you were dying, Gilbert. Oh, I knew—I *knew* then—and I thought it was too late."

"But it wasn't, sweetheart. Oh, Anne, this makes up for everything, doesn't it? Let's resolve to keep this day sacred to perfect beauty all our lives for the gift it has given us."

"It's the birthday of our happiness," said Anne softly. "I've always loved this old garden of Hester Gray's, and now it will be dearer than ever."

"But I'll have to ask you to wait a long time, Anne," said Gilbert sadly. "It will be three years before I'll finish my medical course. And even then there will be no diamond sunbursts and marble halls."

Anne laughed.

"I don't want sunbursts and marble halls. I just want *you*. You see I'm quite as shameless as Phil about it. Sunbursts and marble halls may be all very well, but there is more 'scope for imagination' without them. And as for the waiting, that doesn't matter. We'll just be happy, waiting and working for each other—and dreaming. Oh, dreams will be very sweet now."

Gilbert drew her close to him and kissed her. Then they walked home together in the dusk, crowned king and queen in the bridal realm of love, along winding paths fringed with the sweetest flowers that ever bloomed, and over haunted meadows where winds of hope and memory blew.

The End